BONE VALLEY

A Jack Kendall Mystery

When profits come before lives,
justice becomes personal

JAY B. GREENE

Acknowledgments
The author would like to express deep gratitude to the *Sarasota Herald-Tribune* and the Lindsay family for graciously allowing me to use their names in this story. I also consulted with several local environmental and phosphate experts to develop the technical descriptions for this book. If there are errors, they are mine, not theirs. Their contributions in their respective fields have been significant, and their influence has enriched this book's narrative.

Dedicated to Olga Greene, my children and grandchildren, my Sarasota-Bradenton friends, environmental advocates, and others who have inspired and supported me in bringing this story to life.

ISBN (Paperback): 979-8-9902256-6-4
ISBN (eBook): 979-8-9902256-7-1

Cover Design and Interior Book Formatting by Adam Hay Studio, UK
E-Pub Formatting by Steve Mead Graphic Design

Printed in the United States of America

Contents

Chapter 1:
James Brewster

7 a.m., Monday, July 12, 1982

James *Brewster* and Dan Rumsfeld drove to the giant phosphate gypsum pond in an old, rusted company Chevy pickup truck.

"Where was the leak you saw last night?" asked Brewster, Granger Station Phosphate Co.'s 32-year-old chief mining engineer.

"It's up ahead," said Rumsfeld, a 22-year-old mining technician who had been on the job only a year after graduating from Manatee Junior College in nearby Bradenton.

"What did you see exactly?" Brewster asked calmly as he tried to understand the latest breach in the 200-foot-high earthen berm that contained 250 million gallons of gypsum wastewater and toxic slime.

"Well, as I made my final trip around the stack, I saw a steady trickle coming from a crack in the wall. When I got out to look, the dirt was soft and damp all around the crack," said Rumsfeld as he looked at his notebook. "I noted it in my log and told Mr. Grousland. I thought I'd better report it directly when you came in."

Brewster grimaced. Pierre Grousland, Granger Station's plant manager, had refused to repair the weakening gypstack wall all year. The wastewater in the stack, built primarily of sand and clay, was rising to a dangerous level.

Brewster knew a significant spill into the nearby Terra Ceia Bay ecosystem and adjacent neighborhoods could cause catastrophic environmental damage.

An anomaly in the phosphate industry, Brewster was a brilliant structural and mining engineer with an environmentalist's mind. Coworkers saw him as a talented, conscientious, friendly, supportive, and dedicated professional.

His math background gave him a mastery of statistics and economics. But it didn't take a genius to figure out that the more ore trucked to the Granger fertilizer processing plant, the more money the company could earn—and that meant higher bonuses in the executives' pockets.

Granger Station was the area's oldest and most notorious phosphate fertilizer processing plant. It was located several miles south of Piney Point in far northwestern Manatee County, close to Terra Ceia Bay, and in the middle of several housing developments that had grown around it over the years.

"Grousland should have called me last night. You were right to come to me," Brewster said. "I've been worried about the strength of the gypstack walls and the rainfall and water levels in the pond all summer. There must be a fissure inside the wall that's getting through the berm."

While Granger's main phosphogypsum holding pond—called a gypstack in industry terms—was considered small and outdated, it still contained a hazardous mixture of radioactive gypsum and toxic wastewater byproducts from the adjacent fertilizer processing plant.

Like many fertilizer plants and mines in Central Florida's Bone Valley phosphate region, Granger Phosphate Co. faced the challenge of managing massive amounts of gypsum waste, an unusable byproduct of fertilizer production.

By 1980, Florida's 20 gypstacks had already accumulated nearly 900 million tons of gypsum, with an additional 30 million tons added annually—a growing environmental and logistical burden.

"Mr. Brewster, what do you think would happen if the walls ever collapsed?" asked Rumsfeld as they drew closer to the problem area. "These leaks seem to be getting worse."

"It would be a catastrophe for this neighborhood. The runoff to the bay also would be highly destructive," said Brewster, his voice filled with concern.

"When too much nitrogen and phosphorus get into our waterways, it can lead to harmful algae blooms," he added. "These blooms can suffocate marine life and are linked to red tides that can cause respiratory problems, skin irritation, rashes, and burning eyes."

"I've been reading about heavy metals from phosphate mining," Rumsfeld said.

"Lead and mercury can stifle growth in plants and animals, mess with their reproduction ability, and even lead to neurological issues. It's up to you and me—and our team— to prevent this sludge from getting out into our ecosystems," said Brewster, relishing the teaching opportunity.

"What about radioactivity from mining and processing?" Rumsfeld said. "We are warned about it as employees, but the industry seems to downplay its risks."

Brewster didn't respond immediately. He stared past Rumsfeld, his jaw tightening as memories surfaced—his parents' coughing fits, the smell of damp earth, and the hollow silence that followed their passing.

Finally, he spoke, his voice low but firm. "You're right. The industry downplays it because admitting the truth would shut them down overnight. They don't want you—or anyone—connecting the dots," Brewster said.

He paused, his gaze hardening. "So, when they tell you the risks are minimal, or the radiation is harmless. That's not caution—they're covering their tracks. You'd better believe it's dangerous, not just for employees but for every family living near these sites."

Rumsfeld shifted uncomfortably. He hadn't expected such a weighty answer.

"I appreciate you leveling with me. I have to tell you, it always amazed me how the county could allow this fertilizer company to build this plant so close to Terra Ceia Bay," said Rumsfeld as he scanned the tall gypstack walls for the slightest sign of cracks.

Brewster looked at Rumsfeld and smiled. He was happy to have him on his team. Rumsfeld was a conscientious worker who cared for the environment.

When Brewster had taken the job at Granger a year earlier, he also wondered the same question. Phosphate spills into Terra Ceia could cause immense harm to an environmentally sensitive bay. Then there was the damage and the serious health problems a spill could cause for families in the adjacent neighborhood.

But when the plant opened in 1965, the property had been an aging orange grove in a primarily agricultural area with only a few houses and barns nearby.

Due to affordable housing, the working-class and retirement neighborhoods had expanded to more than 300 homes and 1,000 residents, including men, women, and children.

Brewster had met some of the neighbors when Grousland was unavailable. He listened to their complaints about the plant's smell and the noise that sometimes echoed around the clock.

They asked him what would happen if a disaster struck and the gypsum stack collapsed. While he explained that a gypstack collapse was unlikely, he said fissures in the walls could open, and wastewater could seep into the perimeter ditch.

If that happened, Granger's three holding ponds would begin to discharge wastewater into several underground pipes leading to Terra Ceia until the cracks in the gypstack could be sealed, primarily with cement.

Brewster had not informed the neighbors about the potential danger, but a collapse of the gypstack wall could result in a surge of wastewater up to 10 feet high, flooding nearby homes. This imminent threat kept Brewster awake at night, prompting him to repeatedly urge Granger to improve maintenance and strengthen safety measures for both the gypstack and the holding ponds.

"Mr. Brewster, I see the leak. It's up ahead," Rumsfeld said.

"I see it. It's coming out very fast!" Brewster called out as he saw a stream of white toxic wastewater running across the access road at the base of the containment wall and into the perimeter collection ditch.

"It wasn't leaking as much last night, I swear. I would have called you at home," Rumsfeld said.

"We have a significant leak," Brewster excitedly said.

"Yes, this is it," said Rumsfeld in a shaky voice. "Did I screw up? I didn't think the crack was going to break open like this. It's only been 10 hours since I first saw it."

"It's not your fault, but we need to get this fixed immediately," Brewster said with a frown. "We need to mobilize the maintenance team and start sealing the crack as soon as possible."

Brewster looked down at the wall as far as he could and saw no other leaks.

"We need to do a complete inspection of the entire berm. Where there's one leak, there could be more. I've been warning about this," said Brewster, stopping the truck. "I'm going to take some measurements and pictures."

As he left the truck, he grabbed his tape measure and walked over to the hole gushing wastewater. He measured the gap's diameter. It was about 18 inches across.

"Dan, get me three or four of the small Pyrex sample bottles," said Brewster as he looked up at the top of the wall and realized where he was.

Brewster had noticed a dark discoloration at the top of the bulging wall two weeks earlier. He informed Grousland, and the repair crew patched the spot. However, the situation had worsened, and it was now clearly waterlogged. This development concerned him, mainly because it was directly above the hole leaking white, acidic water.

While the bulge at the top of the wall was troubling, he was most concerned about the fissure leaking wastewater slime at the base of the containment wall. If not repaired immediately, the leak could cause a significant breach.

He poured samples of the white, foul-smelling liquid into

three small bottles, then marked the location and date. He would later test them for phosphorus, fluoride, solids, and radium-226, and compare the results with EPA surface water standards. Previous tests showed that Granger's surface discharges exceeded EPA standards, and he expected the same here.

As he finished sampling, Brewster began to consider what he would say in his daily report to executive management. His reports were usually met with irritation. No one wanted to hear bad news that could slow down production.

But this leak was severe, an apparent emergency. Action needed to be taken immediately. Brewster snapped several pictures with his Polaroid camera and wrote down the date and the time on the border of each print.

"Dan, we need to measure and document the flow out of this hole. This wastewater is coming out at a fast rate," Brewster said.

Rumsfeld got the flowmeter, the device Brewster used to obtain a precise reading of a breach, and handed it to the engineer, who took several quick initial measurements. The gauge read 200 gallons per minute, higher than last year's leak rate.

"After we're done, I'd like you to monitor this leak every two hours until we can repair it," Brewster said. "Make sure the next shift knows about this in case of delays. I will let Grousland know what we have here."

Brewster stood and stared at the flow of highly acidic wastewater crossing the access road and into the perimeter ditch surrounding the gypstack.

A hundred feet away, the perimeter ditch connected to three smaller retention ponds, which, based on Granger's discharge permit, could be pumped into Terra Ceia in emergencies to reduce overflow.

"What will happen now with all this wastewater coming out? Is it as toxic as it looks?" Rumsfeld asked.

"Yes, it's highly toxic, acidic, and poisonous. Please don't get any of it on your shoes. I'm sure Grousland will want to pump it into the bay unless we can stop it," Brewster said. "You say this is worse than last night?"

"Yes, much worse," Rumsfeld said. "I can't believe it."

"Can you get a repair crew out here today?" Rumsfeld asked. "I've seen management shoot you down on other repairs."

"Grousland has to order a repair. This leak is the worst we've had this summer," Brewster said.

"What if Grousland decides to discharge into the bay? He's done it before," Rumsfeld said.

Brewster shook his head as he reached for his walkie-talkie. "He could do it. He has a state permit for a two-million-gallon-per-day discharge. But this leak could get worse, way beyond his permit, if he doesn't fix it."

"Pierre, this is James. Do you read me? Over," Brewster said.

After a brief delay, Grousland replied, "What is it? Over."

"We have a serious breach on the east wall," Brewster said. "We need a repair crew out here ASAP. Over."

"How much is it? Over."

"We have a hole discharging 200 gallons per minute. As you were informed, it's been steadily increasing. Have you been out here?"

"I'm aware of it."

"Well, you should come out and see this for yourself," Brewster insisted. "We need to get this fixed before it gets worse, and it will unless we do something."

"I'll come out later. I'm discussing options with corporate," Grousland replied. "When you finish, return to the office and give me your written report."

"But Pierre, this is serious. The wall could breach. It's soft up to the top. We need a crew out here now," said Brewster, wondering how Grousland could be so calm about the leak.

"I'm on it. Don't worry, write up that report," Grousland said.

"Are you going to order a repair? Over," Brewster asked.

Grousland didn't answer. The line went dead.

"Did he answer you? Are we getting a repair crew?" Rumsfeld asked.

"He's talking with corporate about it," said Brewster, voice tinged with disgust. "Wait here. I need to take a closer look at the bulge up top."

As he started climbing the 35-degree slope, Brewster thought it odd that the bulge was above the hole at the base where the leak was flushing wastewater. He suspected the whole wall was weak from top to bottom.

Over the past month, he'd observed the bulge extending outwards, growing several inches daily. He'd attributed that to the intense summer rain, which increased the stack's water level. It looked even worse today, indicating further instability in the wall.

It was clear to him that the sheer volume and weight of the water were becoming too much for the containment wall to bear, especially since the 15-year-old stack was an old design built without polyurethane protective liners, a precaution many newer walls featured.

After examining the stack's top and water level, Brewster returned to the truck. He opened the door, took out his notepad, and jotted down his observations.

"How did it look?" inquired Rumsfeld.

"Worse than before," Brewster said. "We have problems up and down this section of the wall."

"I watched the leak, but it didn't seem like it was getting larger or coming out faster," Rumsfeld said.

"I want you to watch this section all day," Brewster said. "Every hour, I want you to measure the height and width of that hole and take flowmeter measurements. Take water samples every two hours, one at the base here and the second where the stream empties into the perimeter ditch. Now, let's drive around to the north wall."

"May I tell you something?" Rumsfeld asked.

"What is it?"

"Many workers think Mr. Grousland isn't doing enough to make the plant safe. They hear you sometimes arguing with him," Rumsfeld said. "Is that about the water levels?"

Brewster nodded. He wanted Grousland to slow production at the processing plant and reinforce the containment walls.

"Do you think the boss is doing enough?" Rumsfeld asked.

"I shouldn't talk about what managers discuss in meetings, but I will say this: you aren't wrong," Brewster said.

"There is a lot of talk about a disaster coming. I have friends who live around here, and they're super worried, especially with the rains getting stronger and the number of leaks we've been fixing," Rumsfeld said.

"It's not rocket science what we're doing," Brewster said. "The more rain that falls in the stack and ponds, the higher the water levels rise and the greater the pressure on the walls becomes. You combine that with higher amounts of groundwater pumping to run the fertilizer processing plant, and that's a recipe for disaster."

"Can't they just slow production until we fix these walls?"

"You'd think it would be that simple, but that would mean Grousland would have to tell corporate to slow phosphate ore shipments from the mine in Polk County," Brewster explained. "Do you think he'd want to be responsible for lower quarterly profits?"

"I don't know. Did you ask him?" Rumsfeld asked.

"Of course. No chance."

"Sell more fertilizer. Is that all they care about?"

Brewster shrugged and continued to steer the truck along the shell road, looking for signs of problems.

It was only a matter of time until one of the leaks he had been fixing for the past couple of months would burst open. The rain had been steady and, at times, heavy the whole summer. It was highly likely to continue as hurricane season neared its peak in August and September.

Weather forecasters always said the Sarasota-Manatee-Tampa Bay region was due for a big hurricane. Even if a Category 1 storm with a minimum of 74 mph winds came within 50 miles of the plant, the high winds and rain, and the additional stress against the walls, could cause a terrible disaster, Brewster believed.

For weeks, Grousland had been telling Brewster not to worry about the containment walls and to keep monitoring them. He argued that the odds were against a major Category 3 hurricane striking the plant.

It was true that such a storm had not made landfall in the Tampa Bay area since the 1920s. In recent years, the worst had been Hurricane Donna, which hit Sarasota-Manatee on Sept. 11, 1960, with 100 mph winds and dropped about 20 inches of rain.

Despite Grousland downplaying the risks, Brewster monitored news from the National Weather Service for tropical waves developing in the eastern Atlantic or northern Caribbean Sea. Early July storms could be surprisingly ferocious. He constantly worried that one could become a major hurricane and threaten Bone Valley.

As Brewster drove along the east wall, looking up at the berm for leaks or other problems, he asked Rumsfeld to look down at the perimeter ditch for anything unusual. Two minutes later, Brewster was satisfied there were no other problems in this section.

"Let's drive around to the north wall. Let me know if you see anything," Brewster said.

After a few minutes, Rumsfeld spoke up. "Do you see what I see? Another leak ahead. This wasn't here yesterday."

"I see it," said Brewster as he drove closer to the leak streaming across the perimeter road and into the ditch.

"Look at the top. Is that another bulge?" Rumsfeld asked. The soil was dark and damp, just like the bulge on the top of the eastern wall.

"I was afraid of this. This looks almost as bad as the other one," Brewster said as he surveyed the leak.

"What is causing this all of a sudden?"

"There has been strong wave action inside the stack for weeks with the rains and wind," Brewster explained. "The water is so high in the gypstack that it sloshes the sides, weakening it from the inside, pushing out the walls and creating fissures."

Brewster continued as he turned the vehicle. "Dan, let's drive back to the office. Then you can take the truck and come back. I need to write my report, and I want you to take measurements here and inspect the west and south walls. If you see any leaks or bulges, document them with photos and their locations and report them to me immediately. We will be working overtime until we get these leaks documented and—hopefully—fixed."

Brewster sat silent during the ride. He wondered what he would do if Grousland ordered a discharge to lower the water levels in the retention ponds surrounding the gypstack.

The protocol required that Manatee County be notified if the company began discharging phosphate wastewater. If Grousland refused, he would have to make the call.

A few minutes later, Rumsfeld dropped him off by the trailer office. Overall, it had been a bad morning. Brewster had a terrible feeling as he walked into the office.

He entered the office to confront Grousland, but no one was there. It felt as if the Granger manager was deliberately avoiding him.

For the next two hours, Brewster worked on his report. He knew Grousland would reject his recommendation to temporarily shut down the plant while repairs were made.

But he had no other choice. All the signs of a significant breach were present: fissures, leaks, bulging walls, and a lack of storage space in the gypstack and holding ponds.

During times like this, Brewster felt like the proverbial Dutch boy holding his finger in the dike. But this time, he thought, it might be too late to prevent a collapse and an environmental catastrophe.

Chapter 2:
A Shocking Act of Unity

11:15 a.m., Monday, July 12, 1982

Jack Kendall sat in front of his computer screen, busily typing another story about Estech's four-year-old plan to build a mine and fertilizer plant on 10,400 acres of land in east Manatee County.

It had been eighteen months since Jack Kendall's wife, Becky, was murdered in Bogotá by Gordon Gecht, an act of violence that closed one chapter of his life without ever really ending it. He had tried to save her. He would always believe that. But he also carried the quieter regret—that he hadn't done more, hadn't seen the danger sooner, hadn't understood how desperate she was to escape the life closing in around her. Grief didn't fade for Jack; it settled in, becoming part of how he saw the world and the stories he chose to tell.

Jack had come back to Sarasota bruised but not broken, a reporter who had already learned what power looked like up close and how ruthlessly it protected itself. After recuperating, he took on a new beat—healthcare and environmental reporting—not because it was safer, but because it mattered.

Over the past year, Jack had written several articles about Estech's permit application. The company had often identified property rich in phosphate deposits beneath the beautiful grasslands, pine trees, palmettos, and scrub oaks.

However, Estech's proposed $100 million mine was in an environmentally fragile watershed area of the Manatee River. Local politicians, environmentalists, and the business community expressed concerns that a spill could threaten the water supplies of hundreds of thousands of people in Sarasota and Manatee counties.

In an unusual resolution that morning, what Jack described as a "shocking act of unity," Sarasota, Charlotte, and DeSoto counties approved a legal and marketing plan to support Manatee County's ongoing efforts to prevent Estech from operating in the Manatee River Watershed.

Kendall quietly chuckled at the alliance with Manatee County because neighboring county commissioners rarely missed an opportunity to tease or criticize each other in the press. Highly competitive, most commissioners cared deeply about their interests and the welfare of their constituents, and they jealously guarded their political territories.

But Sarasota feared the potential threat to the Lake Manatee reservoir from Estech's above-ground 480-acre phosphate slime pond. The county purchased 12 million gallons of water per day from Manatee County for its north-county residents.

In the Sarasota County Commission meeting, Chairman

Bob Anderson said Estech's proposal to mine phosphate in the Manatee River Watershed was "tremendously dangerous" to Sarasota.

"We understand property rights," said Anderson, a lifelong Republican who'd campaigned on a pledge to fight against phosphate mining, in an interview with Jack after the meeting.

"Estech correctly quoted section 380.8 of Florida statutes, which prohibits any government from imposing undue property restrictions," said Anderson. "But we also have a right to protect public property, public health, and the environment from unnecessary threats. If this slime pond bursts and destroys our water resources, we will have allowed an even worse problem for our people and county."

Jack also included quotes from interviews with Manatee County commissioners, which he'd conducted a day earlier.

Manatee County Commission Chairman Dalton Dickers was always colorful. He'd vowed in life-or-death terms to never allow Estech or any phosphate company to start mining ore in the county under his watch.

"I am strictly opposed to phosphate mining," Dickers said. "I've been campaigning against people like this as long as I could walk. I will never agree to phosphate mining in Manatee County. I will not even negotiate with them. My mind is made up."

While all five commissioners were concerned about Estech's plans, two felt they were fighting an expensive battle they would ultimately lose against the deep-pocketed and politically connected phosphate industry.

"I'm going to vote against them, but I don't like how they're trying to use their money, influence, and power to run over us," said County Commissioner Fred Fance. "If it turns out we can't stop them, and if they end up mining here, they're going to mine by our rules."

Before Estech's proposal, Manatee adopted two mining ordinances far beyond state and federal requirements. Phosphate engineers and lawyers complained, but managers quietly agreed, knowing the paltry fines and weak oversight would do nothing to deter their profitable business model.

County Commissioner Wanda Wood said she would reluctantly support the Estech plan with additional local regulations and oversight. However, she was fatalistic about the county's ability to stop phosphate mining.

"It's inevitable," Wood said. "I'd really like them to disappear, but it's inevitable. We've got three on the books, two in the wings, and four or five other companies own land out there, and they are fully intending to mine someday. We are talking about two-fifths of the county."

But Dickers promised to do whatever he could to stop any phosphate company from getting a chance to strip-mine the land and potentially pollute the Manatee River Watershed.

"What I'm talking about here is safety," Dickers said. "The only asset we've got is good drinking water. If they have an accident out there, we all lose. They can't convince me it's safe. I don't trust them. Let me put it that way."

Jack knew what Dickers was talking about.

In the Central Florida counties where phosphate had been mined for over 70 years—Polk, Hillsborough, and Hardee—companies had a poor track record on environmental protection, water use, and land reclamation.

Dickers, who grew up in Polk County, a neighboring county called the "phosphate capital of the world," knew firsthand what happened to the land and water resources when phosphate companies started strip-mining ore.

"When I was a kid, it took them five years to mine 1,000 acres. Now, with just a few swipes, they can do that. There are regulations, but I've seen spring after spring and lake after lake dry up after they were through."

Dickers wasn't an environmentalist; far from it. But he was right. *You'd have to be blind, dumb, or ignorant not to see what was already happening in Manatee*, Jack thought.

Experts said Estech's planned Duette mine site and processing plant could double the environmental danger to Manatee, Sarasota, and Charlotte counties.

While there were opponents of Estech, there were also supporters. Some would've called them enablers of the phosphate industry, but they were not enthusiastic about the company's plans. They were the bureaucrats who strictly enforced state and federal rules on what a company needed to do to mine phosphate on the property it paid taxes on.

When the bureaucrats examined the applications and heard the phosphate lawyers speak, they concluded: Why shouldn't a company be allowed to use its land?

Conversely, as Anderson and Dickers argued, how a mining company uses its land is essential.

Like freedom of speech, people have a right to talk, but does their speech infringe on other people's right to pursue happiness? Technically, constitutional rights should be equal for the speaker and the listener.

The same is true for property rights issues. A company has the right to use its land, but shouldn't people who live near a phosphate mine, downstream of it, or are affected by it also have a right to live in peace, safety, and happiness? Protecting the property rights of adjacent landowners could be just as necessary, especially if there was a danger that one right might be extinguished or diminished.

These were all tricky questions that lawyers would have to argue in court.

During interviews, Jack carefully listened to the positions on the permitting process taken by Estech, its executives, lawyers, and the Florida Phosphate Council, the industry trade group. They maintained that they strictly followed local, state, and federal regulations. They alleged Manatee County was illegally trying to control how they used their property.

Those voices appeared to have won out, at least in the preliminary rounds.

After Manatee rejected Estech's preliminary application, the Florida Cabinet, sitting as the land and water adjudicatory commission, approved Estech's mining permit.

In another stunning blow, Manatee County's own Planning Commission recommended approval of the mine and adjacent fertilizer plant.

Despite the headwinds, most members of the County Commission, led by Chairman Dickers, were firmly against permitting another phosphate mine and plant to operate in Manatee.

Jack had enough officials quoted for the story. Still, he needed to talk with a few people affected by phosphate mining.

Suddenly, the telephone rang.

"*Herald-Tribune*, Kendall here."

There was a slight pause at the other end.

"Is this Jack Kendall, the reporter who writes about phosphate mining?" asked the caller in a shaky voice.

"Yes, what can I do for you?" Jack answered as he automatically reached for a pencil.

"I'm calling about the phosphate plant at Granger Station. I've got a story for you," said the caller nervously.

"What is it?" Jack asked.

"There are two leaks in containment walls in the gypstack, and unless something is done immediately, they will burst, flooding the neighborhood and polluting Terra Ceia Bay."

Chapter 3:
Insider Tip

11:30 a.m., Monday, July 12, 1982

"What do you mean, the walls will burst?" Jack asked politely.

"Just as I said. They'll burst. You need to write about Granger Station," the caller said, still nervous. "Something is happening there that will become a disaster unless it's stopped."

"I've written about Granger Station, so I know they have problems. All right. You've got two minutes. Give me the headline and a quick summary," Kendall said, trying to get the caller to the point.

"The headline," said the caller sarcastically, feeling more confident, "is this: *Gigantic Phosphate Gypsum Pond spews 100 million gallons of toxic slime into Terra Ceia, destroys marine life for miles.*'"

Now, Jack wondered if the call was a prank. He occasionally received fake news tips, and this one sounded outlandish.

"Are you serious? How does something like that happen?" Jack asked.

"There are two fissures in the containment wall that are leaking toxic wastewater. Management isn't doing anything about it and is making the situation worse. A major breach could cause a toxic spill into Terra Ceia unless someone stops it. It could be very destructive," the caller said.

Jack sensed that the caller had some knowledge about phosphate mining. He was aware of Granger Station, the county's oldest and most notorious phosphate fertilizer processing plant. Located several miles south of Piney Point, it sat near Terra Ceia Bay and was surrounded by housing developments that had emerged around it over the years.

"Okay, you've got my ear. So, why won't they do anything?" asked Jack, who started writing in his notebook.

"Management has been withholding maintenance on the wall to save money. Now that leaks from the gypstacks are draining into the retention ponds, managers want to allow a major breach to relieve pressure on the wall. But that could cause millions of gallons of extremely hazardous and highly toxic wastewater to run into a ditch and a pipe that discharges into Terra Ceia," the man said.

"Yes, I got it, go on," Jack said.

"Do you know what that means?"

"Sounds like a disaster."

"Now you have the picture. Millions of gallons of toxic phosphate wastewater will create uncontrolled algae blooms, fish kills, pollution in pristine waterways, and untold economic losses in the commercial and sports fishing industry," the man explained. "Then there are the heavy metals and radioactivity that will cause long-term damage to the seafloor in the bay."

"How do you know this?"

"I know because I work there, but that is off the record."

"Do you have any evidence?" Jack asked.

"Yes. I have proof that the company is cutting corners and committing fraud and other crimes. They know the pond walls are failing. They want it to fail to dump wastewater and process more ore," the man replied. "Can you do a story this afternoon before they start dumping?"

Jack looked at the wall clock. It was 30 minutes before the deadline for the *Sarasota Journal,* the *Herald-Tribune's* afternoon paper. He had no time to write a story for the *Journal,* especially with an anonymous source and no documents.

"I'm past the deadline for a story today. Why don't you come in, go on the record, and bring your evidence?" Jack said.

"I can't, at least not right now," the caller said.

"What about after six tonight?" Jack asked. "We can talk about it, and I might be able to write a story for the morning."

"Not right now," said the caller. "I'd rather give you information so you can write a story to stop the discharges."

"Have you reported this to the county?"

"Not yet. You've covered the phosphate industry very closely, and if you write a story, you can stop them."

"Possibly, I could in time, but I have a journalistic process I must follow. Is there anyone you know who will talk to me about this?" Jack asked. "I need confirmation. I can't write a story with one anonymous source."

"Some others feel like I do at the plant, but I can't give you their names right now. Will you do a story? A large breach into the bay could happen very soon," the man said impatiently.

"I told you, I don't have time today. We're past our deadline. Besides, I need some proof, and then I would need to call the plant manager to confirm they have cracks in the walls," Jack said.

"It's going to happen," the caller insisted.

"It's not that I don't trust you, but my editor would never allow a single-source story from someone who refuses to identify themselves," said Jack as calmly as possible. "Can you understand?"

"What I understand is that Granger is going to do what they want, and nobody is going to do anything about it," said the caller, clearly frustrated.

"Let's meet and talk. Just come by later and tell me what you have. I'll make some phone calls, then if it pans out, I know people on radio and TV; maybe we can get something on the news later tonight?" proposed Jack, wondering if he could pull that off. He had never worked on a scoop with television or radio, even though he knew everyone in the news business in Sarasota-Manatee.

There was a pause on the other end of the line, as if the caller was thinking.

"If you can't come tonight, maybe tomorrow?" Jack offered.

"Tomorrow could be too late," said the man. "This spill will be nothing less than a complete catastrophe for the environment, the people, and the local marine life and animals. You *must* write a story this afternoon so people will know."

"I understand what you want, but it's impossible. Just let me call you after my deadline. I'm writing a story about the Estech proposal in East Manatee County, and it's due in 30 minutes," Jack said.

"I know about the Estech mine. That could be another catastrophe for the Manatee River watershed."

"I'm covering everything, and I want to investigate this.

At least give me your name and a way to contact you. I will keep it confidential."

"I can't give it to you now," said the man. "I don't have much time. Other things are going on as well that you should know about."

"I'd like to talk with you more about it, but you should have come to me sooner. Please give me your number. I will call you back in a few hours, or we can meet tonight after my deadline," Jack repeated.

Suddenly, Jack heard the phone line click. Jack blinked and shook his head. Had he ticked the guy off? He hoped not. He'd done everything he could think of to accommodate him.

And the tip sounded strong and promising. An intentional, illegal discharge at Granger Station to cover up structural problems with the earthen dam? That would be awful for the community, but it would be a great story if he could confirm it.

Chapter 4:
Phosphate Mining's Destructive Legacy

11:45 a.m., Monday, July 12, 1982

Jack was nearly done with his Estech story, but the anonymous call bothered him. He'd gone way out on a limb to get the man to go on the record and tell his story. It sounded serious and legit.

Jack remembered several discharge problems at Granger Station last year. Maybe Steve Tracy, the county's phosphate coordinator, knew something, so he placed a call.

"Steve, this is Jack at the *Herald-Tribune*. Do you have a minute?"

"What's up?" Tracy said.

"It's about Granger Station. Remember that bioassay you did last year on the Granger leak and its discharges into the county ditch that ran off into the bay?"

"Yes. What of it?"

"You said the tests showed a clear violation. Did they ever pay a fine?"

Tracy didn't hesitate. "We fined them. And no—we're still waiting to be paid."

Jack let that hang for a moment. "Was there ever any corrective action? Anything that forced them to discharge cleaner wastewater?"

"We ordered them to double-lime any discharges. Just between us, they aren't doing it."

Jack circled "no double-lime." He coughed, "I've got to report that."

Tracy's jaw tightened. "It's in the plan they submitted. You can request a copy," he said. "On paper, it was fine. New monitoring protocols. Voluntary adjustments. Promises."

"But?"

"But nothing changed," Tracy said, the edge now unmistakable. "They kept discharging the same wastewater, at the same levels. The state doesn't have the teeth—or the will—to shut them down, and the company knows it. Fines get appealed. Enforcement gets delayed. And meanwhile, the pollution keeps moving downstream."

He leaned back, shaking his head. "That's the part people don't understand. The violation isn't the problem. The problem is that there's no real consequence. Just paperwork, patience, and the assumption that eventually everyone will stop paying attention."

"Why hasn't anything been done to hold Granger liable? The state can penalize them at least $1,000 a day."

"You don't understand. The state refused to do anything, and Granger is still violating the toxicity standard in its discharges," Tracy explained. "I can't go on the record with this, Jack. We are working through channels."

Jack shook his head. He knew Manatee and Granger disagreed over test locations and regulatory requirements, but now Tracy was telling him the state wasn't backing the county.

"What's being done?"

"We complained to the local inspector about it. He said the discharged water was within quality standards. We disagreed, of course, but the county didn't want to press the matter up the chain of command now."

"So, nothing happened?" Jack asked.

"Not yet. I've told commissioners about the problems I see at Granger. They haven't agreed on what to do yet. We've got our hands full with this Beker situation and the Estech mining proposal going on, as you know," Tracy said.

"Believe me, I know. I'm spending more time on phosphate mining stories than I ever thought possible when I took over this beat," Jack said.

"I don't know how you have time to do it all."

"Thanks, but what about Granger? What is the county going to do?"

"We're compiling a list of problems and going to do something big, but I can't discuss that with you."

"What do you mean?" Jack asked.

"I can't say anything now," Tracy said. "Let me check with Commissioner Fance to see if I can tell you the actions we're considering."

"Thanks. Say, when was the last time you were out at Granger for an inspection or any other reason?" Jack asked.

"It's been a while. Why?" Tracy asked.

Jack laughed. "Let me tell you the reason I called. I got a tip from an anonymous source at Granger who says there are two leaks in the gypstack, that wastewater is running into a ditch, and the company isn't doing anything about it."

"Two leaks in the gypstack?" Tracy exclaimed. "I haven't heard anything. I'll call the plant manager."

"Please let me know if there are any issues out there. Call me at home if it's late," Jack said. "The source was certain that a disaster was imminent. I'm on deadline and don't have time to go out this afternoon."

"Sure will. Given what else is happening in the county with Estech and Beker, we've been watching Granger as closely as we can," Tracy said.

"If I don't hear from you, I'll call you in the morning."

"Yes, I'll talk with Commissioner Fance tonight, and I'll call Pierre Grousland right away and check on this leak tip."

"Remember, it's anonymous, so don't say you got it from me," said Jack.

"Right, talk with you later," Tracy said.

As Jack contemplated the anonymous tip about Granger Station, he opened a large envelope containing newspaper clips of the biggest phosphate disasters of the past 20 years. The stories reminded him of what could happen if the caller was correct and the gypstack at Granger burst.

He found his story last year about the Granger leak and the discharges that violated the company's surface-water discharge permit. The breach, patched after several days of discharging into Terra Ceia, originated from the containment wall of a smaller holding pond containing concentrated radioactive process wastewater.

Jack's story described the discharge as toxic to small animals and fish. The county cited the company because the wastewater effluent wasn't treated with double lime before it was released into the environment.

The Granger Station fertilizer plant leak was just one of many articles on phosphate mining that Jack found in the clip files.

Another egregious example occurred in 1962, when a gypsum stack dike at the American Cyanamid Phosphate Complex in Brewster, a small town in eastern Hillsborough County, broke. Some three million gallons of sludgy, contaminated wastewater were released into the Alafia River, which then emptied into Hillsborough Bay.

The phosphate spill in Brewster triggered immediate and catastrophic fish kills that left miles of water choked with dead wildlife and stripped of oxygen. It inflicted long-term ecological damage, poisoning sediments and vegetation, decimating fish and shellfish populations, and destabilizing the river's ecosystem for months—and in some areas, years—after the discharge ended. The company and the town collapsed, its residents scattered as the industry moved on. American Cynamid was forced to surrender the deed to Brewster to the state of Florida as partial compensation for the environmental damage—an acknowledgment of the lasting harm left behind.

But that wasn't the worst phosphate disaster—not even close.

In early December 1971, a giant earthen dam in Fort Meade collapsed, releasing nearly two billion gallons of sludgy and slimy phosphate wastewater into the Peace River, according to the *Herald-Tribune*'s front-page story.

The article, "Peace River Struck By Phosphate Spill," documented the worst phosphate disaster in Florida's history. For nearly two weeks, highly toxic phosphate slime flowed more than 100 miles from a Cities Services Co.'s slime pit in Polk County to Charlotte Harbor north of Port Charlotte and Punta Gorda.

Jack knew the Peace River phosphate spill story first-hand, as he was in high school when it happened. It was one of the reasons he studied environmental science and later became a reporter.

The massive phosphate spill turned the Peace River and Charlotte Harbor the color of chocolate milk, killing millions of fish and animals. The spill also spread toxic phosphate wastewater and slime into adjacent pastures and wetlands.

After the Peace River spill, the Sarasota County Commission began spending millions of dollars on legal fees to keep phosphate mining as far away from the fast-growing tourist, cultural, and retirement haven as possible.

Another article Jack read was about Beker Phosphate suing the *Herald-Tribune* in 1976 for $10 million, alleging that the newspaper had harassed it through articles and editorials opposing phosphate mining. The Sarasota County Commission was also sued on similar grounds. When a real estate brokers' group organized a speakers' bureau to inform the public about the dangers of phosphate mining, Beker threatened legal action against the group.

Jack shook his head as he scanned through story after story about phosphate mines and fertilizer plants in Bone Valley that polluted rivers, streams, and the groundwater by dumping sludgy wastewater.

He nodded when he came across an article he had written a week earlier. Weakened by heavy rains and winds, Beker Phosphate's massive Wingate mine in east Manatee County had burst, discharging millions of gallons of slimy wastewater into Wingate Creek, a tributary of the Myakka River. To repair the berm wall, Beker asked Manatee County to increase its four-million-gallon-per-day discharge permit to 15 million gallons per day. As Jack read the article, he realized the caller's warning about the Granger Station gypstack could lead to a similar situation.

Jack had written about how evasive Beker engineer John Lerro was about the condition of the slime pond.

"If you claim the clay settling pond is in no danger of collapsing, why do you need to pump 15 million gallons of wastewater into Wingate Creek?" asked Steve Tracy.

"Lowering the water levels in the pond is necessary to perform maintenance, that's all," replied Lerro.

"How weak are those walls?" Tracy asked.

"We need to do the maintenance," Lerro said.

"Are they in danger of collapsing?"

"There has been some damage to the walls. We are within acceptable structural integrity," said Lerro, refusing to answer Tracy and the commissioners' direct questions.

Disgusted with Beker, Dickers ordered Tracy to inspect the containment walls to assess the potential danger.

Jack's story reported two days later that the County Commission voted 5-0 to notify Beker that it had violated water quality standards at its Wingate Mine. The company was also warned that its operating permit could be suspended unless it made improvements.

In his next article, Jack quoted Tracy as saying that Beker continued to discharge wastewater above its permitted limit of 4 million gallons daily. As usual for Beker, the company declined to comment.

Jack looked at the clock. It was 12:15 p.m. He needed to finish his Estech story for the afternoon edition of the *Sarasota Journal*. He typed a few more sentences, did a quick read-through, and sent the story to the desk.

"Hey, Rick, you have the commission story for the *Journal*," Jack blurted out.

Rick waved at him. Jack returned to his desk and reviewed his notes about the morning's commission meeting. He needed to make a few more calls for a more in-depth story for the next morning's *Herald-Tribune*.

He thought he'd also gather comments on the Estech proposal and the Beker Wingate discharge. If he had time, he would make some calls about Granger. He sensed something would happen out at that fertilizer plant in Palmetto.

His first call was to hydrogeologist David Montgomery.

"David, Jack Kendall here. What do you think about Beker's request to increase discharges to 15 million gallons daily into Wingate Creek?"

"So, you want to know my take on Beker's slime pond? If the county allows that, it won't be long before the pollution reaches the Manatee River's watersheds and Myakka River," Montgomery replied.

"Is that why Charlotte and DeSoto counties are getting involved with Sarasota and Manatee?"

"Yes. Phosphate companies are also talking about moving south to follow untapped ore reserves. Mining techniques have improved, and it's now more efficient to extract lower-quality matrix in Sarasota and DeSoto counties."

"I've heard them talk about that," Jack said.

"With the discharges now from Wingate, the chances double, maybe triple, for the Peace River, the Myakka River, and Charlotte Harbor becoming dumping grounds for phosphate sludge," Montgomery said. "And if they start mining in Sarasota and DeSoto, we're talking about a substantial decrease in water quality."

"What about the Estech proposal?" Jack asked.

"There is no doubt that Estech could pose significant dangers for the Manatee River watershed," Montgomery replied. "Now, Estech is a responsible company. It's nothing like Beker, but accidents happen all the time in the phosphate industry. The pressure to maximize profits for shareholders and owners is strong even for the best companies."

"Thanks for the comments, David. Talk with you later," said Jack as he hung up.

Next, Jack called homeowner Gary Remy, who lived close to the Wingate Mine and whom he had met the previous weekend at a commission meeting.

"Hi, Gary. Jack Kendall from the *Herald-Tribune*. Do you have a few minutes?" Jack asked.

"A few," Remy said. "How can I help?"

"Are you concerned about the Estech mining proposal?" Jack asked.

"Another damn phosphate mine. That's what I have to say. Like I told you Saturday, my neighbors and I worry about radiation when radium, radon, and everything else are exposed during the mining," Remy said in a strong Southern accent.

"Are you going to talk with a lawyer?"

"We're thinking about it. Who's going to pay my medical

bills in 10 years if we get cancer?" Remy said. "Beker will be gone. Estech will be gone. We'll be left holding the bag."

"What do you think about Beker's request to discharge 15 million gallons daily?"

"Beker should be shut down. Phosphate mining has no benefit for our county," Remy insisted. "We saw what happened in 1971 when the Peace River turned to garbage with that phosphate slime. The company that did it used lawyers and the courts to avoid cleaning the river.

"Mark my words, if we continue to allow Beker to dig up phosphate—and Estech to mine even closer to Lake Manatee—this will come home to roost with us, just like the Peace River," Remy said. "Nobody wins except the phosphate companies and their investors."

"Thanks, Gary. Let me know if anything changes out there."

"It's changing right now with Beker discharging millions of gallons of slime into Wingate Creek."

"Manatee just cited Beker for water quality violations and threatened to suspend their operating permit," Jack said.

"The county talks a lot, but they can't stop them," Remy said. "Beker's lawyers will delay until they get what they want, or they'll just dump and pay a small fine."

"That seems to be the pattern. Well, take care," said Jack as he hung up.

As Jack began to write an updated commission story for the morning paper, he wondered how Sarasota, Charlotte, and DeSoto could help Manatee keep Estech from mining in the watershed. After all, Manatee hadn't had a sterling record of keeping phosphate companies out—Granger, AMAX, and Beker were three prime examples of that failure.

However, the four neighboring counties felt an alliance

was a logical and necessary next step in their ongoing fight against the phosphate companies. Most of the 20 county commissioners believed it was their duty to provide clean water to citizens, ensuring the region could sustain steady population growth and development.

They knew Manatee County was on the front lines in the fight to keep phosphate mining out of Sarasota, Charlotte, and DeSoto counties. If the alliance could help Manatee prevent a fourth phosphate mine from gaining a foothold in the county, it could also stop, or at least delay, phosphate mining along the southern edges of Bone Valley.

Ironically, the two phosphate mines and three fertilizer plants already in operation in Manatee County were, perversely, helping Sarasota, Charlotte, and DeSoto counties justify fighting the companies and their lobbying flacks, the Florida Phosphate Council.

But up until now, all of Jack's articles on phosphate mining had been academic. He had spoken with old-timers who remembered the damage caused by major phosphate spills, but he had never covered one.

Jack looked at the clock. It was nearly 5:30 p.m. He needed to finish his story for the morning paper. He gave one more read-through and sent it to the city desk.

"Hey, Rick, you have the updated commission story," Jack said in a voice that reverberated throughout the newsroom.

Wiseman nodded and waved goodbye. "I'll call you later if I need anything."

Jack looked around to see if Bobbie Jackson, the cop reporter, was still working on a story. She was on the phone in a deep conversation, hand running through her wavy blonde hair.

He jotted a note, walked over, and put it on her desk. Bobbie flashed her pretty blue eyes at him, smiled, and mouthed, "See you later."

As he drove home, Jack turned on his radio and heard a weather report about a tropical wave that had formed off the west coast of Africa. The National Weather Service predicted the wave would soon develop into a tropical depression as it moved across the North Atlantic Ocean.

Jack wondered if this might be the season's first hurricane. Already, this summer had been one of the wettest and hottest he could recall. He made a mental note to stop off at the grocery store to stock up.

Chapter 5:
James and Elizabeth

8 p.m., Monday, July 12, 1982

James drove to his sister Elizabeth's apartment in Bradenton after a long, frustrating day. His mind was a whirl of anxiety and anger over the Granger gypstack leaks and his inability to convince anyone to take the problem seriously. He had done what he could—documenting the dangerous situation, filing his report, and even giving an anonymous tip to Jack Kendall about Granger's potential illegal discharge into Terra Ceia Bay. Still, nothing felt like enough.

He knocked twice on Elizabeth's door and immediately braced himself. His sister's moods could shift unpredictably, and he never knew which version of Elizabeth would greet him: calm and focused or tense and irritable. He hated putting his stress on her, but he needed her input.

When she opened the door, her piercing gaze locked onto him. "James, what's wrong?"

"Elizabeth, we need to talk. Things are worse than I thought," he said, stepping inside.

Her apartment felt suffocating—dim lighting, heavy curtains drawn tight, and piles of papers and half-read books scattered across the room. He caught a faint whiff of cigarette smoke, even though she insisted she'd quit months ago.

She motioned for him to sit, but her movements were jittery, her fingers tapping a nervous rhythm against her thigh. "What are they doing now?"

James paced instead of sitting, trying to organize his thoughts. "The gypstack walls are leaking. There are two small breaches already; if they're not patched soon, they'll give way."

Elizabeth's face remained neutral, but her hand rubbed the back of her neck—a telltale sign she was on edge. "I'm not surprised. Granger is the worst phosphate company in Florida," she said with forced calm. Her voice, though steady, carried an undertone of tension. "That's why we're here. What else?"

James hesitated. "Two leaks are bad enough, but it gets worse."

Her eyes narrowed. "Go on," she said sharply.

He hesitated again, glancing at the messy coffee table, where an ashtray with a single stubbed-out cigarette sat like an accusation. "Elizabeth, have you been smoking again?"

"Yes, I'm sorry. The stress is coming back. The meds aren't working again," she explained mournfully. "Just tell me what's going on."

James sighed, recognizing the warning signs: her clenched jaw, the way she gripped the couch's edge as though it anchored her to reality. He pressed on.

"Nothing is being done to fix the breaches. And on my lunch break, I called Jack Kendall—anonymously—but if Granger figures out I tipped him off, they'll come after me."

Elizabeth stood abruptly, her anger rising to the surface. "They'll come after *us*, James." Her voice rose slightly, and she began pacing in a mirror of his earlier movements.

"I know," James said softly. "That's why we need to figure out our next step. Together."

James walked over and placed a hand on her shoulder. "Hey, we'll figure this out, okay? I need you to stay with me on this. Focus."

Elizabeth inhaled deeply, steadying herself. "I'm with you," she said, but her eyes betrayed the storm of emotions swirling beneath the surface—anger, fear, and something darker she didn't dare name.

"It seems to me Granger could use these leaks as an excuse to illegally dump millions of gallons of phosphate wastewater into Terra Ceia Bay," James said, his voice heavy with anger.

Elizabeth's fists clenched, her knuckles whitening. "Terra Ceia? Those bastards."

"I tried talking with Grousland about it. He won't order maintenance to fix the leaks," James said.

"He's a scumbag. They're all criminals. But why do you think they will do it now? After all, you've fixed many leaks in the past year," said Elizabeth, getting angry. The anger seemed to balance her and focus her. Strangely, she looked calmer.

"Yes, but before, at least, they had maintenance start repairs. They haven't done that this time. Grousland talks about contacting Bartow for help, but he's stalling," James explained, sitting down, exasperated.

"What do you want to do?" asked Elizabeth, giving him the first chance to propose a plan. He suspected she had an idea.

"I'm not sure what I can do now," James said. "I don't have any proof, but I suspect they'll pretend it's an emergency discharge."

"Did Bartow send anybody?" Elizabeth asked as she sat down next to him.

James shook his head. "No, I waited until dark, and no one showed up."

"Do you want me to take care of it?" Elizabeth asked pointedly.

"No, I don't want you involved yet," he replied, placing his hand on hers.

His sister's voice darkened. "What are you going to do? Just let the walls burst and the phosphate slime run into the bay?"

"I know you didn't want me to do this, but I called Kendall at the *Herald-Tribune*," James said.

She shook her head. "I heard you say that before. You know how I feel: newspaper reporters are useless."

"I know, but let me explain. Kendall has written many articles about phosphate mining in the past year and knows Grousland and Granger."

"I believe you're doing what is right. But what can he do? He is just a small reporter."

"I know, but he listened, and his columns reach a lot of people. He wants me to meet with him and go on the record with what I know," James said. "He also wants documents, photos, and other evidence before he can write anything."

"We've talked about this before," Elizabeth said as she stood up and stared at him. "When are you going to let me get the hard evidence? Grousland has everything at his house.

Let me break in and find it."

"Not yet," James said.

Elizabeth began pacing the small living room. "Not yet? When will you be ready to take action? You've been writing the state about how Granger has been falsifying your reports, and they haven't done anything. You've talked about reporting it to the county, but they keep approving new phosphate mines. Like everyone else, including Kendall, they're probably in Granger's pocket."

James sighed. "I don't think Kendall can be bought. And Mr. Cooper is on our side."

"I hope so, but nothing is happening with the class action lawsuit he filed to bring justice to our parents," Elizabeth growled in disgust.

"You heard what he said. He's trying, but the judge who will decide the case doesn't believe phosphate causes cancer," James said.

"Exactly my point. We need to take drastic action to stop Granger. They are greedy, evil people who killed our parents. What more evidence do you want?"

"I talked with Jack Kendall. He is our best bet to alert the public and get Manatee County to enforce its regulations to stop Granger from this major discharge."

Elizabeth stopped pacing and turned to face him. "You believe those asswipes will do it this time?"

"Yes," James said firmly.

"Well, all right, you contacted Kendall, and if he needs more evidence, you must get it yourself," she said. "I have an idea how to do it."

James looked at her, his face filled with worry. Typically, he wasn't as daring as his sister. "What are you thinking?"

She crossed her arms, her expression resolute. "You need to get some rest tonight. Go home and get some sleep. Then, early in the morning, before dawn—5 a.m., before Grousland gets in—search his office. There must be documents on his desk or in his file cabinets that Kendall might find valuable. Then call the reporter and meet with him."

James hesitated. "Elizabeth, I considered taking more documents, but it's dangerous. I copied the maintenance expense reports last month, but Grousland has gotten more suspicious as I've become more outspoken."

"It's time we took the gloves off," she said, her voice firm. "Mom and Dad told us the fight to expose them would be difficult, but they implored us to fight hard. We've been watching and waiting for our chance. We need to act now before something horrible happens."

"We need more than just evidence," James replied. "We need allies—and Jack Kendall might be a good one. He knows other people, too. People who can take action."

"I'm not sure I trust him, but I trust you, and we need more evidence. You need to get it," Elizabeth insisted. "Go home and get some sleep."

James nodded. As he left, he hugged and kissed her on the cheek. "You've been healthy and strong lately, Lizzy. I'm very proud of you."

Elizabeth smiled. She liked it when he called her "Lizzy," just as he had when she was younger, when their parents were alive. Talking with James always lifted her spirits. He would gather the documents while Kendall would write a story to stop Granger. If that plan didn't succeed, she had something else in mind.

As James drove home, Elizabeth's words rang in his ears.

"It's time we took the gloves off." He smiled as he realized exactly what to do.

Chapter 6:
Slime Spill

8 a.m., Tuesday, July 13, 1982

Jack left for the newspaper the following day in his brand new red 1982 Ford Mustang GT. His special order had come the week before, and he'd been so busy with work that he hadn't had time to take it on a long drive.

Jack loved his GT "Boss." It was a dozen steps up from his 1976 Gold Oldsmobile Cutlass Supreme and miles better than his first car, a dark green 1966 Mustang with a V6. The Boss's 5.0L engine was super-fast, going 0-60 mph in less than eight seconds.

He drove the five miles to the paper in the mostly legal time of 12 minutes. He had to be careful not to drive too fast because the car rode like a dream, and he didn't want a speeding ticket. He parked his new beauty and walked to the front door of the *Herald-Tribune*.

It was too early to call Tracy, but he wanted to review his

notes from his interview with the anonymous source and do more research on Granger Station, Manatee County's oldest phosphate-processing plant.

Even in its early years, Granger Station had a terrible safety record. In 1965, Granger's previous owner was caught dumping toxic, untreated wastewater into Terra Ceia Bay, angering the public and commercial fishermen.

As he dug deeper into Granger's story, Jack realized this facility was far worse than other phosphate plants in the county and had serious problems.

For example, Piney Point dumped phosphate slime into Tampa Bay in well-publicized spills in the years after it opened in 1966. Like Granger, the spills regularly threatened the adjacent neighborhood with toxic leaks.

Since 1979, when Granger took over the Pebble fertilizer plant, spills, leaks, accidents, improper discharges, fines, and neighbors' complaints had increased. Its noisy, dirty industrial processing operation seemed to run 24 hours a day.

As Jack read over the latest clips, he wrote down the names of people he would call for comments on the plant, just in case of a spill, as the caller had warned.

First was Angus Miniver, the phosphate mining inspector with the Florida Department of Environmental Protection. He had been quoted often over the past five years.

Jack made a few notes to ask Miniver about the latest maintenance records on the mine and plant. He jotted down other questions. Have there been any recent citations or fines? How much does Granger spend on maintenance per month? What is the current condition of the containment walls? Finally, are there any dangers associated with the plant that the public should know about?

Next, Jack wrote down the name of Gloria Barton, the chairwoman of the environmental group Suncoast Protectors. Her nonprofit was active in several areas of growth and development, but phosphate mining was its primary focus. A volunteer board of experts led the group. It also paid consultants to review tests conducted by the county and the state on Granger and Terra Ceia.

What would Barton say about an anonymous source reporting leaks in the containment walls and a sizeable unannounced discharge at Granger? Jack was sure she'd give him a great quote.

Jack made a note to call Pierre Grousland, the plant manager at Granger Station. However, before calling Grousland, he needed to speak with his insider source again. He hoped the man would call back soon.

In addition, Grousland would likely deny everything, as he had on several prior occasions. He had called Jack regarding Jack's environmental stories and the use of academic and consulting sources that criticized the phosphate industry. Jack reminded him that he had given the industry ample opportunities to share its perspective.

Jack looked at the clock. It was 8:30 a.m. He decided to try Tracy.

"Hi Steve, this is Jack. Did you talk with Commissioner Fance about Granger?" he asked.

"Jack, what a coincidence you called yesterday about Granger. I'm headed over there right now. There has been a major discharge into Terra Ceia Bay. The leak started overnight. Do you want to meet me there?" Tracy asked.

"What happened?" asked Jack, shocked but not surprised that a discharge had happened as precisely as his source had warned the afternoon before. He felt the caller knew his stuff and immediately felt terrible that he hadn't been able to do anything about it.

"I got an anonymous message from a worker early this morning that Granger has a suspicious containment wall leak. The caller said the manager failed to fix the issue when he was told about it," Tracy explained. "He also said they're discharging millions of gallons of toxic wastewater from the main gypstack and overflow retention ponds into Terra Ceia."

"I bet your caller was the same one who tipped me off about the leak yesterday," Jack confidently said. "He said the same thing, and he was absolutely right. He also said management was making it worse by doing nothing about it."

"Definitely sounds like the same guy. I called Grousland last night, but he never called me back. I just talked with him a few minutes ago," Tracy said. "He confirmed they have begun to discharge from the stack to alleviate pressure off the berm."

"Did he say anything else?"

"He said he had to begin to discharge because the stack could collapse."

"Hold on, let me make sure I understand what you're saying: Grousland told you he's pumping wastewater from their holding ponds into the bay to avert a collapse of the containment walls?" Jack said.

"Pretty much, yes," Tracy confirmed.

"That is exactly what my source said he would do intentionally because the manager refused to fix the breaches," Jack recounted. "I'm starting to believe what my source said: that Granger wants to dump excess water to relieve pressure on the wall and maximize production."

"Jack, we'll make a full inspection. I'll talk to Grousland and his employees," Tracy said.

"Look closely because my source said the company wants a major breach to relieve the pressure on the walls," Jack suggested. "He implied it was part of a big plan to get rid of wastewater so they could resume full production in a couple of days. This is exactly how the Peace River spill happened in '71."

"Could be, but I hope not. I'll certainly check that out. Off the record, I wouldn't put it past Granger. They're worse than Beker, and you know the problems we've had at Wingate Mine," Tracy said.

"Sounds like a similar situation is brewing at Granger," Jack said.

"I've warned Grousland about the weak containment walls and the high water levels this summer. Are you going to quote your source?" Tracy asked.

"He isn't ready to come forward. This is just between us. I've got to get this guy on the record to put him in the story," Jack replied.

"I understand," Tracy said. "I'd better get going."

"See you in about 30 minutes," said Jack.

* * *

After leaving the message with Tracy before 7 a.m., Brewster drove back to the plant. Rumsfeld was waiting for him in the parking lot.

"Morning, Mr. Brewster," Rumsfeld said.

"Have you seen any Granger repair trucks?" Brewster asked.

"I saw one drive away when I got here a little while ago.

They must have been here all night. Maybe Grousland fixed the leaks?"

"I doubt it. Let's get in the truck and check out the east wall. I have a bad feeling about this," said Brewster. "You drive."

Rumsfeld took the keys from Brewster, fired up the old white 1975 Ford pickup, and skillfully maneuvered along the dirt road.

"Look at that leak! It's gushing! It didn't look like that yesterday," Rumsfeld exclaimed, shaking his head.

"No, this is very different. Check out the contour. That's not natural. It looks cut, sharp on the edges," Brewster said. "I've never seen a leak shaped like this before."

"What should we do?" Rumsfeld asked.

"I'll take more pictures, and then we can compare with yesterday. See if you can measure the breach," Brewster instructed. "I want all this documented."

"It looks a lot bigger than yesterday," murmured Rumsfeld. After measuring, he realized the breach had doubled in size to 24 inches by 36 inches. "It's pouring out twice as much as before."

"Let's get over to the north wall. I have a feeling we'll find the same. We can measure with the flowmeter later to get precise readings," Brewster said.

Rumsfeld drove quickly around the gypstack to the north side.

"Look at the top. The bulge. It's leaking, too," he said.

"I'm not surprised. Look down at the leak at the base. See the crack? Again, just like the east wall, it is cut and sharp. This is not normal, not at all," Brewster said. "It's intentional, just as I feared."

"What do you mean by intentional?" Rumsfeld asked.

"I shouldn't say anymore," Brewster replied. "We may need the police out here."

Chapter 7:
Birth of a Conspiracy

Before dawn, Tuesday, July 13, 1982

Before other employees arrived for work, Granger Station plant manager Pierre Grousland met with executives Herbert Cross and Louis Decker in the trailer office to discuss the ongoing discharge.

"How much have we removed from the stack?" asked Grousland, a small, wiry man with sharp features and a balding head.

"Nearly 20 million gallons. We can get out more today if the county doesn't stop us," Cross said.

"Good. I sent a man to Bartow to get equipment to fill the breaches. I told him to take his time. He should be back this afternoon. We should be able to unload another five million gallons, at least," Grousland said.

"But boss, Tracy is bound to ask why we don't have the necessary equipment—a backhoe, fill, and concrete to fix the leaks," Cross said.

"I'll simply tell him there was a miscommunication with the company about the equipment. He'll realize we're making excuses, but it will buy us time to continue pumping water out of the gypstack. Granger authorized paying whatever fine we get," Grousland said.

Cross shook his head. "I'm not sure these excuses will work," he said. "They're going to bring their inspectors and see everything."

"You both did a good job getting our people from Bartow out last night to cut out and drill bigger holes in the containment walls that Brewster wanted fixing," Grousland replied.

"They worked fast. They dug out the one on the east and north sides with a backhoe. The leaks are much worse than when Brewster reported it," Cross said.

"Good, but I don't want the entire wall to collapse—just a steady flow. We will keep the pumps running, discharging effluent out to the bay. Later this morning, when Tracy arrives, it will be much worse. We can't be blamed for the discharge because we have two breaches. It will prove we need to lower the water level to repair the walls," Grousland explained. "Finishing the job should take three or four days of discharging. Then we can ramp up production bigger than before."

Cross and Decker looked at each other but didn't respond.

"I know, I know. We're pushing our luck. I don't care. You know our problems with the wall. We had no choice. The issues would become even worse if we don't get that wastewater out," Grousland said. "This is an opportunity, not a disaster."

"Just so you know, the two maintenance men on duty didn't like what we were doing with the backhoe," Decker said. "I had to pay them $3,000 to keep quiet."

"We have that in petty cash," Grousland replied with a cold smirk. He leaned back in his chair, tapping a pen against the desk. "Do they know what will happen to them if they change their minds?"

The room fell silent. Cross and Decker understood what he meant.

"Yes, I told them," Decker said.

"Anything else?" Grousland asked.

"We're saving money on maintenance, but the stack and holding ponds are unmanageable," Decker reported. "There is too much water in them. Brewster is telling us that, and telling the state the same, using those letters he thinks we don't know about. Once we get these discharges done, we'll need to upgrade the walls."

"Don't get cold feet on me now. Brewster is getting to be a pain," Grousland said. "His reports are hysterical. I've told you to restrain him. With the heavy rains and hurricane season getting to its peak after we fix these breaches, we've got to get out another 75 million gallons, and we don't want him causing any delays."

"Why don't we tell him to stop writing the state? Miniver is blocking those letters from getting to higher-ups, but he isn't sure how long he can do it," Decker said.

"I'm considering my options regarding Brewster," Grousland muttered. "That is all I want to say on the matter."

"Brewster is right about the stack and the ponds getting so full. We're heading toward a major collapse unless we complete the repairs or reduce the water levels," Cross said.

"We've got to relieve the pressure off those walls. We need a little more time.

"It may be time to give him a bonus so he will look the other way, like we did with that idiot, Miniver," Decker added.

"Brewster is not greedy like Miniver. It's one thing to bribe a state inspector who has no scruples. It's another thing to pay off a man like Brewster. We may have to take other action to silence him," Grousland said.

In a darkened adjacent room, James Brewster overheard the conversation among the plant's top three executives. As he switched off his tape recorder, he nodded and smiled. He had both what he needed to report the spill to the county and the proof that Jack Kendall wanted.

Chapter 8:
Polluting Terra Ceia

9 a.m., Tuesday, July 13, 1982

When Jack arrived at Granger Station, the parking lot was crowded with vehicles. Several people were standing in small groups. There was a mild acid smell in the air.

Jack noticed Steve Tracy talking with Grousland. He slowly headed over to them to eavesdrop.

"You say you can't do anything to stop the leaks? And you're dumping untreated wastewater into the bay because you don't have capacity in your gypstack?" Tracy asked Grousland loudly, clearly perturbed that the county wasn't notified before the company began discharging above its permit.

"We are doing the best we can. I decided to authorize the pumping due to two serious wall problems. You can see water pouring out into the ditch," Grousland replied.

"You should have had the backhoe, concrete, and all the repair equipment on hand. You know the walls are weak and the ponds are high," Tracy insisted.

"We've got to pump because we don't want these holding ponds to overflow or the containment pond to collapse and flood the neighborhood," Grousland said. "Your people can confirm the breaches, the weak walls, and the water levels in the holding ponds and gypstack."

Tracy shook his head. "Unbelievable," he muttered. "Even with the two breaches, you realize that authorizing discharges of this magnitude was a decision for the county and state to make, right? You should have called me yesterday and requested an inspection of the breaches and an emergency permit for the discharge."

"We didn't have time."

"Remember what you promised the County Commission? You're supposed to report all problems immediately and get special permits for treated discharges above the two million gallons daily maximum the state allows."

"We followed state law. We didn't discover the leaks until this morning. By then, the holding ponds were starting to overflow," Grousland said. "I had to make a quick decision."

"The county will review what you've done. How many total gallons have you dumped?" Tracy said.

"About 20 million."

"Have they been treated with double lime?"

"We didn't have time and ran out of lime."

"You ought to have been ready, Pierre," Tracy remarked, looking at Grousland while jotting down notes. "When did the leaks begin?"

Grousland didn't answer. He only shook his head.

"Are you admitting that you violated regulations by exceeding your two-million-gallon daily limit, failing to treat it, not reporting it, and not obtaining an emergency permit immediately?" Tracy asked, disgusted.

"I'm not admitting anything," said Grousland, his voice starting to rise. "My engineer told me the pond wall could fail at any moment. We protected the neighborhood from a large-scale collapse by continuing to pump."

"When are you going to get a repair crew out here?" Tracy asked.

"I should have a crew on site later today to make necessary repairs on the containment walls, and then we should be able to slow the flow."

"When will it be completed?"

"I hope by tomorrow morning at least 60% will be done," Grousland said. "We need to lower the water pressure on the upper walls to reduce the wave action."

As Grousland was speaking, Jack was furiously writing down notes.

"Pardon me, Mr. Grousland, may I ask a question?" Jack interrupted. "I understand this dump could have been prevented if you had shored up the walls weeks ago. You knew leaks were springing for several days. Is that true?"

"Well, well, the reporter has something to say. That is incorrect, Mr. Kendall," Grousland stated with disdain. "We were aware yesterday, based on my engineer's report, that the wall had structural issues in at least one area, possibly two. This morning, I learned that these problems had worsened overnight."

"Who's your engineer?" Jack asked.

"James Brewster, but he is not authorized to talk with the

press," Grousland growled. "You can get everything from me."

Tracy interrupted. "Pierre, I'd like to speak with Brewster, your assistant manager, Herbert Cross, and Louis Decker, your financial manager."

"They're busy right now, Steve, but you can talk with them later, maybe this afternoon," Grousland said. "Let's talk privately in my office, away from the press."

With that, Grousland turned, and Tracy followed him.

"Please, Mr. Grousland," asked Jack. "A few more questions. Is it true that you have withheld major and necessary reconstruction on the pond walls this past year to hold down expenses?"

"It is not true," said Grousland, turning to face Jack with a scowl. "I don't know where you get your information. We've been doing repairs as needed all along. I don't have time to talk with you. This interview is over."

"But, Mr. Grousland, people want to know if it's true that you've been aware for several weeks that serious problems have been found with the pond wall and that the wastewater is at dangerously high levels behind the stack because of the heavy rains. Can you comment?"

Grousland didn't answer. He continued to walk toward the trailer where the plant's office was located.

"Okay, Mr. Grousland, I'll check with you later. I need more answers because I'm writing a story about this huge pollution discharge in a couple of hours for the afternoon edition," Jack said loudly enough for Grousland to hear.

Tracy turned back and added, "Jack, let me find out some more, and I'll get back to you. I'll ask to look at the engineer's daily reports and talk with him and the others."

Jack nodded and looked back at the parking lot.

Photographer Alex Mahoney had arrived.

"Alex, get as many photos as you can of the side of the east pond wall with the biggest leak. The north side has a smaller leak. Then, follow the water flow and pipes to the ditches, where you should also find the larger pipeline leading to the bay where the wastewater is spewing out," Jack instructed. "I'll join you shortly."

"Sure," Alex said.

Jack walked around to see if he could spot the engineer, James Brewster. He wondered if Brewster had tipped him off yesterday and called Tracy earlier this morning.

He saw a man sitting in the cab of a pickup truck, clicking into a calculator, and sensed it was Brewster.

"Are you James Brewster? I'm Jack Kendall with the *Herald-Tribune.*"

The man looked up with an angry stare. "A little late coming here, aren't you, Kendall?"

"I got here as soon as I could. Can you talk?" Jack asked.

"Yes, but this is off the record," said Brewster, looking around. "I can't be seen talking with you. They're watching me."

"Who is watching you?"

"They. Company stooges," Brewster replied. "You have no idea what is happening, do you? I told you this would become a problem. You could have stopped this."

"I understand you are upset, but I'm here now, and I need a few minutes," Jack said. "Did you expect it to happen so soon?"

"No, to be honest, I didn't, not until this morning," Brewster said, looking around again. A few workers stood by their cars in the parking lot, talking, but they didn't seem to be watching.

"Okay, here's an answer, off the record. I'm angry with what happened last night. I didn't expect the two small breaches

I told you about to become this big a problem today. It all happened after I turned in my report and left the plant at 6 p.m. They never contacted me about this discharge last night or this morning before I came into work, and I'm the chief engineer!" Brewster snarled in disgust. "Now that they've started to pump from the gypstack, two holding ponds, and two retention ponds, they won't stop until the police or the county forces them to."

"What are they trying to do?" Jack asked.

"They see this as an opportunity to lower the water levels in all the ponds and get back up to maximum production. It's just what I told you last night."

"I see. I'm sorry. I wish you'd contacted me earlier about all this. We could've met and talked."

"We can't talk here. I'll call you later."

"Quickly, tell me how this happened."

"How? Because these bastards are corrupt!" Brewster angrily shouted.

Jack took a moment to size up the engineer. He saw a passion in Brewster that he had never encountered in any other phosphate industry worker. He wasn't a big man—quite average. He had intelligent dark eyes, dark hair, and a serious, tanned face and arms. He spent a lot of time outdoors.

Brewster continued to write notes in his notebook.

"James, you say they will continue discharging?" Jack asked. "Grousland told me he would slow the discharges this afternoon after they repair the walls."

"He's lying, but that's off the record. They'll keep the pumps going all day and night," Brewster said. "They plan on dumping 100 million gallons over the next several days. I heard them say that."

"They told you that?"

"No, I heard them."

"One hundred million is more than 40% of capacity in the gypstack and the ponds," said Jack, his voice rising. "How long will it take them to discharge that amount?"

"Quiet. If we have to talk, follow me," Brewster instructed as he led Jack to a blind spot behind his truck.

When they'd found privacy, he continued. "Let me explain. Write this down. The 100 million they plan on pumping into the bay includes about 10 million from the holding ponds. And that 10 million is the most toxic. Management finally took my warnings seriously about too much volume in the stack, but I didn't expect them to dump so much when I talked with you last night."

He paused. "Mr. Kendall, the catastrophe will be ten times greater than I believed yesterday. They don't care about the marine life in the bay," he added with a look of extreme anger and frustration.

"My photographer is out there by the discharge pipe. I will tell him to stay all afternoon to take pictures and record the time," Jack said.

"At least you'll write a story," Brewster said. "Maybe the county can stop them."

"Listen, James, I'm sorry I didn't have more time to talk with you yesterday. I must write this story for this afternoon's edition in a couple of hours, so I need a little more information," Jack said.

"I can't tell you much more now. I must dig deeper into their plan. We can't be seen talking anymore now, and I can't get off duty until later tonight," Brewster said. "This spill is terrible news. Worse than you know."

"Worse? How so?"

"Couple reasons. First, the effluent they started discharging originates from the main gypstack and a pipe on the west side, closer to the bay. But it doesn't stop there—they've also initiated a second and third discharge from two smaller holding ponds. This wastewater is the most toxic and radioactive from the fertilizer plant. Those ponds contain ten times more radioactivity than the main containment pond, where I discovered the cracks."

"What does that mean?" asked Jack as he furiously wrote down as much as possible.

"High levels of radioactive wastewater are devastating to marine life and threaten human health and local economies," Brewster explained. "We're looking at long-term contamination risks that disrupt ecosystems, harm seafood safety, and demand costly, extensive environmental remediation."

"I wish I could quote you on this," Jack lamented.

"You can't, so don't even think about it," Brewster snapped.

"Grousland didn't say anything about higher radioactivity or toxicity. He said the wastewater being pumped comes from the gypstack. You said they are also pumping from the holding ponds. So, he is lying?" Jack asked.

"Yes, they do that for a living," Brewster replied, his voice low and tense. "They're pumping from all four ponds and the stack. You can walk around and count the pipelines. I know much more, but I can't say anything else now. You have to leave. You're putting me in danger. I'll contact you later."

"Danger?" Jack asked, leaning closer.

Brewster nodded grimly. "What they've done with the leaks is intentional. And I have proof."

Jack froze. Brewster had just accused Granger of deliberately creating the leaks to discharge radioactive wastewater into Terra Ceia Bay. He had to find a way to get him on the record.

Before Jack could respond, Brewster turned and started to walk away.

"Wait!" Jack called after him as he scribbled down his phone number. "Here, take this. Call me later. Any time. It's my home phone number."

Brewster stopped and turned. With a quick nod, he took the note, stuffed it into his pocket, and walked across the parking lot toward the massive gypstack.

Jack watched him go. The weight of Brewster's words sank in. If what he'd said was true, this wasn't just negligence—it was far worse.

Jack had come looking for answers. Now, he had even more questions—and a dangerous truth waiting to be uncovered.

Chapter 9:
The Sludge Thickens

10 a.m., Tuesday, July 13, 1982

As Brewster walked away, Jack noticed two men in their mid-20s in Granger overalls standing behind a car.

Jack wondered if Brewster was right about the company watching him. He decided to walk over and find out who these men were and what they were doing.

"Hey, I'm Jack Kendall with the *Herald-Tribune*. Mind if I talk with you two?" he asked.

The two employees, one tall and thin and the other short and stocky, waved him off.

The taller man said, "We can't talk with you if you're a reporter."

The stockier one added, "We can talk, just not here. We don't like what's going on today."

"Do you think the company started these leaks?" Jack asked softly as he approached them.

The stocky worker waved his hands back and forth to stop Jack from talking.

Jack moved closer, understanding they didn't want to draw attention. "What do you two do here?" he whispered.

"We work in maintenance. We can't be seen talking with you. We'll call you later. I saw you talking with Mr. Brewster. I have some information," said the stocky man as he nervously glanced around.

"Right," said Jack, handing him a business card. "Call the paper. Ask for Jack Kendall."

The two men nervously walked away. Jack didn't see anyone else in the parking lot, so he headed to the other side of the plant to look for more workers.

Everyone he talked with seemed surprised by the wastewater dump in the bay and the two breaches. Several said they'd heard about two minor breaches the day before, but nothing out of the ordinary for Granger.

"We were only told that the plant is offline and we should go home. They're bringing in Granger workers from Bartow," said one older employee in his mid-40s who declined to give his name.

Jack handed out several more business cards, thanked them, and walked to the office to try to talk with Grousland again before leaving for the paper. He wanted to find out how long the dumping would continue.

He also wanted to confirm the events that led to the spill. Were all four ponds being pumped, or just the gypstack? He also needed to verify whether the holding ponds were more radioactive and toxic than the gypstack.

Jack turned the knob on the office door, but it was locked. He knocked a few times.

Grousland finally opened the door. He looked at Jack and said, "No more comments, Mr. Kendall. We'll give you a statement later."

"I just have three more questions. I need them answered before I write my story for the afternoon edition," Jack said.

"You have everything I can tell you until we finish our investigation and repairs," Grousland said. "This was an accident. Bye."

He slammed the door shut.

Jack was accustomed to people getting upset when he sought the truth behind a story. Grousland was doing his best to downplay the circumstances surrounding the spill, but Jack sensed he was being dishonest about several aspects. He decided to find alternative methods to get his questions answered.

But first, he needed to find Alex. He spotted a 24-inch discharge pipeline from the top of the gypstack and followed it along a ditch toward the bay. He noticed several other pipelines leading to the ocean from the other ponds.

After a five-minute walk, he saw Alex taking photos of a disgusting sight: greenish-yellow wastewater pouring out of the pipe and mixing with the blue-green saltwater of the bay.

It was a disheartening scene. Jack knew the wastewater contained heavy metals that would settle on the seafloor. The toxic elements would eventually kill crabs, clams, oysters, seagrasses, and mangroves. From talking with biologists, he knew that elevated nutrients such as nitrogen and phosphorus in the wastewater would also cause massive algal blooms, reduce oxygen levels in the bay, and kill fish for miles.

"Alex, is there any way you can get out in the bay and see how far the sludge is spreading?" Jack asked.

"We'd need a helicopter to get an aerial shot of that," Alex said. "When are they going to stop discharging?"

"Not for a few days. I don't know. Grousland won't answer many of my questions."

"I can't stay out here much longer. I've got another assignment in Sarasota."

"Can you get some backup? I want to know if the pumping slows later today."

"I'll call to see if Julie or Carlson can come out, but I need to get back and develop these pictures to meet your afternoon deadline."

"Okay, what about that summer intern?"

"I'll check," Alex replied.

"Thanks, see you back at the paper," Jack said.

Jack walked back to the parking lot. He saw Grousland talking with some of the idle employees.

"Mr. Grousland, can I have a few more words with you before I leave to write my story?" Jack asked.

"Very quickly, Mr. Kendall," he said.

"When are you going to stop pumping?"

"We hope to slow it down later today, after we repair the east wall. We need to relieve more pressure on the stack," Grousland replied. "We don't want to see this situation get worse."

"You said you're pumping effluent from the gypstack. However, I traced two discharge pipes back to the source, which could also be from the two holding ponds and two retention ponds. Is that true? Are you draining all four ponds?" Jack asked.

"We had to run an emergency pipe from the main stack, which is now leaking at the top and the base of the north wall. Have you seen that?" Grousland said.

"Yes. What about the two holding ponds? Are you pumping those out? I saw the pipes running out to the bay," Jack pressed.

Grousland didn't answer.

"The effluent going into the bay seems very strong. How toxic and radioactive is that wastewater?" Jack asked.

"You're wrong, Mr. Kendall," Grousland objected. "The wastewater is within regulations. End of interview."

He turned and walked away.

"I was told the two holding ponds have much higher radioactivity than the main pond. Can you comment?" Jack continued.

Grousland didn't respond.

"And you're supposed to be treating these discharges with double lime. Why don't you have enough to comply with state law?" Jack shouted.

The plant's manager pretended not to hear as he neared the office.

"Mr. Grousland, did you intentionally worsen these leaks to lower the water levels in the stack?" Jack shouted again.

Several workers in the parking lot couldn't help but hear Jack's questions. They turned to see if Grousland would respond.

"That is a damn lie, Kendall," he said, glaring at Jack for a moment, then turning to enter the office and slamming the door behind him.

Jack hadn't wanted to yell his question, but he needed an answer. Grousland denied intentionally breaching the gypstack, while Brewster claimed he'd heard Grousland admit they purposely worsened the leak.

Grousland also didn't deny that the two holding ponds contained higher concentrations of radioactivity and pollutants than the main gypstack.

If Brewster was correct about the toxicity, why would Grousland blatantly lie? Surely, Tracy would test the effluent and report the concentration levels. Grousland must've been stalling. He knew the truth would come out eventually.

Either way, Jack hated not being told the straight facts the first time. He knew he would get to the bottom of what had happened with the spill, one way or another. It was only a matter of time, especially having an inside source like Brewster.

Walking to his car, he saw Brewster talking with another employee. They got into an old truck and headed out by the gypstack.

Jack didn't have time to search for more information. It was 10:30 a.m., and he had been at the plant for 90 minutes. He needed to get back to the paper. When he reached his GT, he saw that its red exterior was covered in a fine layer of white dust.

"Damn phosphate plant. No wonder the neighbors hate it," he grumbled as he got in his vehicle. He wondered if he had time to get a quick car wash. He still had to talk with Tracy and make several other calls before his deadline.

As he started the engine, he realized the story would be difficult to tell because Brewster had provided several pieces of information contradicting Grousland's account.

Jack knew he would have a problem using Brewster as an anonymous source for much of his powerful revelations. The newspaper's policy was to confirm everything an anonymous source claimed through two independent sources before it could be published. Without this verification, Brewster could be dismissed as a "disgruntled" employee, putting Jack at risk of a libel suit.

He hoped that either Tracy or one of the workers could verify or support some of Brewster's claims. Tracy could provide information about the toxicity and radioactivity of the holding ponds. Still, evidence of the intentional breaches in the gypstack walls would need to come from Brewster, the only person with that crucial information.

Jack wondered whether Brewster could really obtain evidence of corruption. Jack needed more facts to write a major scoop exposing the truth.

Chapter 10:
Afternoon Spill Story

Noon, Tuesday, July 13, 1982

After a 30-minute drive to the newspaper, Jack quickly walked to his desk and called Steve Tracy.

"Steve. I'm on deadline and need to confirm a few things for my story."

"I'll try. I didn't get much more information from Grousland. We're going back this afternoon with equipment for a full inspection. I am trying to get the state to help," Tracy explained.

"Can you confirm the discharge into the bay came from the main gypstack, the two toxic wastewater processing holding ponds, and the two gypstack overflow retention ponds?" Jack asked.

"Did you ask Grousland?"

"I did. I want to know what you think."

"Based on my initial observation, the discharge came from all five sources you mentioned," Tracy replied.

"All five? Not just the gypstack?" Jack asked.

"No, Grousland was discharging from all the ponds."

"Grousland didn't answer my question about whether he was discharging from all ponds *and* the stack."

"You can quote me that he was," Tracy said. "We'll have an estimated flow per hour for the stack and all the ponds later this afternoon. Get back to me before your deadline."

"Two more things. First, Grousland denied that the two holding ponds were more toxic and radioactive than the gypstack. Is that true?" Jack asked.

"The holding ponds are always more toxic and radioactive than the gypstack," Tracy answered.

"Are they above EPA's allowable limits?"

"They've been way above federal maximum limits for a while. Remember, we cited them about that."

"That's what I thought," Jack said. "Did you test the discharge pipes?"

"I got a few samples from both discharge pipes, the individual ponds, and the bay. We won't know the preliminary results until later today. Still, I can tell you from experience that the discharges into the bay are more than double the maximum allowable limits," Tracy replied. "We'll go back this afternoon, test the water in all the ponds, and then compare."

"Grousland denied the discharges are violating water quality standards."

"He always disputes our tests," Tracy said. "We're investigating everything at this point."

"Will you have the preliminary results for my deadline tonight?" Jack asked.

"Call me after seven, and I'll let you know."

"Did you find out when the pumping started?"

"He said it started about six this morning when they discovered the leaks, but I have a feeling it started much earlier."

"I had a source tell me the pumping started after dark, about 9 p.m. the night before."

"We will talk with workers. Maybe our mutual source will come forward," Tracy said.

"Second question. As I mentioned before, my source said Granger intentionally worsened the leaks, and he has proof. Did you see any evidence of sabotage?" Jack asked.

"The two breaches I looked at were strange, that's for sure. I'll take another look at it later," Tracy replied. "Right now, we can't say one way or another."

"Last question. I promise. Is there a structural problem with the main gypstack?" Jack asked.

"It's passed previous tests, according to the state. Our tests last month showed that the walls were weak. I'm trying to get the state to reinspect it and thoroughly evaluate the breaches and other possible weak spots," Tracy explained. "I saw a few problems with the walls and the leaks at the base of the east and north walls. There are bulges above both those leaks we're concerned about."

"Steve, do you believe the stack is safe?" Jack pressed. "Grousland said they dumped to avert a catastrophe."

"Well, the water in the gypstack and the four smaller ponds is high. I can see why they might have been worried," Tracy replied.

"Could the gypstack walls collapse? My source said it is very possible."

"Let me put it like this," Tracy said slowly. "Unless Granger makes serious repairs and slows its processing…if we get a hurricane or even a major tropical depression with 10 inches or more of rain, the gypstack and the smaller ponds could overflow or collapse."

"That bad?"

"Yes. I agree with your source, whoever it is. If the stack collapses, Granger will lose control of the plant and have to shut it down. At this point, they have every incentive to prevent a collapse."

"Can you tell if they are trying to fix the leaks?"

"They are supposed to get a crew from Bartow out to the plant this afternoon. I will check on that when I go back," Tracy said. "I don't know why Granger delayed fixing the leaks for 24 hours. Their excuse about miscommunication with the home office doesn't make sense. We'll find out about that soon enough."

"How much do you think they will discharge?"

"That's a good question. With the discharges today, they should be in better shape regarding the volume in the big pond and in the smaller ones," Tracy replied, hesitating for a second.

"What, Steve? What were you going to say?"

"I probably shouldn't tell you before I tell the County Commission, but I believe Grousland did not want to get permission to discharge this much because they knew we would ask hard questions about their lack of proper maintenance of the stacks and the pace in mining and fertilizer production," Tracy said.

Jack furiously wrote down every word. He could tell the phosphate coordinator was getting angry with the morning's events as he talked.

"You should write this—Granger Station is an old plant, and the gypstack and holding ponds are full. The whole operation should be retired. You can only put so much gypsum and water in these things," Tracy said.

"Good quote. You plan on inspecting the gypstack and ponds, right?" Jack asked.

"We'll be out there the rest of the week. I don't care what the state says. The walls are still weak and may pose problems. I'll find out how they plan to strengthen them."

"Thanks, Steve. That's all I need for now. I'll check with you later. Let me know when the report or summary is available," Jack said.

Jack wrote up a quick story about the incident for the afternoon paper. He noted all the facts about the discharges, the two breaches in the walls, and the lack of maintenance Tracy mentioned.

He included Grousland's denials that the company skimped on containment wall maintenance. He highlighted that Grousland and Tracy disagreed on when wastewater pumping started and on the toxicity and radioactivity of discharges from the holding ponds.

Jack knew there were too many unanswered questions and conflicting opinions. He concluded the story by stating that the county and Granger had initiated investigations.

"Are you done with it yet?" asked Rick Wiseman, Jack's longtime editor.

"Almost. Give me one more read," Jack said.

Five minutes later, Jack hit the send button on the computer. "Rick, it's over to you now."

"Got it," Rick replied. "Stand by for a few minutes."

Jack leaned back in his chair and scanned the newsroom for Bobbie. He wanted to find out if she had eaten lunch, but she was still out on her rounds at the police stations.

After getting a hot cup of coffee and using the restroom, Jack started to think about a more extended version of the story for the next morning's paper.

He had a few hours to kill before he needed to start making more phone calls for his next story. He expected to talk with Tracy again after seven to get the latest data and information on the spill.

While he didn't need Brewster to go on the record for the first two stories, Jack hoped he would call to set up a meeting. He needed to convince Brewster to go on the record and turn over the evidence of corruption.

Chapter 11:
Toxic Slime

Later that afternoon, July 13, 1982

At 4 p.m., Jack was at his desk when the newsroom secretary laid down a copy of the afternoon paper.

As a veteran reporter, Jack never got tired of the aroma of a freshly printed daily newspaper. The scent was distinct and evocative, comforting and exciting. The earthy and musty newsprint reminded him of damp wood and freshly cut lumber.

He looked down at his desk. Breaking news was never dull. Capturing events that had occurred just hours earlier in physical form felt surreal. It almost confirmed reality.

On A-1 of the *Sarasota Journal*, his article on the spill was the main story with photos and a two-line, 36-point headline:

GRANGER PHOSPHATE LEAKS TOXIC SLIME INTO TERRA CEIA

Below the headline, the 24-point deck further explained:

CATASTROPHIC ENVIRONMENTAL, ECONOMIC DAMAGE TO BAY, EXPERTS WARN

The story jumped to page three.

The afternoon article featured six of Alex's photos of the containment wall, leaking toxic wastewater into ditches and the surrounding neighborhood; the milky, sludgy pipeline discharges into Terra Ceia Bay; and headshots of Tracy and Grousland.

For the morning edition, Jack would gather more details about the discharge's sequence of events, the environmental damage to the bay, the probable fine, the conflict over how much radioactivity was spilled into the bay from the fertilizer plant's two holding ponds, and reactions from various stakeholders.

But lingering concerns filled his mind.

Would Brewster call him as promised? What evidence did he have to prove that Granger manufactured the spill to drain the gypstack and ramp up fertilizer production?

He expected the County Commission to hold an emergency hearing on the Granger spill in the coming days. Grousland and Miniver would testify, and Tracy would give his report to the commission. The public, led by Gloria Barton and Suncoast

Protectors, would certainly weigh in.

As Jack contemplated his next steps, he wondered if he would truly uncover the truth behind the disaster. He felt uncertain; the likelihood of fully explaining a corrupt company's actions, particularly those related to environmental accidents, was slim.

Jack shook his head as he leaned back in his chair. He had written two good stories for the afternoon paper. What more did he want? Mermaids? He chuckled at that. He'd heard someone say that once and thought it hilarious.

Still, Jack had something special—an ace up his sleeve he never had before in any phosphate story: an inside source. Brewster gave him confidence. He wanted to expose Granger as much, if not more, than Jack.

Not only did Jack have an insider, but he was also a manager who promised to provide hard evidence about the spill and corporate corruption. At least two plant workers had also promised to give him information on what they saw in the hours leading up to the spill.

He looked at the clock. It was 5 p.m., time to start making calls to gather the latest information for the morning edition.

James Brewster probably wouldn't call until much later in the evening. He'd mentioned that he needed to gather evidence of Grousland's plan and minimize the ongoing damage.

First, Jack left a message with Tracy. His secretary said he was still at the plant with other pollution control officers and wouldn't return until after 7 p.m.

He called Miniver and the state DEP office supervisor to request a comment and to let them know he was on a deadline. The 24/7 operator said she would try to contact one of them by pager.

Jack decided to see if Alex knew anything more about the discharges. He walked over to the photo department.

"Hey, Alex. Have you heard from our intern about Granger?" Jack asked.

"She called me about six o'clock. She said the wastewater was still being pumped out at the same rate as earlier," Alex replied. "They weren't slowing up, as far as she could tell. She'll be back by seven thirty."

"Anything else?" Jack asked.

"I told her to watch for a Granger crew from Bartow coming to repair the leaks. She told me she didn't see any repairs being made, but they chased her away from the gypstack and couldn't get a great look," Alex said.

"Thanks. By the way, you shot some great photos. Do you have any others for the morning?"

"A few. Oh, shoot, how could I bury the lede? Mr. Lindsay approved a helicopter to shoot some photos of the slime spreading out into the bay," Alex said. "Carson is developing them now. He said he has some amazing shots. Hold on, let me show you a few."

Jack was pleased that Mr. Lindsay was getting involved. He could use the front office's support for this story, which he knew would become controversial, since he needed to use an anonymous source.

David Lindsay Jr., a fiercely principled newspaperman and longtime opponent of phosphate mining, had encouraged Jack to write articles explaining the environmental hazards of phosphate sludge spills in the Myakka and Manatee watersheds.

Once, to duplicate what Lindsay and his son, Bob, saw as they flew over phosphate mines and slime pits, Jack hired a helicopter and assigned Alex, his favorite photographer, to do a photo essay. Jack's award-winning story, which featured Alex's photographs, described how mining unnaturally altered the terrain. Phosphate companies crudely strip-mined the ore from the ground, turning the picturesque countryside into barren moonscapes with massive gray gullies, rutted, jagged hills devoid of wildlife, flora, and fauna. The story drew attention from a public often oblivious to the environmental impacts of development and industry because those impacts were hidden in rural areas.

Alex returned with three photos. "What do you think?"

"These are sensational, Alex. Thanks so much for following up on the helicopter," Jack said.

"I didn't call him. Mr. Lindsay called Carson and told him to be ready to fly in an hour," said Alex with a laugh. "Mr. Lindsay is ticked off at Granger."

"That's great. I'll thank him personally when I can. Drop off some copies of what Carson has when you get a chance," Jack said. "I hope to get some preliminary data to show how toxic the wastewater discharge into the bay is compared with state standards."

"We might be able to do a graphic to illustrate that. Tell Rick your thoughts. We're going to meet with him in about an hour," Alex said.

"Thanks, I'll do that. Keep up the good work. I'll talk with you later," Jack said as he started to leave.

"Hey, Jack. Did Granger purposefully dump that sludge into the bay? Everyone's talking about it," asked Alex.

"Is that right? Gossip travels fast. I haven't reported anything like that yet," Jack replied. "Still waiting on evidence."

"The phosphate slime in the bay is enough for me. Let

me know if you need anything," Alex said as he turned and headed into the dark room.

"Sure, thanks," Jack said as he returned to his workspace. It was after 7 p.m., and Tracy had not called back.

∗　∗　∗

Walking back to his desk, he noticed that Bobbie had returned from her precinct rounds. He'd missed her for lunch and hadn't spoken with her much because of the breaking news.

"Hey, Bobbie. What's up? Been busy today?" Jack asked.

"Working. Say, you're on to a big story today! I read what you wrote about Granger and Terra Ceia. How much poison will the county allow them to dump into the bay?" Bobbie asked.

Jack shrugged slightly. "I'm not sure how the county can stop Granger. I might ask an environmental attorney if the county could get a temporary injunction to halt the dumping."

"How much have they dumped so far?" Bobbie asked, already bracing for the answer.

"I'm hearing they've already discharged more than 20 million gallons in the past 24 hours, maybe more," Jack replied. "They raised the possibility that the walls could collapse if they aren't allowed to dump millions of gallons into the bay to relieve pressure off the gypstack."

"That's not good. Are they exaggerating?" Bobbie asked.

"They could be."

Bobbie watched his face as he spoke—focused, tight, already a step ahead of the next deadline. "Sounds like you're going to be here a while," she said. "Do you want to have dinner later?"

"I'm hungry," he admitted, "but I'll be here past 10. I'll

probably go home and grab something from the fridge."

"I'll be heading out after my last story," she said. "Call me at home if you decide you want to go out later."

"All right," Jack said.

She nodded, smiled, and watched him walk away, already pulled back into the gravity of his story. He was still holding back, she thought. It had been more than eighteen months since Becky's death—and Bogotá, and everything that followed. She knew he cared about her; she had never doubted that. She'd been patient, deliberately so, but she wondered how long it would take for him to see her more as a woman than a good friend and trusted colleague.

She had been ready for something more almost from the day she met him, seven years ago now. For five of those years, he had been married to Becky. Back then, she had put her feelings aside without resentment. She'd kept them there ever since.

Bobbie took a slow breath, turned back to her screen, and told herself to get back to work.

*   *   *

Jack returned to his desk, tapped his keyboard, and opened his working file. It flashed on the screen. He looked it over and began typing notes where he needed updates to the information and data.

After 30 minutes, the phone rang.

"*Herald-Tribune*, Jack Kendall here."

"Hi Jack, it's Steve. If you're ready, I can give you the latest, " Tracy said.

"Just in time."

"We took tests and measurements all afternoon," Tracy explained. "Based on the flow of the three pipes, we estimate between 18 and 25 million gallons were pumped into the bay, depending on whether the pumping started at 9 p.m. the previous day, as workers told us, or six that morning, as Grousland said."

"Can I quote you as saying, 'What workers said?'" Jack asked. "They told me the same but didn't want to go on the record."

"Yes, you can quote me," said Tracy. "Off the record, I told the commissioners that there's no doubt Grousland is lying about the spill." He was clearly ticked off at Grousland and was in no mood to cover for him.

"Were you able to test the discharge going into the bay for violations?" Jack asked.

"Do you want all the numbers?"

"Give me the important ones."

"Here they are. All measurements are twice the standard levels. Phosphorus was measured at 200 milligrams per liter, compared to the EPA standard of 105; fluoride at 150 mg/L, exceeding the EPA's 75; and solids at 300 mg/L, against a standard of 159," Tracy said.

"Yes, I see," Jack said as he wrote down the numbers.

"The water's pH was 1.2. Very acidic and toxic. We have many more numbers and data points, but this should be enough for you now."

"What about radioactivity?"

"It's too soon to know how much radioactivity went into the bay. It will also take us a few days to test for that," Tracy replied. "Until Granger stops dumping, we won't know how many tons of phosphorus, fluoride, heavy metals, and other things were ultimately deposited into the sea."

"So, by my rough calculations, if 25 million gallons of wastewater went into the bay the first day, that is only 10% of the total volume in the stack?"

"That's correct. Let me cut to the chase. When I left, Grousland only slowed the east leak by half. He said he would get both cracks done tomorrow. I expect another 25 million gallons will be released by then. You can quote me on that," Tracy said.

"That will be 20% of the stack discharged?" Jack asked.

"That's right."

"My source told me he doesn't believe Granger will stop at 50 million gallons. They will ask the state to let them lower the volume of wastewater in the stack by 100 million gallons," Jack said. "I won't have that in my story because I can't confirm it with anybody, and my source won't go on the record yet."

"Jack, we'll announce this in the morning. You can put this in your story. The County Commission will hold an emergency meeting on Monday morning to talk about the spill and hear an explanation from Granger," Tracy said.

"Will the county do anything else?"

"Off the record, the commission will consider fining Granger for what they've done so far, order the company to stop discharging, and take them to court if they don't," Tracy said. "I hope you have enough for your story."

"Plenty, thanks, Steve," said Jack.

"Good. I've got to go," Tracy said as he hung up.

Jack had enough to finish his story. At 9:30 p.m., he gave it one more look, then sent it to the city desk.

He searched for Bobbie, but she had already gone home. It was too late for dinner, so he called and told her he was still at the office. He planned to stay a little longer to talk with Wiseman before heading home.

After answering a few questions, he left the paper a little after 10 p.m. Rick would call him if anything came up.

Jack drove home in silence. He thought about turning on the radio to get a weather report, but he was frustrated that he wasn't getting into his spill story more.

He thought about Brewster and hoped he would call later. Why didn't he know more about him? He didn't have a phone number or address. He should ask his detective brother, Ed, to do a background check on him. His $50,000 investment in Ed's agency covered things like that.

Brewster had gone out of his way to contact Jack, but he wanted anonymity. Still, he had already told Jack many things about Granger. He felt he was in danger because of that, but he also seemed willing to go the distance to get the truth out.

Granger earned millions by boosting mining and fertilizer production when prices on the market were high. What measures would they take to protect this revenue stream? How far would they go?

As Jack drove home, he knew he had to learn more about his new insider source and what was happening at Granger Station.

Just then, Jack spotted the neighborhood car wash up ahead. He finally had time to stop and get a quick clean. He hated the pasty white dust on his new GT.

After a 10-minute wash, Jack still wasn't happy. There was still much more to do. He didn't like publishing incomplete stories with so many unanswered questions and conflicting accounts. He had to get to the bottom of the Granger Station conspiracy.

Chapter 12:
Brother and Sister Bonds

Later Tuesday night, July 13, 1982

James Brewster had another long, frustrating day. From his point of view, the massive spill into Terra Ceia Bay had been very preventable. The destruction to the environment, the damage to the area's economy, and the death of so much sea life were unnecessary.

Before leaving work at 9 p.m., he met with Grousland, Cross, and Decker. He asked why they hadn't called for an emergency crew on Monday morning—24 hours before the spill reportedly began—when he had informed them that repairs were needed to plug the concrete fissures at the base of the east and north walls to stop the leaks.

"And why didn't you ask for a permit from the county to discharge the wastewater on Tuesday morning?" Brewster asked.

"We didn't have time. You told us the gypstack could collapse," Grousland replied.

"I also told you to get a repair crew out to fix the leak Monday morning, but you didn't do that either," said Brewster, frustrated. "Those repairs should have been made weeks ago. Then, if you did have to discharge, you could have done it at a much lower volume."

"James, calm down. It's not Pierre's fault. Corporate wants us to maintain production," Cross said.

"Just one day of intensive repairs with two crews—that's all I asked. Then you could have continued production at that rate," Brewster said. "You know how the afternoon rains have increased pond water levels."

"We asked for the equipment two days ago," said Grousland. "There was some mix-up in Bartow, but it's coming."

"What, Wednesday? You promised Steve Tracy the crew would be out this afternoon!" Brewster shouted.

He was angry. He knew Grousland was lying because earlier that morning, he had heard them admit to intentionally worsening the breached walls.

"This discharge was unnecessary!" Brewster added. "You all know it!"

"We had no choice. Based on your reports, corporate ordered me to discharge wastewater from the gypstack," Grousland said.

"My reports? I warned you weeks ago about the weak walls and rising waters. You conveniently ignored my ongoing recommendations to patch the leaks with concrete and reinforce the stack ridges with polyurethane liners," Brewster shouted, waving his hands.

Grousland went quiet.

"James, what's done is done. Let's work together now to lower the water level, fix the leaks, and get back to normal operations," Decker said.

"Will you promise me to at least double-lime the discharges?" Brewster asked.

"We are liming," Cross said.

"Not enough. My tests today showed the water was very acidic and the lime count was low," Brewster said. "I will run more tests in the morning. We need to double or triple the lime or slow the discharges."

"Let's talk in the morning. Everything will be better," Cross said.

"I'm leaving now. Call me at home if there are any more problems," said Brewster, slamming the door as he left the office.

"Pierre, what are we going to do about Brewster?" asked Cross. "He's on to us."

"Don't worry. I'm taking care of it," Grousland replied confidently.

*   *   *

As Brewster walked to his Ford pickup, he thought Grousland might lie about how the leaks had become breaches. He could also lie about when Granger would repair the walls. However, Brewster possessed an audio recording detailing how and why they did it.

Besides, any amateur detective could deduce that they used a mechanical device, such as a backhoe or a boring machine, to cut holes in the gypstack walls. The state inspector might ignore it, but Steve Tracy and the county would certainly notice it, especially after Brewster told them and Kendall.

Moreover, if needed, he had two witnesses: Dan Rumsfeld, who had seen a Granger truck at the plant earlier that morning, and Manny Hernandez, who had photographed Granger workers destroying the gypstack wall the night before. He also knew of other workers who would come forward with damning testimony.

*   *   *

When James Brewster returned home after 10 p.m., his sister, Elizabeth, was waiting for him. She had heard about the phosphate slime spill on the radio and came over.

"What have they done to Terra Ceia?" she asked, her voice sharp with worry. "It was all over the news."

James sighed heavily as he set down his bag. "Sorry I didn't call you. What did you hear?"

Elizabeth's jaw tightened. "I read Jack Kendall's story and saw all those pictures of the green slime spreading into the bay... They had radio and television reports. It made me sick."

James shook his head. "I'm sorry, Lizzy. I tried. How are you feeling?"

"I feel better today. I saw the doctor this morning, and he adjusted my medication," she said, adding angrily: "We have to do more to stop them!"

Brewster sat on the sofa, closed his eyes, and shook his head.

"James, are you all right?"

"I'm all right," he reassured her, though the exhaustion in his tone betrayed him. "I stomped my feet, yelled, and threatened them. They don't care."

"I was worried. When I didn't hear from you, I thought something might have happened. Did you go in early and get more documents?"

"Yes, I got everything, but I'm tired, and it's been a long day. I'll tell you the story in a few minutes. First, I'm starving. There's some chicken in the fridge. Can you make me a sandwich?"

"Yes. Be right back," Elizabeth said as she went into the kitchen. A minute later, she returned with the food and a glass of apple juice, setting it on the table before him.

James took a bite, his shoulders sagging with weariness. "It's worse than I expected. I arrived at 4 a.m. before anyone else, just as planned. I found two documents in Grousland's desk to prove they falsified my reports to the state."

"It's enough to convince Kendall?" she asked.

"Lizzy, I have a tape recording of them admitting everything," James replied, a slow smile creeping across his face.

"What did they say?" she asked, tone turning positive.

"They admit to ripping open the two small leaks I told you about last night," he said grimly. "The leaks are three times as big now, and the slime is pouring into Terra Ceia through four pipes."

Her hands clenched into fists. "Those bastards! Have you had enough of their lies yet? Can we do something about this crap?"

James nodded, his gaze steady. "Yes. Here are copies of my report and the recording of the stupid, criminal things Grousland, Cross, and Decker said about why they polluted the bay."

Elizabeth reached for the tape. "I want to listen."

"You can, but I need you to make copies of the report

and the tape," James replied. "I've got to call Kendall at the *Herald-Tribune*. I saw him today and promised to tell him the whole story."

Elizabeth reacted skeptically. "Well, he can write a good story, but I'm not sure it'll do any good. Newspapers are powerless against these phosphate slime companies."

"I told him that," James said, setting down his chicken sandwich. "But he seems sincere about getting to the bottom of this conspiracy."

"Oh, sure, he's sincere—but he's still completely powerless," Elizabeth muttered.

"We need his articles to alert people to what's happening. If we can get the public behind us, maybe they can demand the county and state stop the environmental damage to the bay and the surrounding neighborhood," James said.

"How bad is the spill?" she asked, her voice dropping to a whisper.

"They probably pumped out 25 million gallons," he said, leaning forward, "but their plan is 100 million. We don't have as much time as I thought."

Elizabeth inhaled sharply. "I agree, but is getting Kendall to write a story all we're going to do?"

"For now," James replied firmly. He held her gaze. "Promise me you won't do anything unless I ask."

Her lips thinned, but she nodded. "I'm ready, and I've got a plan."

James shook his head, his expression grim. "We must be careful what we do because Mr. Cooper wants to file a state and federal lawsuit against Granger for violating the Clean Water Act and falsifying compliance reports. We don't want to do anything that hurts the county's chances in court."

Elizabeth exhaled loudly. "You and I know that lawsuit has problems, not because of the facts, but because of the judge overseeing Polk County. I don't see how anything we do could cause more problems."

James glanced down at the tape, his fingers brushing its edge. "Listen to this. Grousland and his flunkies talked about bribing me, just as they had the corrupt state inspector. Grousland even threatened me again."

"Would he try to hurt you? I wouldn't like that."

"Just keep the documents safe. It's our proof of what they've done—and our best protection," James said quietly. "You knew this would get dangerous. It's the risk we agreed to take."

"You're taking all the risks, James," Elizabeth said, lowering her voice as well. "I've got the originals in a safe deposit box at my bank. I'll make copies and put these in there."

James nodded, but the weight of the day showed in his eyes. "We'll talk more after I leave Kendall a message."

As he dialed the number for the *Herald-Tribune*, Elizabeth lingered nearby, her gaze locked on the tape recorder. The phone rang and went to the automated answering machine. James left a detailed message, his voice steady but tinged with urgency.

When he hung up, he turned to Elizabeth. "Let's hope Kendall shows up."

Elizabeth pressed her lips into a thin line. "He should, with that last part about the tape. But James, you're taking a big chance. If Grousland finds out you're leaking information..."

James cut her off with a sharp glance. "If he does, you know what to do."

She nodded slowly, her resolve hardening. "I know. Just be careful."

An hour later, Jack's work phone rang again. One of the maintenance workers he spoke with earlier in the day left a voice message.

"I've lived here all my life, Mr. Kendall. I don't like what this company is doing. The night before the discharge, I saw a truck drive in with a backhoe. The Granger workers—I saw their shirts—went out to the gypstack and used the machine to dig bigger holes in the wall," the worker slowly said. "I took pictures.

"Just so you know," the man continued, "Grousland is behind everything wrong at this plant. He gets his orders from Bartow. I don't think Cross and Decker like it, but they do what they're told.

"Don't say I work at the plant if you use anything else. I can't give my name right now. Maybe we can meet this weekend. I'll develop the roll of film I took of the Granger workers with the backhoe. I can tell you more then," the worker added. "I might have broken some laws and need legal help. I can't keep quiet any longer."

Chapter 13:
Neighbors in Arms

Wednesday morning, July 14, 1982

The following morning, Jack awoke refreshed. He entered the kitchen, poured a glass of O.J., drank half, and walked outside to get the paper.

His next-day story on the Granger Station spill and investigation dominated the front page. It had a strong headline, *"Granger Phosphate Spill Poses Severe Threat to Terra Ceia Bay,"* and great aerial photos of the green phosphate slime in the bay. Despite the black-and-white photos, you could still make out the water's discoloration. It was shocking but far from complete. He needed more to nail Granger Phosphate Co.

Another story appeared on the bottom half of the front page: *"Tropical Storm Amos Builds Strength."* Jack remembered hearing about it the previous day. Amos had begun as a tropical wave that moved off the west coast of Africa near the Cape Verde Islands. Now, it was showing 40 mph winds as it went through an eyewall replacement cycle. According to the article that urged people to prepare, this could lead to rapid intensification as it passed over Haiti and approached the Bahamas later in the week. He wondered if this one might come near Sarasota.

Jack recalled his experiences with the last significant hurricane as he walked into his house. In August 1980, Hurricane Allen approached Jamaica. He was at GoldenEye in Oracabessa Bay, waiting for word from Becky. He remembered being on one of the last planes out of Montego Bay before Allen's landfall.

He shook off the memory and began to think about his busy day ahead. He wondered if Brewster had tried to contact him at the newspaper, so he dialed his work number to check for messages.

The first message was from James Brewster. He promised to tell Jack all about the spill and give evidence he could use in a story. He wanted to meet at J.R.'s Old Packinghouse at 6 p.m. that evening.

The next message was from Manny Hernandez, a maintenance supervisor. "I met you at the plant the day after the spill. I left a message before without giving my name. If Mr. Brewster goes on the record, I can confirm many things, but we have to meet first," the worker said.

Manny accused Granger of making the breaches worse by punching holes in the containment walls. He said he had photos of the men at work and offered to share more information over the weekend. "I will call you this weekend," he said.

Jack was ecstatic. Having a single inside source on a story was a significant advantage for getting to the truth in the news business. However, having two or more at different levels of responsibility was best.

As they said in the news business, the Granger Station story was developing "legs."

Jack got dressed, and a little before 8 a.m., he slid into his GT and drove to the newspaper. He parked his car near the building because he knew he'd leave soon for interviews.

Opening the front door, he saw that the large, spacious lobby was nearly empty. The security guard, Curtis Nettles, a 45-year-old former Bradenton police officer, was at his post, as was Kathy Hopkins, the middle-aged receptionist.

"Morning, Jack," said Curtis.

"Hi, what's shakin' today?" Jack asked.

"Not much. My arm's a little sore from bowling that 300 last night."

"Oh, right, how many games did it take?" Jack returned. They both laughed. It was a routine exchange between rival players in the newspaper's bowling league.

Kathy waved at Jack as he passed. As usual, she was talking with a visitor. Jack looked at the table where she sometimes put the messages for the newsroom. There was nothing for him, so he walked on.

He took the elevator to the 5th floor and went straight into the newsroom.

Rick Wiseman was in early as usual.

"Rick, do you have a few minutes? I want to talk about an idea for a Sunday story," Jack said.

"You mean about talking with the neighbors at Granger Station?" Rick asked.

Jack's expression turned puzzled. "Did I tell you about that already?"

"No, but I figured that was it unless you have another scoop going about the spill."

"Nice, you got me. I hope to have another follow-up on that tomorrow. Tonight, I'm meeting with my anonymous source, James Brewster, Granger's chief mining engineer. I should have a smoking gun we can use to expose the whole conspiracy," Jack explained.

"Can't wait. So, what about the neighbors?" Rick asked. "Should we get a photographer to go out with you?"

"If you want," Jack replied. "I don't know exactly what I'll get."

"I'll send her out now. It'll be a good learning experience for her."

"I also want to go to Captain Joe's Marina to talk with some boat captains and fishermen."

"I'll talk with Carlson to see if Erin is available for three or four hours," said Rick, who was always thinking ahead.

Jack chuckled. Rick was a man of action. If you gave him an idea of what you wanted to do for the day, he would visualize it and sometimes plan the photography, graphics, and even the headline, all in a flash.

It usually worked out, but it sometimes put too much pressure on the reporters to meet his expectations. Jack had had a few heated discussions with Rick over how to play stories based on the editor's ideas and what he had gathered to write. The disagreements mainly stemmed from Rick's unrealistic expectations over the story's size and whether he visualized it for the front page. Usually, though, after discussing it, they found common ground. However, there were times when

Rick and other editors demanded more, which meant many more phone calls to flesh out angles, assuming they were there and just hidden.

While waiting to hear from the photography editor about Erin's availability, Jack reviewed his list of contacts near Granger Station.

Then he would see Joe Cassidy, the owner and manager of Captain Joe's Marina, about the toxic spill. Jack knew fishing and tourist boat captains like Captain Joe would have colorful quotes and opinions about the spill and its impact on their livelihood. Most had seen phosphate spills before, but this one seemed worse than the others.

Suddenly, a female voice interrupted his thoughts.

"Hi, are you Jack? I'm Erin, the intern. Carson sent me over," said Erin Jovinich, a pleasant-looking, dark-haired young woman of about 21.

Jack looked up. "Yes, I am. Glad you could come along on short notice," he said. "Ready to go?"

"I am if you are," she replied, hefting the large photographer's bag over her shoulder. She followed Jack out to the parking lot.

"This is my new Mustang GT. I barely have 100 miles on it. What do you think of it?" Jack asked.

"Very sporty! Looks fast," Erin said with a smile.

"I've been wanting another 'Stang for a long time. You like the color?" Jack asked as he unlocked the passenger's side.

"Very bright," Erin replied as she got in.

"It is pretty bright. I might have it repainted dark green. I'm not sure I want to draw this much attention. This GT model is called 'The Boss.' It was designed for Edsel Ford, who insisted Ford rework the Mustang for this year."

"Interesting. Just drive carefully."

Jack walked around the car and got in. "Buckle up," he said.

Pulling his car from the *Herald-Tribune*'s parking lot, Jack headed toward Bradenton on U.S. 41 to the Granger Station neighborhood.

"Carson said we were going to talk with some people who live near the Granger phosphate plant?" Erin asked.

"That's right. I'm not sure what they'll say, but I've met a few at commission meetings, and they have had many complaints about spills and industrial accidents over the years," Jack replied. "Last year, I wrote a story about a 33,000-gallon sulfuric acid leak from a holding tank at the fertilizer plant that forced about 100 people to evacuate because of the toxic gas that drifted around the plant. Some nearby businesses also were in danger, and employees had to leave for the day."

"That's awful! Do you think we'll talk with some of these people?"

"We might. I have a few names on my list to contact. I have someone in mind we'll start with first."

"Should I take pictures of everyone you interview?"

"Yes. Get some headshots and close-ups of people who talk, and make sure you get their names and ages. I always ask, so keep track of them in your notebook. You know the drill, right? Take any photo you think might be good. I might ask you to take this or that picture, but I mostly want you to blend into the scene. You don't need to talk," Jack explained.

"Where are we going first?" she asked.

"I want to start with Mrs. Chiquita Barkley," Jack said. "We may just have to knock on doors. It might take some time."

* * *

When Jack and Erin arrived at the neighborhood at about 9:45 a.m., he drove to the closest house to the plant, about a quarter mile away. On the third knock, an older woman, about 70, answered the door.

"Hello, Mrs. Barkley. Remember me? Jack Kendall with the *Herald-Tribune*?"

"Yes, I do," she said, her smile quick but strained, as if she'd been waiting for him.

"I'm here to talk with you about yesterday's spill at the Granger phosphate plant," Jack said. "This is Erin, my photographer."

"You brought a photographer?" Mrs. Barkley said, eyes widening. "Good. People need to *see* this. Come in. Do you mind if I call a few neighbors?"

"No, ma'am. I'd appreciate it," Jack said, already sensing the weight of what was coming.

Mrs. Barkley ushered them inside. "Give me a minute," she said, flipping open her address book. "These people have been living with this fear for years. They deserve to be heard."

Jack nodded. He'd learned long ago that homeowners told the clearest stories—because they lived with the consequences.

"Coffee?" Mrs. Barkley called from the kitchen.

"That would be great," Jack said, smiling. He'd picked the right house. He knew homeowners were sometimes the best sources of information and often the best storytellers about their neighborhood.

He recalled several years before when he wrote a story about runway expansion plans for the Sarasota-Bradenton Airport. He met at a house with several neighbors, and three hours later, he had talked with more than a dozen upset people.

Mrs. Barkley returned with mugs and sat across from him.

Her hands trembled slightly as she set them down.

"Before anyone else gets here," she said, "you need to understand what we lost. I've lived here thirty years—before the mine, before the permits. This was a peaceful place. We raised children here. We trusted the land."

Her voice hardened. "We begged the County Commission not to approve that plant. We told them people lived here—kids, seniors, families who couldn't just pack up and leave. They nodded, thanked us, and voted yes anyway. Someone made money, and we paid the price."

She gestured toward the closed windows. "Now the air burns your nose. Some days it smells like chemicals, like fertilizer and rot mixed. We get these white dust storms—phosphate dust—from the plant and the gypsum pond."

"That dust settles everywhere," she said. "On our cars. On our furniture. In our lungs. I stopped hanging laundry outside years ago. I don't open windows anymore. I'm afraid of what I'm breathing."

Just then, there was a knock on the door. Mrs. Barkley excused herself and returned with six neighbors, ranging from a teenage boy to an elderly man with a cane, all wanting to talk with Jack.

"Mr. Kendall," she said, "these are the people living with Granger Station."

Jack scanned the group as they sat down in the living room. They looked on edge, worried. He wondered how they could stand to live so close to the fertilizer plant. He could smell chemicals in the air. Jack thanked them for coming and reminded them they were on the record.

"I spoke with you last year about the acid spill," said Jeremiah Jones, his voice low but steady. "I've evacuated three times. Three. Each time wondering if I'd come back to a house—or a toxic mess."

"I've got five dogs," added the retired county school bus driver. "They're family. You can't just grab them and run when the sirens go off."

"What about the current spill?" Jack asked. "Are you worried the gypstack could fail?"

Jones didn't hesitate. "Of course I am. That stack fails, and this neighborhood is done. Granger knows it. They've known it. They make millions and gamble with our lives." His voice and demeanor darkened.

"They should've shut it down already. Not tomorrow. Not after a hearing. *Yesterday.*"

Ben Gervin, a Tropicana retiree, was the next to speak. He stood up, anger breaking through his calm. "I've lived next to that pile of poison for years. It leaked before. They patched it just enough to keep operating. Now it's leaking again."

Gervin walked to the front plate-glass window and pointed toward the plant, where a white plume of smoke could be seen.

"They're dumping poison into the bay so they can keep producing fertilizer. We're expendable. That's the message."

Tanya Prior, an elementary school teacher in Palmetto, spoke next, her voice shaking. "We're right on the evacuation line. Half a mile. One decision away from losing everything."

A tear ran down her cheek. "What happens when that wastewater seeps into my yard?" she asked. "My well? My soil? Am I supposed to wait years to find out if I'm sick? For the first time in my life, I made out a will."

She described her visit to Granger's offices. "Grousland talked to me like I was stupid. Like, I didn't deserve answers. Like my life was an inconvenience." She paused, letting that sink in.

"I left shaking. Not just angry—scared."

Jones said he also once talked with Grousland. "As Tanya said, he's a real jerk. He didn't want to explain the environmental dangers of their operations or what we should do if something happened. It's like we're invisible. There are so many new houses and people here. They look right past us. No consideration at all."

"Have any of you spoken with James Brewster? He's Granger's chief mining engineer," Jack said.

"Yes, I have," replied Prior. "I went out there a second time and talked with James. He was extremely polite and nice. I sensed he was embarrassed by how dirty the plant was. But he explained how he's trying to shore up the walls and keep the facility safe."

"What about the plant itself?" Jack asked. "Does anybody have any thoughts about what goes on there?"

Gervin said he sometimes sneaks onto the Granger property to look at the water in the holding ponds. "I haven't seen any fish in the ponds in years. I used to see little fish swimming around the big gypstack and even in the smaller holding ponds," he explained. "Now, they're dumping that toxic water into the bay?"

Jack looked over to Tim, who had been quiet. "What would you like to tell us, Tim?"

The boy swallowed hard before speaking. "Mr. Gervin took me out a couple of times. The water in the pond was brown. It smelled like something died. There were no fish. Nothing."

He paused. "We climbed the gypstack once. It's like a mountain. Mr. Gervin said if it breaks, everything rushes downhill—toward our homes."

When Tim finished, the room was silent.

Jack stood. "You've all helped more than you know," he said. "People need to understand what's at stake here."

As he handed out cards, Mrs. Barkley asked, "When will the story run?"

"It's scheduled as a Sunday feature story with Erin's pictures from today and Alex Mahoney's pictures of Granger Station and the sludge spill in the bay from yesterday," Jack said.

He and Erin thanked Mrs. Barkley and the others again, then headed out.

"Those were nice people," Erin said as they walked to the GT. "Do things go as smoothly as that for you all the time?"

"I wish. Rarely," Jack said with a laugh. "But you never can tell. People sometimes surprise you. Depends on the story."

Erin adjusted her shoulder case. "One thing I sensed is how terrified they are. I hope I caught that on film."

Jack nodded. "I hope so too. And they have every reason to be afraid. This isn't theory or politics or talking points. This is what happens when warnings are ignored—and ordinary people are left living beneath the consequences."

Chapter 14:
Captains React

Early Afternoon Wednesday, July 14, 1982

Jack raced down the road in his GT to Captain Joe's. He loved the acceleration of his new car, but he also wanted to finish the interviews and return to the newspaper to check if James Brewster had called.

It wasn't long before he saw the wind-battered sign and pulled into the parking lot surrounded by a chain link fence.

He and Erin walked into Joe Cassidy's office. "Hi, Joe, Jack Kendall from the *Herald-Tribune*. How've you been?"

"Why, it's Jack Kendall! I know why you're here. Tell me this: why do I only see you nowadays when there's a disaster?" asked Cassidy, who'd opened his marina in the early 1950s.

"Captain Joe, I'm always amazed you remember me from when I came here in high school to get gas for our ski boat," Jack replied.

"You always came with your girlfriend. I remember her father, George White. He owned a boat and kept it in a slip here. George was a friend. Do you know he passed away a year ago?" Cassidy said.

"No, I didn't," Jack said. "I lost touch with Joni 10 years ago, after high school."

"Before we get to why you're here, who is this nice young lady you have with you?" Cassidy asked.

"Sorry, Joe, bad manners. This is my photographer, Erin. She's one of our summer interns, so be easy on her," Jack teased.

"No problem. Hello, Erin. I'm glad to meet you," said Joe as Erin nodded and started taking pictures. "I take it you want to talk about Granger Station."

"You got it. It's the third day, and phosphate sludge continues to pour out," Jack confirmed. "I'd like to talk with you about it, and anybody else I can find on the docks."

"I'll share my thoughts, but first, let me check if any captains are moored. They would typically be out on a summer morning, but this spill has disrupted their plans," Cassidy explained.

"I know. I am running a little late today. I've been talking with the Granger Station neighbors."

Cassidy nodded and walked behind the cashier's counter, grabbing the microphone connected to the loudspeakers on the docks. "Attention, captains! Jack Kendall is here from the *Herald-Tribune*. He wants to interview any captain who is willing to talk about the Granger spill. He will be here for about an hour," Cassidy announced. "Over and out."

Cassidy hung up the microphone and looked at Jack. "Good enough? Don't ever say I don't take care of you," he joked.

"Sure," said Jack, laughing. He couldn't believe the luck

he'd had today. Usually, it took a lot of pleading—just short of begging—to get people to do interviews. Today, he had Joe Cassidy at the docks and Mrs. Barkley in the neighborhood to promote his interviews.

"Let me tell you what I think," Cassidy said. "When word got out that Granger was dumping, some of the captains started to plan to work out of other marinas in the area, even going down to Marina Jack in Sarasota. They had clients lined up this week and wanted alternative plans. Some clients wanted to take a ride out to see the spill."

"How many do you think left?" Jack asked.

"I would say about ten boats," Cassidy replied. "I went out with Captain Mike later that morning just to scope out the flow of the sludge. Do you want to see some pictures?"

"Sure, what do you have?"

Captain Joe reached into an envelope and pulled out a dozen photographs. "Look at this green and white crap. The tide was going out, and the sludge spread all over for 1,000 yards from the discharge pipe in just four hours."

"This is amazing. The green slime almost looks like it's glowing. That's a good picture."

"Yeah, that's a photo I took of two brothers fishing. You can see the clear blue water on one side of their Whaler and the white foam and green slime on the other."

"Can I keep this copy?" Jack asked.

"Sure. Do I get credit if you use it?" Cassidy countered.

"Of course. Do you have the names of the brothers and any other information?"

"Yes, I know Steve and Nick Chootas. I will write down their names, some other information, and their phone number, which I think I have."

Just then, several men entered the marina office.

"Is this Jack Kendall from the *Herald-Tribune*?" one man wearing a captain's hat asked in a deep voice. "I'm Captain Jaspar. What do you want to know?"

"What did you see out in the bay by the Granger Station spill?" Jack asked.

"It's disgusting! Thick greenish-yellow sludge, all pushing out hundreds of yards every day," said Jaspar, standing over 6 feet tall and weighing at least 300 pounds. "We are going to lose a lot of sealife because of those carpetbaggers!"

"Captain Jaspar. How do you know?" Jack asked.

"It's common sense, son. When you dump that amount of phosphorus and nitrogen in the water, you'll lose seagrass and sponge beds, then fish, clams, and dolphins," said Jaspar, who owned three fishing boats and a tour boat. "It's inevitable. These things *will* happen, just as sure as I'm standing here."

"How does this discharge compare with some of the others you've seen over the years?" Jack asked.

The other two men shook their heads and looked to Jaspar.

"This one's horrible, mostly because of the volume. We'll have algae blooms that will suffocate fish and other creatures for miles," Jaspar said.

"There is something else," he said, pausing. "The last time we had something close to this bad, we had some bizarre organisms in the water. It turned the water red. I saw more dead, floating fish and two dying manatees. It was sad, and there was an awful smell in the air that my customers complained burned their eyes. I haven't seen that yet, but I'm sure it's coming."

Captain Justin Less, a tour boat guide, walked in just as Jaspar finished. "I know what the big guy's talking about. I talked with a marine biologist the other day. He told me he believes there is a definite connection between that red tide and phosphate spewing into the bay."

"I just don't know how much more these bays can take. It's more than Granger; it's also Piney Point. Both regularly dump sludge into the water. They have state permission. Why, I have no idea," Jaspar grumbled. "They should close those cursed phosphate plants."

Jack asked if the phosphate mines were cutting into the fishing and sightseeing business.

"I took a full boat of tourists to the area where the wastewater was being dumped. They wanted to see the pollution, but some complained about the smell, and two got sick," Less said.

"Overall, sports fishing and commercial fishing will be hurt for weeks, if not longer," Jaspar said. "You can tell it's not healthy for sea life. The water normally is clear this time of year, but now it's greenish yellow."

"There are no birds, hardly any mullet. You can tell the fish are sensing it and moving away from it if they can," Less added.

Erin snapped pictures of all the captains as they talked.

"Thank you all for telling me about what you've seen out there," said Jack.

"Don't be a stranger! Stop by anytime," Cassidy said.

"Thanks. Hope things get better out there soon," Jack said, waving goodbye.

Chapter 15:
'Smoking Gun'

Wednesday evening, July 14, 1982

At J.R.'s Old Packinghouse, a small neighborhood café in northeast Sarasota near Cattlemen Road, Jack waited at a table toward the back for James Brewster.

Ten minutes later, James strolled in and sat across from Jack, who had ordered two beers. Jack estimated that James was about 5 feet 8 and 150 pounds, with short, dark brown hair. He was dressed casually in a light blue shirt and blue jeans.

"Glad you could make it. Do you want a cold one? This one might be warm," Jack said.

"Thanks, this is fine," said Brewster, taking a small sip. "I can't stay long. I have some documents and a tape recording I made of the plant's top three executives discussing what happened. You'll recognize their voices. I need assurances that my name won't be used in any story."

"You are on background until you tell me otherwise," Jack said as he turned on his tape recorder. "I will refer to you as a knowledgeable source; your name will not be used."

"All right, but you can't say I work at the plant. I'm going to trust you because this is so important. Mr. Kendall, it's life or death, believe me," Brewster insisted.

"It would be best if you go on the record, but I want you to be comfortable telling your story," Jack said.

"I can't be exposed right now. I've got more to dig up before they find out about me."

"Are you afraid they'll fire you?"

Brewster shook his head solemnly, frustration etched on his face. "This isn't just about me; it's about the families who live in the shadow of the plant, the delicate environment that surrounds us, the vibrant sealife that thrives in the bay's sparkling waters, and the looming uncertainties that future generations will inherit. We must consider the potential dangers created by Granger's actions today and the impact they will have on those who come after us."

Jack eyed him with wonder. He clearly wasn't blowing the whistle for selfish reasons. "This is important to you. I get it. I want to help get your story out there."

Brewster nodded. "You do? Your story this morning was pretty weak."

"I'm trying, believe me," said Jack. "I've got to have two corroborating sources for everything you tell me as an anonymous source. Steve Tracy, the county phosphate coordinator, disputes some of what Grousland says, but he doesn't know everything you do about the inner workings at Granger."

"The corruption starts with Grousland and Granger Station,

goes to Bartow at Granger Phosphate, and to Tallahassee with at least one inspector at the DEP," Brewster explained.

"You can prove that?"

"I have evidence that the state inspector assigned to Granger, Angus Miniver, has been bribed by Granger to look the other way. He's covering for them."

"Bribery is a pretty big charge. I'll need direct evidence of that to report it."

"I have Grousland, Cross, and Decker admitting on tape that they bribed state inspector Miniver. It's the smoking gun I've been hoping to get on them. I know where there's more evidence of bribes and corruption. It'll take a few more days to get it."

"I'd like to hear more about the tape," Jack said.

"I can provide you with a copy of the recording. This is the crucial evidence. It shows that Granger intentionally dumped the wastewater. Grousland, Cross, and Decker laid out their plan," Brewster explained.

"What exactly is their plan?"

"They admitted to intentionally cutting the leak in the east wall and creating a breach in the north wall," Brewster replied. "Grousland even dared to have Granger's workers use a backhoe, which we typically use to dig underground pipelines. I have a picture where the breaches appear to be cut into rather than pushed out naturally."

"They used a backhoe to destroy the containment walls?" Jack asked, incredulous.

"It's all on the tape. The recording is somewhat difficult to hear because I was in another room, but you can make out their conversation," Brewster said.

"Does anybody else know this?" Jack asked.

"You can get further confirmation about the backhoe from the maintenance workers and my field technician. They witnessed the incident and took pictures. One of them told me that he contacted you," Brewster added. "They're ready to talk."

"I got one message," Jack said. "Who's your field technician?"

"Dan Rumsfeld. Let him contact you, and don't use his name. I don't want him to get hurt."

"I understand. Let's get back to the tape. Start from the beginning. Tell me how you got the tape recording."

"Okay, here's the story. Tuesday morning, before dawn, the day after the spill started, I was in another room when I recorded the plant's top three executives proudly talking about the illegal discharges.

"The first voice is Grousland, then Herbert Cross, and then Louis Decker. You can make a transcript using their voices. Each one is distinctive.

"Grousland thanks Cross and Decker for bringing in Granger workers late Monday from Bartow to cut out and drill holes in the stack so they can ramp up fertilizer production and make more money.

"He describes digging out holes on the east and north containment walls," Brewster said. "He said the leaks were much worse than when I reported it to him Monday morning."

"Grousland said that?" Jack asked incredulously. "That's the smoking gun. You did it, James."

"It's all there. You can listen for yourself and write about it," Brewster said.

"Sure. When I came out to see the spill Monday morning, I asked Grousland when the pumping started. He said he ordered it first thing Tuesday morning after he said he saw how bad the leaks were."

"That's a lie, of course, and we can prove it."

"With the tape?"

"Yes, the tape and the Granger workers from Bartow. Under the direction of Grousland, they intentionally destroyed the walls to make the leaks much worse."

"When did you first see the discharges being pumped out?" Jack asked.

"When I arrived before dawn on Tuesday, I heard them running at high speed," Brewster said. "I went into the office trailer to look for documents. Grousland, Cross, and Decker came in. I heard them talking and hid in the back room. That's when I taped their conspiracy."

Brewster paused and looked at Jack. "Mr. Kendall, everything I've told you here...the deal is the same with the tape and the documents," Brewster said. "No mentioning my name. Not even that you got it from a Granger employee."

Jack nodded. "Of course, I'll be discreet and protect your identity," he promised. "Do you think they're still watching you?"

Brewster glanced around. "They don't trust me because I'm the highest-ranking employee not on the company payola account. After these stories come out, and you refer to a tape recording, I know they'll blame me."

"Are you afraid of what might happen?" Jack asked.

"Not afraid, but I've decided to expose what they're doing, no matter the cost," Brewster said with a firm expression.

"You should talk with a lawyer about going on the record as a whistleblower. I know it would mean the end of your job at Granger, but this tape is all you need to shut them down," advised Jack. "Telling your story publicly would be the surest way to stop this company. I can write articles about what you have given me, and I'm sure the national wire services will pick them up."

"I thought about that, but there is more to be done. I can't explain everything to you now; trust that I need another week to do everything," Brewster said. "Publishing this story will stop the pollution and give me time to finish the job I need to do.

"Now, I'll tell you something you can't print. It's totally off the record. No knowledgeable sources."

"You got it. Go ahead," Jack said.

"You have the tape recording with top executives at Granger conspiring to sabotage the gypstack walls, dump toxic wastewater into Terra Ceia, lower the water levels in the stack, and resume max production," Brewster said.

"Yes," Jack said.

"Once you write about the recording, give the police a copy," Brewster said. "The police will investigate and hopefully charge Granger and its executives with crimes. That will force Granger to stop discharges into the bay."

"I'll have to talk with my editor about that, but if you authorize its release, I probably can do it," Jack said. "What else is on the tape?"

"Grousland says on the tape he wants to discharge another 75 million gallons of wastewater and sludge in the next few days. He admits Granger authorized that and is willing to pay any fine the county or state imposes," Brewster said. "That is proof right there of corporate fraud.

"Mr. Kendall, you have to understand that even though they have already discharged 25 million gallons, there are more than 300 million gallons in those four ponds and the stack.

"They'll keep discharging even if they have to pay more fines. They don't care. They want more room in the gypstack to keep mining after the leaks are fixed and while the fertilizer prices are as high as they are. They're making a ton of money, so these measly fines are nothing.

"Mr. Kendall, I want to point out something else for your story. I have not seen any critical repair orders for the recommendations I submitted to them weeks ago," Brewster said.

"I asked Grousland if he was saving money by not doing routine maintenance, and he denied it and told me they do regular repairs," Jack replied.

"All they do is inexpensive repairs, like replacing faulty discharge valves and improving electrical lines. They did some fills last year on the leaking section of a bulging containment wall."

"I wrote that story. The leak that caused an evacuation of residents?"

"They were forced to fix the wall to stop that leak," Brewster said. "They do what they are forced to and hardly anything more."

"Tracy complains about that all the time. He said the County Commission is preparing to do something early next week to hold them accountable," Jack said.

"Good. I hope the commission forces Granger to make repairs. They haven't done much, even though Granger has violated state laws and the county operating permit."

"This spill will change that."

"I can give them a list of violations and repairs that need to be made if they ask for it," Brewster said. "But they need to ensure Granger strengthens and stabilizes the walls for the coming rainstorms we will get in the next two months. That is most important."

"So, what's next?" Jack asked.

"Now that they've been caught discharging more than two million per day without a permit, they will ask the state for permission to discharge 10 million gallons daily to take the pressure off the containment pond walls."

"Ten million? That's a story for me."

"I'm sure that will take time to approve, so they'll discharge higher amounts into the bay daily, up to the 100 million gallons I mentioned earlier," Brewster said. "They want to lower water levels to fix the breaches, process more ore, and make room in the stack for more rain."

"You told me Granger is falsifying water quality reports to the state. How are they doing that?" Jack asked.

"I'm glad you asked. The state doesn't appear interested in doing anything about the fraud and mismanagement at the plant."

"Now, that's an understatement. Tracy complains all the time about it."

"I write monthly water quality and wall maintenance reports and give them to Grousland. They regularly show violations grossly exceeding state and federal standards," Brewster explained. "Last month, when I found out he turned in fudged reports to the state, I wrote George Garvey, the DEP's regional phosphate coordinator, and told him about it. I included my accurate reports. I haven't heard back."

"I know Garvey. He oversees the state inspectors. I'll ask him about the letter," Jack said. "Is it normal for the state or county to require monthly reports? I am not sure Beker or Piney Point are required to do that."

"It was required for Pebble when it opened in 1965 as an operating permit condition," Brewster said. "It passed on to Granger. They must file monthly reports on the maintenance of the containment wall and the quality of wastewater discharge. Not many phosphate plants or mines have such strict requirements. It was the one good thing Manatee County required when they allowed this fertilizer plant so close to the population and Terra Ceia."

"But what's the use if they're falsifying the data?" asked Jack, shaking his head. "James, can you give me an example of what's in the fake report Granger is giving the state?"

"I have a copy of several in my folder for you. For example, under a new state groundwater rule, Granger must obtain a new discharge permit for our gypstack and holding ponds," Brewster said.

"I completed the tests last month for the permit," he continued. "The results were way above EPA's permitted levels, double the level allowed at the gypstack, and five times higher in the holding ponds. I completed the application with the correct numbers. I told Grousland we were well above the allowed limits for every pollution measure in the book. He told me not to worry about it."

"What do you mean?" Jack asked.

"In the application, Grousland altered the test results I signed to match what Miniver reported."

"Miniver backed Granger's false statement? Wow. Any other examples?"

"I have another in the folder that shows Granger has been violating the state's surface-water discharge permit," Brewster said. "Our permit requires us to treat the wastewater effluent with lime before it is discharged. Only a tiny amount of lime is used, which is insufficient to neutralize the toxic acidity harmful to fish and crustaceans."

"That sounds familiar," Jack said. "I reported a few months ago that Granger was cited for having toxic discharge effluent that killed crabs and small fish. Grousland said the test was wrong and disputed where the state sampled the effluent."

"I told my managers they were wrong to dispute that. They couldn't care less about the truth. You've talked with Grousland; you know how he never answers questions with facts."

"I see. Grousland may stonewall a reporter, but how can he get away with saying and doing those things to the state with all its experts?"

"It's easy when you bribe the lead inspector, Miniver. I'm unsure if Miniver's bosses know what Granger is doing or if they're looking the other way," Brewster said. "Are they conspiring with Grousland and Miniver or not? I'm not sure which. I hope to find documents soon to prove this conspiracy goes all the way to the corporate office in Bartow and possibly to the DEP in Tallahassee."

"Hmm, I may need to get Tom Justice, our state government and political reporter, on this story as well. Tom knows everyone in Tallahassee," Jack said.

"Either way, this plant is a pollution machine, and it will worsen," Brewster added disgustingly.

"What do you mean by worsen? How could it get worse?" Jack asked.

"We're talking about a radioactive, phosphorus, and nitrogen-rich spill into the bay, right?" Brewster said. "That's only one of several ticking time bombs."

"What could be worse than that?" Jack asked.

"Granger is a 75-acre gypstack, which is small compared with some newer slime pits twice that size," Brewster explained. "What they all have in common is they sit less than 100 feet above the Florida aquifer system, the multi-layer underground drinking water supply for nearly 10 million people in Florida, right?"

"Go on."

"What if I were to tell you that a sinkhole opening up under the stack could drain every drop of the toxic wastewater and sludge directly into the aquifer?"

Jack froze. The pen in his hand stopped moving, hovering above the notebook as if the words had suddenly lost their meaning. His jaw tightened, and he leaned back slightly in his chair, eyes fixed on Brewster, trying to recalibrate what he'd just heard.

"The whole thing? Sludge, slime, toxic metals, radioactive wastewater? Sucked into the aquifer? That could happen?" Jack asked, his voice higher now, stripped of its earlier certainty.

"Of course, and every city, housing development, farm, and business that gets its potable water from the aquifer is screwed," Brewster said. "Now, it's not just dead fish; it's contaminated drinking water, and medical problems for people like no one has ever seen."

Brewster's warning wasn't far-fetched. Jack recalled reading a recent federal study that showed that Granger's gypstack was slowly leaking gypsum water into the county's surficial aquifer, a porous layer of earth and rock stretching from the surface to about 60 feet underground.

"In my reports, I write about tests we conduct in the monitor wells surrounding the plant," Brewster continued. "Guess what? It showed increasing levels of phosphorus and nitrogen. The groundwater around the plant also contains carcinogens, heavy metals, and radioactive elements that spread in all directions from the gypstack."

"Didn't state law from a few years ago require Granger to build seepage collection ditches around the perimeter of the stack to minimize the spread of acidic water drifting away from the ponds?" Jack asked.

"Yes. We built three holding ponds near the gypstack," Brewster replied. "They collect surface seepage, but my tests show the ponds have much higher concentrations of all pollutants, similar to what we find in the test wells. We know the toxic wastewater is leaching out, even without a sinkhole."

"I can ask Steve Tracy about all this—the falsified reports, the leaching into the aquifer, everything," Jack thought out loud. "Since the county hired Tracy, he's also been working overtime to monitor all the phosphate mining in the county. They're busy with the Beker discharges and the Estech mine proposal."

"I know lots of things are happening at once. Manatee County is on the verge of a phosphate meltdown, and it doesn't even realize it," Brewster said.

"You should talk with Tracy. He's a good guy who cares about the environment."

"I left a message with him on Tuesday morning about the spill. I can give him my original reports."

"You should meet with him in person," Jack said. "I'm sure his samples are similar to yours. He's always complaining about how Granger's reports are wrong."

"Grousland won't let me talk with Tracy," Brewster said.

"Tracy has always been honest with me. He's an old-school

environmental engineer hired by county commissioners to be a bulldog with the phosphate industry. He's skeptical and wants to get to the truth."

"Do you know this county commissioner, Fred Fance? He seems interested in getting to the truth as well."

"Yes, Fance is a good commissioner, and a source of mine. He wants to get to the bottom of why Granger has so many problems."

"I might want to talk with him at some point," Brewster said. "Now, I've got to go. I've spent a lot of time with you. I hope you've got what you need."

"James, thanks a lot. If you get those other documents, let me know. Just be patient. I need to confirm some of what you gave me," Jack said.

"I've laid it out for you. Don't let me down. You have to act fast. The pollution is killing the bay," Brewster said sternly.

"I'll do my best," Jack promised.

Brewster nodded and walked out of the bar quickly. Watching him leave, Jack noticed Brewster had left a thick folder on the chair next to where he was sitting.

He turned around and motioned for Bobbie, who had been sitting at a nearby table for nearly an hour, to come over. She smiled, stood up, and slowly crossed the room to join him.

"Can you at least buy me a cold one?" said Bobbie with a mischievous smile, tapping the beer Brewster hadn't touched.

"If you want. Could you overhear us?" Jack asked.

"Not much. You were pretty quiet."

"That's good. Did you notice anybody paying us attention?"

"No, everybody was fairly engaged. Oh, I did have one guy try to pick me up. I was polite, but I think anyone with similar intentions was also put off," Bobbie said with a laugh.

"Okay, you kept your cover anyway," Jack replied with a similar laugh. "Let's drink our beers and then go home."

"Sounds good to me," Bobbie said with a wink.

Chapter 16

Digging into a Coverup

Thursday, July 15, 1982

Jack was at his desk early the next day with the tape recording from the interview with James Brewster. He also had confidential documents and a recording of the Granger executives discussing the wastewater spill. So far, Jack had gathered evidence of a conspiracy to illegally and fraudulently dump toxic wastewater into Terra Ceia Bay to avoid a temporary plant shutdown for costly repairs. This was a violation of the state's surface water regulations and the U.S. Clean Water Act. And then there was the corporate corruption, including bribes to the plant's state inspector, and deliberate destruction of containment walls. All the angles would be big scoops, contributing to a blockbuster report.

He put the tape into his cassette player, plugged in his headphones, and listened as the managers discussed bribes, sabotage, intentional pollution, and greed. It was precisely as Brewster described it: the Granger managers coldly admitted their complicity and guilt.

Then Jack chuckled at the memory of his newsroom joke—that all he ever wanted was a solid story and a few mermaids to make it irresistible. With the recording of the Granger managers calmly plotting the spill, he realized he finally had them: the kind of undeniable, mythical proof every reporter dreams of, turning a strong story into an unforgettable one—with mermaids.

After listening to the 12-minute tape, Jack asked one of the newspaper's summer interns to transcribe it and his 45-minute interview with Brewster.

While reviewing the documents Brewster gave him, Jack noticed a handwritten note: "I have more revealing documents about the corruption at Granger. They are in safe hands."

Jack wondered what Brewster meant by "safe hands." It sounded as if he was collaborating with someone.

Brewster's documents included many monthly reports of water quality inside the gypstack, the three adjacent holding ponds, the adjoining ditches and pipes, and the effluent discharged into Terra Ceia Bay at different points. The comprehensive reports included data from both this year and last. The findings indicated deteriorating conditions, but Jack needed an expert to analyze them and confirm whether Granger's wastewater quality violated state and federal water quality regulations.

Another set of reports evaluated the structural strength of the earthen walls. Jack observed that the data showed the walls steadily weakening, but he still needed to run them past an expert.

Finally, air quality measurements taken at varying distances from the stack and holding ponds, including midway and beyond the surrounding neighborhood, revealed worsening conditions.

There was another report labeled confidential analysis. This sounded promising.

While the three previous reports contained raw data, this one was a narrative that explained what it all meant.

Brewster had compared state and federal standards with the trends in Granger's stack and the holding ponds' surface and discharge water quality, the structural strength of the containment walls, and the air quality.

He listed vital data in a pullout chart with straight-line trends and bar graphs. This was incredibly revealing and potentially useful in Jack's stories.

According to Brewster's report, the surface water standards for wastewater discharged into the bay exceeded the state's standards and were more than double the EPA's allowable limit.

Jack quickly reviewed all the charts. The trend lines steadily increased for almost all measurements: gypsum stack, holding ponds, bay discharge points, and air quality.

The only measurement that decreased was the structural strength of the containment walls, which made sense given the two breaches.

It was shocking to observe declining surface water quality across all sampling locations. The reports indicated that Granger Station was deteriorating under the company's ownership. If the walls collapsed, the highly contaminated effluent could cause catastrophic damage as it surged through the neighborhood and into Terra Ceia.

Jack now needed interviews to clarify the reasons for these actions—aimed at increasing profitability—and the methods behind them, which stemmed from insufficient investment in maintenance and from continuous mining and fertilizer production.

After reviewing his clips and the reports and jotting down a rough story outline, Jack saw it was 9 a.m. and decided to try Tracy at his office.

"Steve, good morning. I'm working on a follow-up story on the Granger spill. I need copies of the county's quality and safety reports on Granger. Can I pick them up this morning?" Jack said.

"I have several reports going back a couple of years. I'm still investigating the current spill," Tracy replied.

"That's good. I'll stop by in about an hour. Can you have the copies made for me?"

"Sure, you just have to fill out a few forms. I'll have my secretary prepare everything for you," Tracy said. "What are you working on?"

"I'll talk with you more about this later. However, I have information from my anonymous source inside Granger that the company has filed falsified reports to the state. That could be why your data is so different from what the state has and why the state hasn't taken any action," Jack explained.

"That's interesting."

"Can you comment on this once I sort it all out?"

"I'm not sure. We're working on a presentation for Monday to the County Commission. Let's talk later, okay?"

"Yep. What is the latest on the current spill?"

"As I expected, Granger's lawyers asked the state's

permission to release up to 10 million gallons per day to take pressure off the walls," Tracy said. "The commission is going to meet next week to discuss this request. I will recommend up to five million gallons, but only if Granger commits to spending money to strengthen the walls and use sufficient lime, as required by law, in the discharges. I've hired a local engineering firm to evaluate the walls, but Granger is objecting. We probably need a commission vote to mandate it."

"What about the discharge? Did you find anything illegal or improper?" Jack asked.

"Still investigating."

"How much was discharged?"

"The first day, we estimated about 22 million gallons. The second day, another 10 million gallons, and the third day, eight million gallons."

"Wow, that's 34 million gallons above their permit over three days. Are they planning to dump more today?"

"Yes, as far as I know. I'm headed out there again pretty soon."

"What about environmental damage to the bay?" Jack asked. "Any general estimates?"

"We're already seeing some fish kill. The cumulative damage will be tremendous because of the volume discharged, the high toxicity of the wastewater, and the accompanying radioactivity," Tracy said. "It's way more than the bay can absorb. But this is just a preliminary assessment; it will take a few more weeks to get the final results. We're still testing, but the amount of dead fish and sea life will be significant."

"What about fines?"

"So far, $3,000. According to the permit, the daily rate for exceeding discharge limits is only $1,000. The commission must vote on the amount that exceeds federal and state pollution guidelines. It's just a drop in the bucket for a company like Granger."

"Okay. Thanks for the update. After reviewing your reports and analyzing my documents, I'll need to talk with you later. Will you be around?" Jack asked.

"Sure, just give me a call," said Tracy as he hung up.

Setting down the phone, Jack looked over to Rick Wiseman's desk. He spotted his editor and walked over to update him on his story.

"Morning, Rick," Jack said. "Did you get a chance to read my reaction story about what the neighbors and boat captains think about the Granger spill?"

"I read it first thing. I liked it," Rick replied. "I slotted it for Sunday on the front page, unless something else comes up. Erin did well with the photos, documenting with cutlines, and matching the names. We also have pictures of the bay from Alex and some of your captains. A lot of material to choose from."

"Great, I worked it up pretty fast because I wanted to get started on my big story for tomorrow."

"What's that?"

"I've got a good investigative story on corruption at Granger Station," Jack said. "It will only take a few minutes to explain because I'm in the middle of interviews."

"Sure, what do you have?"

"I've got an inside source who, while asking for anonymity, has given me internal documents and a tape recording of top executives talking about how the wastewater discharge two days ago was a planned event intended to cover up lack of maintenance on the gypsum stack wall and a desire to keep processing ore at maximum production."

"You know this source?"

"I've met him. He tells me the containment walls are on the verge of collapsing. He gave me an internal company report that had been withheld from the state, which supported that claim. He told me a collapse would release hundreds of millions of gallons of untreated, acidic wastewater into the Terra Ceia Bay."

"You have a name?" Wiseman asked.

"Yes, of course. I suppose you want it?" Jack asked, furrowing his brow.

"Just between us," the editor replied.

"James Brewster is Granger's chief engineer—a pretty sharp young man who is frustrated with Granger."

"How so?"

"He says—and the reports back it up—that Granger has been filing false monthly reports to the state Department of Environmental Protection about the water and air quality and the condition of the containment walls."

"I see. Who else have you talked with about this?" Wiseman asked.

"So far, Steve Tracy at the county. I'm headed over there now to get all their reports on Granger," Jack said. "Tracy told me he's disputed the company's reports for months because they don't match what he sees.

"Tracy had asked the state about the discrepancies, but hadn't gotten far. He seems happy I found out about this, and he may bring it up with the commissioners at the meeting next week," Jack said.

"What else have you got?" Wiseman asked.

"I've got internal Granger company reports that show the

water and air quality and the strength of the containment walls at Granger Station plant have been steadily getting worse over the past several years under Granger's ownership."

"Good," said Wiseman. "Will it be done today?"

"I'm not sure. I'm following up on a few other leads. I still have to talk with the state DEP, Suncoast Protectors, a county commissioner, probably Fred Fance, and Granger," Jack explained.

"Make sure you get confirmations of everything your anonymous source tells you and run everything past Granger."

"Okay. Thanks, Rick," Jack said as he walked to his desk.

It was 9:30 a.m., and several reporters and editors wandered the newsroom, drinking coffee and chatting.

Jack grabbed his notebook and headed for the door to pick up the Granger reports at Tracy's office. He spotted Tom Justice, the paper's 34-year-old political reporter and a good friend, arriving.

"Hey, Tom! How was your vacation?" Jack said.

"The Bahamas was very nice—no Jamaica for Susan and me. You had enough excitement there for both of us," Tom replied sarcastically.

"You've told me that joke at least ten times, and it still isn't funny," Jack grumbled.

"Sorry, old boy. I miss anything?" Tom asked with a quizzical look.

"As usual, gossip moves fast in the newsroom. You have a lot of catching up to do. Maybe we can drink after work this week."

"Sounds like a plan. You still spending time with Bobbie?"

"She has been so helpful. Yes, we spend much of our off-work time together," said Jack with a smile. "Maybe you and

Susan can come to the house one weekend, and I can invite Bobbie. I've put in a dynamite game room and entertainment center with a fully stocked wet bar."

"Can't wait to see that. I know you spare no expense these days."

"Listen, I'm headed out now to get some county documents," Jack said. "We on for drinks and appetizers? Maybe Friday?"

Tom nodded. "You got it! See you soon."

Jack walked down the stairs and out of the newspaper office. It was a short drive over to Tracy's building.

Arriving 10 minutes later, Jack entered the office where Tracy's secretary greeted him.

"Hi, Jack. He left this envelope for you," said Gina Meyer, a petite, brown-eyed county worker. "Just fill out this form. It's going to cost $25. Should I send the bill to the newspaper?"

"Yes, thanks, Gina," said Jack as he quickly took care of the paperwork.

"The spill was horrible. I hope you get to the bottom of what Granger's doing," Gina said. "I have an uncle who lives in the neighborhood. Maybe you'd like to talk with him?"

"I've already been out there, but could you give me his name and number in case I need more?" Jack asked.

"Sure," Gina replied as she wrote down her uncle's information and handed it to Jack.

"Thanks. Tell Steve I'll call him later," said Jack, picking up the envelope that contained what felt like more than 50 pages of reports on Granger. He walked back to his GT and began speed-reading the material.

For 15 minutes, he carefully reviewed the water quality documents from Granger Station. The data clearly showed that Brewster's state reports were significantly worse than

Granger's. Furthermore, although the county's data were less comprehensive, they closely mirrored Brewster's findings. It became evident that both Brewster's and the county's reports indicated a decline in water quality.

No wonder Tracy had talked so strongly with Grousland the other morning. He was questioning everything. Jack was sure Tracy knew Granger was fudging the data, even faking it. He needed a firm quote from Tracy on that. No more "looks bad" or "preliminary results show concerns."

As Jack drove back to the paper, the story's lead and outline began to take shape in his mind. He arrived at the paper and started writing the piece on a legal pad.

After writing the first five paragraphs he had in his mind, he called Grousland. He'd left several messages that morning. He hoped the plant manager would return his calls; he didn't want to waste an hour driving to and from the plant just for an interview. However, he needed Granger's comments because the story would suggest that the company unlawfully provided the state with falsified data.

Jack also needed to ask Grousland about insider information he'd received from two employees—especially the accusations that the company had drilled out the weak spot at the top of the northwest wall to justify the large wastewater dump into the bay.

Chapter 17:
Expert Opinions

10:15 a.m., Thursday, July 15, 1982

Before typing the story's first draft into the computer, minus the quotes he would need, Jack began calling all the sources he needed to gather reactions and paint a picture of what the ongoing discharges from Granger Station could mean for people and the environment.

He first called Suncoast Protectors Chairperson Gloria Barton, one of his best sources on phosphate mining and the environment. Founded in 1970, Suncoast Protectors was the region's leading independent environmental consumer group.

Once she began appearing at County Commission meetings, Barton quickly became reporters' go-to source for environmental opinions. She recruited a team of volunteer experts in the life sciences, medicine, law, and the environment. Because of her contacts and voracious reading of federal, academic, and even industry reports, she sometimes knew more than industry and government experts.

"Good morning, Gloria. This is Jack Kendall at the *Herald-Tribune*. Do you have a few minutes to talk about the spill at Granger Station yesterday and any concerns you have about a larger collapse of the gypsum containment wall?"

"Hi, Jack. I was hoping you'd call. As you know, we've been issuing warnings about Granger Station and Piney Point for years," said Barton. "It was one of the reasons we created Suncoast Protectors."

"Yes, ma'am," Jack replied.

"We knew the industry could not ensure safe phosphogypsum disposal because it contains radium with a 1,630-year radioactive decay half-life," Barton explained. "This spill, the worst in Manatee County history, is what we feared would happen one day."

"Steve Tracy said the wastewater contained nearly triple the EPA's maximum allowable radium count in water. What effect will this have on the bay?"

"Phosphate processing wastewater is highly toxic and dangerous to plant and animal life. We're just collecting the data, but no doubt the effects will last for years."

"What about the Granger discharge?"

"I'm not sure I know the details yet. Has there been a report released?" Barton asked.

"Tracy is working on one for the commission. I was there this morning," Jack said. "Granger said it was an accident caused by two breaches in the wall; then, they said they started pumping more out because they needed to alleviate the pressure. What do you think of that?"

"Do you want something quotable or what I really think?" asked Barton, a hint of sarcasm in her voice.

"I can imagine what you really think. No, I want a quote. We're a family newspaper," Jack said with a chuckle.

"Oh, I didn't mean that, but you're always teasing me, Jack Kendall," said Barton. "Let me see. All right. What Granger has done is nothing short of criminal. When Granger bought the plant three years ago, the Pebble phosphate fertilizer plant was already in bad physical shape.

"As you know, it's one of Florida's oldest and smallest phosphate plants. Why county commissioners approved it in the early 1960s, so close to the bay, is beyond me. But Hillsborough approved that fertilizer plant in Riverview, just as close to Tampa Bay.

"With Granger, it was clear to everyone that restructuring was needed on the gypstack walls. They have done nothing to reinforce the containment walls that protect people from contamination and the environment from serious, possibly irreversible damage," Barton said.

"Should the state order Granger to shut down?" Jack asked.

"Absolutely. Granger should be closed until repairs are done on the gypstack. It should not be reopened until it receives an independent body of experts and the state deems it safe," she said.

"Now, listen," said Jack. "Based on my sources, Granger has also been submitting false reports to the DEP about the condition of the walls. What do you think?"

"We've said all along that Granger's environmental reports were on the low side regarding danger to the environment," Barton replied. "While not as extensive, the county's studies regularly contradict Granger's reports to the state."

"Are you surprised about the allegation of falsification?"

"No. I know no other reason why the data sets are so

different, other than that Granger is fudging theirs.”

“That’s putting it mildly.”

“The gypstack is ready to collapse. Granger is right about that. As I said before, the walls have been in bad condition for a long time, and there’s too much wastewater and sludge in the gypstack,” Barton explained. “I’m not even talking about the radioactivity problem.”

“But the Florida Phosphate Council insists that phosphate companies do everything they can to mine safely. I take it you don’t believe them?” Jack asked.

“Absolutely not. First, FPC’s track record is terrible. Every time they say that, we have another spill that contradicts them. They claim an act of God. How many times can they say that? God appears to be targeting the phosphate industry, if you believe them, which I don’t.

“No matter what they do, one of the most serious, long-term problems associated with the phosphate industry is the gypsum waste produced at phosphoric acid plants that is pumped into these giant gypstacks,” she said.

“What do you mean?” Jack asked.

“At present, no federal, state, or local regulations require the industry to safely dispose of the tons and tons of phosphogypsum waste in an environmentally acceptable manner.”

“Right, it’s like the nuclear power industry. Phosphate companies have no long-term solution to radioactive nuclear wastes.”

“Good analogy,” she said. “It’s very similar. There have been no realistic proposals other than to cap the gypsum stacks, wait, and hope nothing happens.”

“Thanks, Gloria. See you at the next meeting,” said Jack.

"I look forward to your article. We all appreciate what you do. Bye," Barton replied, hanging up the phone.

Next, he dialed the state Department of Environmental Protection.

"Hi, this is Jack Kendall with the *Herald-Tribune* in Sarasota. May I speak with Inspector Angus Miniver?" Jack asked. There was a pause. "He isn't there? What about George Garvey? I've left messages for the past two days."

"What is this about?" asked the state DEP operator.

"It's about the phosphate spill at Granger Station in Manatee County."

"Hold on, let me connect you with Mr. Garvey's office," the operator said.

After a moment, a new voice came on the line. "Hello, this is George Garvey. Is this Jack Kendall?"

"Yes, Mr. Garvey. I've been trying to contact Mr. Miniver. I'm on deadline for a story about the Granger spill. I have some questions, if you have a few minutes," Jack said.

"I'm not sure how much I can help. Mr. Miniver isn't here, and the accident is under investigation," Garvey replied.

"I understand, but I have questions about the reports the state has been getting from Granger for several months. I've been told by a reliable source that there may be discrepancies in the reports Granger is giving you. I was also told you have been alerted to these discrepancies. Have you?" Jack asked.

"No, not that I am aware of. Why?"

"There are several reasons. First, the county's data greatly differs from the monthly reports you get from Granger. Are you aware of this?"

"I'm not sure that's correct. Mr. Miniver is the inspector at Granger, and he hasn't told me anything about discrepancies."

"You're saying Mr. Miniver hasn't brought discrepancies in the water quality reports you've received from Granger and the county to your attention?" Jack asked.

"No," Garvey replied.

"I see. Steve Tracy with Manatee County tells me they have been complaining for over a year about the questionable data Granger submits. Just for the record, then, can you confirm or deny whether there is an investigation into the Granger reports?"

"I know of no investigation. For what? I don't follow you," Garvey said.

Jack wished he could drop James Brewster's name. After listening to Garvey, he wondered if he hadn't seen the reports that Brewster had mailed him. Or, perhaps Garvey was playing dumb. Jack had clearly stated the reason for an investigation.

"It is my understanding that Mr. Miniver has been asked why the county's data is so different from Granger's and the state's," Jack said.

"I don't know anything about this," Garvey replied. "You will have to speak with Miniver."

"He won't return my phone calls or respond to Steve Tracy of Manatee County. Will you ask Mr. Miniver why there are discrepancies in these reports?" Jack asked.

"I can't promise a reporter this, but I will take it under advisement," Garvey said.

"Fair enough. Just so you know, I will be writing about this," Jack said. "I have another question about the Granger spill. What will the state do about the 40 million gallons of phosphogypsum wastewater flushing into Terra Ceia?"

"Mr. Kendall, we take the spill at Granger very seriously and are working with Granger and Manatee County to resolve the problem," Garvey replied. "Our inspector, Mr. Miniver, is there gathering information and data. It's too early to draw any conclusions. You should go out there and talk with him."

"I've tried. I will again. One more question, then a request," Jack said.

"Fine."

"Have you received an emergency permit request for Granger to discharge 10 million gallons per day of effluent into the bay? And if so, when will the state decide?"

"We received that request this morning. We usually have 30 days to decide. But since it's an emergency, we hope to decide by early next week."

Jack then asked Garvey to FAX the *Herald-Tribune* all the water and air quality reports from Granger for the past year.

"You must submit a FOIA request on that," Garvey said. "I assume you know how."

"Yes, I do."

Jack thanked Garvey and hung up. He sat back in his chair and wondered, *even if there were an investigation, Garvey probably wouldn't have confirmed it. But he denied knowing about it. Maybe he's taking bribes just like Miniver?*

Still, it was interesting that Brewster had said he'd mailed his original reports to the state DEP, copied Garvey and Miniver, and hadn't heard back. It sure seemed that a cover-up was underway, but based on what Brewster told him, it was just a guess. He had nothing definite on Garvey.

Jack still hadn't heard from Grousland. He decided to call Commissioner Fance for a quote.

"Hi, this is Jack Kendall at the *Herald-Tribune*. Is Fred there?"

"He has someone in his office right now. Can I ask him to call you back?" said Paula Black, the main receptionist.

"Paula, could you tell him I need a quick word before I head out to Granger Station?"

"For you, Jack, sure," Paula replied. "Hold on."

The line went silent for a few seconds.

"Jack, it's good to hear from you. It's been a while since we've seen you around," Fred Fance said.

"You know I've been busy with this Granger Station spill and lots of phosphate-related issues the county and Sarasota have been dealing with," Jack said.

"We appreciate all the digging you've been doing. I wish I could tell you more about what's happening."

"I've just learned that the spill at Granger was no accident and that Granger has secret plans to dump up to or exceeding 100 million gallons of phosphate sludge into the bay over the next few days," Jack said. "Comment?"

"Jack, I've just been briefed by Steve Tracy. You know my district covers Granger's mine, but Commissioner Doolittle represents the district where the plant is located."

"I know, but you're the one commissioner out front on the phosphate mining issue because the mines, the trucks transporting the ore, and all the so-called 'reclaimed' land are out in agricultural country, which you mostly represent," Jack said. "I'd rather talk with you. Besides, Doolittle is completely unquotable."

Fance laughed. "I won't even tell him that because he has no sense of humor. Okay, let me give you some quotes."

"Fire away," Jack said.

"I've been warning, along with Commissioner Wood and other commissioners, about the looming disaster we have over at Granger Station," Fance said. "Based on the facts we've collected through our phosphate coordinator's office, Granger has short-changed safety maintenance that, if completed, would've prevented this unconscionable hazardous phosphate wastewater discharge.

"By the way, we'll be holding hearings next week. We'll call witnesses and take appropriate action to fine and consider shutting down the Granger plant and the mine until further notice," Fance said. "We have such powers, as you know."

"Yes, you do. Fred, do you have a comment about the discrepancies in the data reports that Granger has provided the state and that Steve Tracy and his team have collected related to water and air pollution quality?" Jack asked. "You know about that, right?"

"Yes. We've also been briefed about that for the past few weeks. Let's call them what they are: 'dueling and contradictory reports,'" Fance replied. "Incredibly, Granger submits these reports to the state, which are so different from our county reports, and they won't explain it. Neither will Miniver.

"We need to get to the bottom of this, and I plan on asking the state officials in charge of monitoring the plant and mine to come to the hearings we're scheduling for next week."

"Thanks, Fred, you've been a big help, as usual. Take care," Jack said.

It was late afternoon when Jack finished his interviews and the story's first draft. He hadn't heard from Grousland for the final interview, so he had no choice but to waste an hour driving to the plant. At least he could pin down Miniver if he was there.

Chapter 18:
Grousland Speaks

4 p.m., Thursday, July 15, 1982

When Jack pulled into the Granger parking lot, he saw Grousland talking with several employees in front of the company trailer.

"Mr. Grousland. Just the man I've been wanting to talk with all day," said Jack, interrupting whatever conversation the men were having.

Grousland glared at Jack, then said something to the workers, and they left. "Mr. Kendall, I've been swamped. I suppose you have more questions," he said.

"I've been talking with many people since I last saw you. Yes, I have more questions. Can we have a sit-down in your office?" Jack asked.

"I was mistaken about the pond we were draining the other day. We started pumping the main gypstack earlier than I thought. We drained about 20 million gallons from the gypstack, then switched and pumped another five million from the small ponds because they were filling beyond capacity. Does that cover everything? We even?" Grousland feigned a smile.

"You just learned that?" Jack said incredulously.

"There was some miscommunication on our part," he said, looking down and shaking his head. He didn't seem to want to make eye contact.

"Let's try not to have any more miscommunication, all right, Mr. Grousland?" Jack said. "Never mind, I have more serious questions to ask you. Can we go inside your office?"

"Of course, but I only have a few more minutes," Grousland replied. "The state inspector was just here looking at the discharges and breaches, and I've got to make a few phone calls about them."

"Is that Angus Miniver?"

"Why, yes, it is. How did you know?"

"I called his office this morning, and they said he was here," Jack said. "Is he still here?"

"Yes, he is. Small world, isn't it?" Grousland mused.

"Yes, it is a small world in the environmental field when a company dumps 40 million gallons and plans to dump another 60 million. Is that correct, Mr. Grousland?" Jack flatly asked. It had been a long day, and he was in no mood for mincing words or receiving incomplete answers, especially with Grousland, a proven liar.

"I can explain that. Follow me," Grousland said.

They entered the trailer office. The air conditioner's noise was loud, but the cool air felt welcoming. Grousland gestured for Jack to take a seat.

"You've heard that we've asked the state for permission to temporarily discharge 10 million gallons per day of treated effluent from the main stack?" Grousland said.

"Yes, but how many millions of gallons will you need to dump into the bay?" Jack asked. "I was told you plan on discharging up to 100 million before you're done. You've already dumped 40 million, Tracy says, plus you've probably dumped another 10 million today."

"We need to lower the water levels to make repairs. We might need another 60 million," Grousland replied.

"The county plans to hold you accountable for what's happened. You know that, right?"

"Well, tomorrow, we will announce a $1 million investment to repair several spots in the big stack's containment wall," Grousland said. "We will inject concrete to close the fissures. We need to lower the water level significantly to get at it."

Jack jotted down the development. He knew what Grousland was doing. He was trying to change the subject from disaster, incompetence, and possible fraud to positivity, concern, and environmental protection.

"When will the concrete be injected? And is that all to reinforce the berm?" Jack asked.

"Very soon," Grousland said. "I can't give you a precise hour and day, if that is what you want."

"Mr. Grousland, don't you think that's too late for the bay? You've discharged at least 50 million gallons of toxic sludge that are killing fish and other creatures out there, and you're still pumping."

* * *

Grousland felt the familiar tightening in his chest but refused to let it show. He had learned long ago that reporters fed on reaction—anger, defensiveness, anything that could be shaped into a headline. Kendall was good at that. Remaining calm was the only move.

He folded his hands on the edge of the desk, grounding himself, and measured his breathing before speaking.

"We're as concerned about the bay as anyone, but we don't believe the discharges will harm the ecosystem, and we're still investigating how this spill began. But I thought you would be happy to know we're making repairs," Grousland said.

Kendall barely reacted, just a shrug—casual, almost bored. Grousland recognized it immediately. That was a man fishing, letting silence and indifference do the work.

"It's a good story, yes. I'm sure the County Commission will be happy to hear about it. They'll hold a hearing on Monday, and you'll get to tell your side."

Grousland nodded slightly, as if the hearing were already penciled into his calendar. He had testified before. He knew how these things went.

"Now, you say you'll spend $1 million to fix the stack's walls. But why haven't you finished plugging the fissures with concrete? Experts tell me that it should have been done weeks ago."

There it was—the pivot from cooperation to accusation. Grousland kept his expression neutral, choosing his words carefully.

"We've done some work, but the containment walls are still dangerously weak. Before we do anything, we need to lower the water level," Grousland explained.

Kendall leaned in just slightly, enough to signal he was pressing.

"Yes, but why didn't you take this action weeks ago? I understand your engineering reports warned of dangerous containment wall conditions, actually going back months."

Grousland stiffened, just a fraction. He felt the instinct to push back hard, but he tamped it down. Reporters like Kendall remembered tone as much as words.

"That isn't accurate. Our reports are confidential, but the state has been monitoring our work, and we are complying with the regulations. We're in full compliance," Grousland objected.

Kendall studied him for a beat—long enough for Grousland to know he wasn't buying it, long enough for Kendall to recognize that Grousland had done this dance before.

"All right. I'm going to find Miniver and talk with him," Kendall said. "Do you know where he is?"

Grousland hesitated. He didn't like this turn. Miniver was brilliant, but blunt—an engineer who didn't always appreciate how words could be used against him.

"He's out on the north wall of the stack, but he's working."

"Can you call him in? I've been trying to reach him for the past few days. Tell him it'll just be a few minutes of his time."

Grousland picked up the walkie-talkie, already anticipating the response.

"Angus, can you come back to the trailer? A reporter here says he desperately needs to talk with you."

The reply crackled back almost instantly.

"Is that Jack Kendall? I don't have anything to say to him. Tell him he'll have my report when I'm done."

Grousland lowered the radio and met Kendall's eyes. "You heard him."

Kendall nodded once, as if he'd expected nothing else.

"I'll be back," he said as he stepped out of the trailer.

Grousland watched him go, knowing that reporters like Kendall never really left—they just circled, patient, waiting for the weakest seam.

*　*　*

Jack stepped out of the trailer and back into the oppressive Florida heat. The air was thick with the stench of sulfur and chemicals wafting from the nearby gypsum stacks.

He needed to get Miniver on the record. The state inspector had to be somewhere near the top, overseeing operations or pretending to oversee them. Sweat beading on his forehead, Jack walked along the gravel path leading to the wall. He was irritated with Miniver's refusal to talk over the walkie-talkie, but he needed to speak with him directly.

Jack reached the base of the gypstack and saw him on top of the berm, gripping a clipboard, his hard hat gleaming in the harsh sun.

"Angus!" Jack shouted, his voice echoing against the massive stack. Miniver didn't acknowledge him, but Jack pressed forward. As Jack approached, he finally turned, his face lined with irritation and suspicion.

"What do you want, Kendall?" Miniver barked, clearly annoyed at the interruption.

Jack wasted no time. "I need for you to go on the record. I'm writing a story about the spill. Are you aware that Granger has been falsifying water discharge quality reports to the state?"

156

Miniver shook his head and turned away.

"Is that a denial?" Jack asked. "Tell me."

Miniver said nothing.

"Second question: Are you taking bribes from Pierre Grousland to cover it up and keep other violations at this plant hidden?" Jack asked.

Miniver stiffened, his eyes narrowing. "You've got no proof of that. I don't answer to reporters. You'll get my report when it's finished. Now, leave me alone. I've got work to do."

Jack took his notebook out and started to write down what Miniver had said. He hoped that would spur Miniver into talking more. He was also recording the conversation.

Jack stepped closer, his tone sharp. "You might not answer to reporters, but you'll answer to the public and the sheriff when this scheme blows up."

Miniver's jaw clenched. He shifted uncomfortably, glancing toward Grousland's office trailer in the distance. "I've got nothing to say to you," he muttered as he walked away.

"I'll give you one last chance before we publish. I'll call your boss, George Garvey, to ask about this, and then I'll leave you a message to call me and tell me the whole story. Think about it," Jack shot back.

Miniver ignored him, his body language rigid and defensive. Jack had done all he could to get him to talk. At least he'd spoken directly with him and had quotes for the story. Hot and dirty, Jack turned and began the trek back to the trailer to confront Grousland one last time.

Knocking on the door, Jack entered. Grousland was behind his desk.

"Mr. Grousland, I spoke with Miniver. I have a couple more questions for you," Jack said as he came in and sat in a chair across from Grousland.

"What is it? I'm busy, as you can see," Grousland said.

"You said Granger is in full compliance with all water discharge regulations. Is that correct?"

"Yes, full compliance," Grousland said wearily.

"That's not what your reports or the county say. But let's leave that for now," Jack said with a hard stare. "Here is a fundamental question. I've been told that Granger has been altering reports filed with the state to show you comply, but your internal data shows you're nearly three times the EPA limit for surface water in the gypstack. More than five times in the ponds in many key areas. Is this true?"

"Where did you get this information? Did you talk with Miniver? It's incorrect! You're suggesting we have filed false reports to the state?" Grousland shouted, standing up from behind his desk and raising his voice for the first time.

Jack stood up, towering over the smaller man. "I know there are two monthly reports: an internal report showing you exceed state and federal water quality standards and the one that has been altered, which you file with the state, showing you are within standards."

Grousland grimaced and shook his head.

"Do you deny that there are two different sets of reports?" Jack asked.

"I have nothing more to say. We will sue you if you print this false information."

"But you just denied it. You just said you would sue the *Herald-Tribune* if we printed false information. It is not false. We have evidence of what you did," said Jack, frustrated and raising his voice. "I've seen the reports!"

"You've what? Our attorneys will contact you, your editor,

and your publisher!" bellowed an outraged Grousland, his nostrils flaring as he took several fast steps to the door and opened it.

"Listen, Mr. Grousland, I have other questions," Jack said quickly, stopping at the door. "We're publishing that the night before the spill, Granger workers were seen with a backhoe, which they used to dig wider holes in the two fissures that are now leaking. Will you comment on this?"

"We did what? That is preposterous. Out, Mr. Kendall!" Grousland ordered as he tried to shove Jack toward the open door.

Jack shrugged off the effort easily and glared back at the plant's manager.

"I'm leaving, but before I do, let me ask you one more thing," Jack said. "Can you explain why the reports you file with the state are so much different than the county's reports?"

"Kendall, I'm going to call security to have you escorted out," Grousland said.

"Answer the question."

"It's simple. The county collects samples at sites where concentrations of substances are higher. We follow industry standards in where we sample. Other than that, we are discussing this with the county. I can say that the state completely agrees with us."

"Is that Inspector Miniver who says everything is fine?" Jack asked sarcastically.

"Good day, Mr. Kendall. And if you come back, I will have you tossed out on your ear," he said as he slammed the office door.

Jack walked toward his Mustang GT with a slight smile. He'd ticked off Grousland and Miniver, but he'd also asked the questions and got the denials he'd expected. The only thing he hadn't had the opportunity to ask about was bribing Miniver.

He paused, realizing he needed to return and ask the question, even if the answer would be a denial or a "no comment." Grousland was angry, but Jack felt compelled to ask since Miniver had denied it. He also had Brewster's recording of Grousland admitting he had bribed Miniver. Turning toward the office, he walked quickly to the door and noticed Grousland looking through the window.

Jack knocked three times. Suddenly, the door swung open, and Grousland stood there with a menacing glance. He was on the phone.

"Mr. Grousland, I am sorry, but I have to ask you for the record about Angus Miniver," Jack said.

"What? I'm talking with corporate right now about your stupid, irresponsible questions," the manager growled.

"Have you paid Miniver to falsify reports and ignore safety at the plant?"

"You have some nerve, Kendall! What gives you the right to make these false accusations? My CFO is on the phone, and he heard you. We're going to sue your pants off!"

"We have evidence of everything I'm asking you," Jack said. "What do you say?"

"Our attorneys will contact your editor and publisher. You'll be lucky to have a job after this," snarled Grousland, slamming the door again.

Jack walked back to his car. This time, he had everything he needed for his story. He hadn't expected Grousland to admit to what they had done.

To protect Brewster, he couldn't tell Grousland about the audio recording Brewster had given him that laid out

Granger's criminal plan. But he wondered if Grousland would conclude that the plant's chief engineer had provided him with information about the second set of water quality reports.

Grousland hadn't accused Brewster of being the source. He could reasonably assume it was Miniver because Jack had just talked with him.

As he reached for his GT's door, Jack suddenly stopped. Did he make a mistake in bringing up the second set of reports? Would Grousland really think it was Miniver, the man they'd bribed, who had told him about the false reports? Where else would Jack know about that unless Brewster had told him? He needed to find Brewster and warn him. But he didn't know how to contact him.

He had waited long enough. It was time to get his detective brother, Ed, on the case.

Then Jack thought about Grousland's threat of a lawsuit. He needed to inform Wiseman immediately. A source threatening legal action could chill any editor's spine.

Jack was hot and sweaty and needed to return to the paper. He started the car, turned on the radio and air conditioner, and started driving, curious about the weather system brewing in the Atlantic Ocean.

"Tropical Storm Amos has steadily gained forward speed and intensity, reaching sustained winds of 50 miles per hour with gusts to 60. While its path continues toward Florida, it is far out in the Atlantic and does not pose an immediate threat. This is meteorologist Bryan Norcross reporting."

Jack wondered what a hurricane might mean for Granger Station, Piney Point, and the Sarasota-Bradenton area. Still, he didn't need to worry about that for a few more days. He had plenty of other things on his mind.

Chapter 19:
Lawsuit Threat

Later Thursday afternoon, July 15, 1982

Jack felt an odd mix of elation, concern, and nervousness as he drove his GT back to the *Herald-Tribune* newsroom. He was anxious about the tropical storm brewing in the Atlantic, but his biggest worry was whether Grousland was serious about having his lawyer contact Wiseman and Mr. Lindsay.

As soon as he walked into the newsroom, Wiseman spotted him and waved him over. Jack knew that meant trouble.

"Jack, I don't know what you said to Pierre Grousland, but he's hopping mad. I'm expecting a phone call from Granger's lawyer. He threatened a lawsuit if we run the story you're working on. I told him we didn't have a story yet, and he told me to kill it, or they'll sue us. He even said he'd shut down the paper," Rick said with a chuckle.

"Tell Mr. Lindsay that. He's bluffing. We have the evidence," Jack said.

"What did you ask Grousland?"

"I questioned him about the story. Everything. I asked him if they faked the reason for the discharge, if they withheld maintenance on the walls to save money, and if they submitted falsified reports to the state about the plant's water quality," Jack explained. "I also asked if he bribed Angus Miniver, the state inspector."

"That's all? Jesus, you might as well have asked him if he cheated on his wife and then beat her for having a problem with it," Rick said. "The guy's a jerk, but we must take the lawsuit threat seriously."

"I know, I know. Listen, I have Grousland's comments. He denied everything, and I told him I had people saying otherwise. Let me write up the story, and we can talk about it later."

"I'm going to have to talk with Mr. Lindsay and our lawyer, just to let them know to be ready," Rick said. "It's already pretty late in the afternoon. We might not be able to run this Friday, unless your source goes on the record."

"I don't think he will, but I'll go all out to reach him, and we still have five hours before deadline," Jack replied. "The story is solid. I'll nail it. Let me finish, and I'll try Brewster again."

"Get started on it. I'll get back to you," Rick said.

Jack had a bad feeling about his story. Maybe he was pushing it too quickly. He had an outline and several sections written. Still, the piece had several questionable elements that needed further verification and careful revision.

Jack doubted Brewster would go on the record, and he'd made that clear, especially at JR's Café. He wanted to get more documents, and he was worried about getting outed—

maybe worse.

Bobbie, who was back in the newsroom after making her rounds at police stations, saw Jack talking with Wiseman and knew something was up. She walked over to his desk.

"Hi, Jack, anything wrong?" she asked.

"It's that story on corruption at Granger Station. I've got multiple sources and internal company documents that Brewster gave me the other night to show corruption. You were there. It's just the Granger manager just threatened to sue us if we run the story," Jack replied. "I've got to find James."

"Can you contact him tonight?"

"I don't know. He wouldn't give me his phone number. I'm going to ask Ed to find him. Then, I'll write up a news story on some of the developments I found out today about the Granger spill and finish my longer story later."

"Good idea. Let me know if you need anything," Bobbie said.

"Thanks," said Jack, turning to the notes on his desk.

But first, he picked up the phone and dialed his brother.

"Ed, could you do a rush job finding James Brewster?" Jack asked.

"He's the guy you mentioned to me the other day? The engineer at Granger? How quickly do you need it?"

"Yesterday. I should have asked you right away," Jack said. "I need his phone number, address, and a background profile if possible."

"I'll make a few calls," Ed said.

"Push hard. I've got to talk with Brewster once more for the story and to warn him."

"Warn him about what?"

"I might have tipped off Grousland that he's my source," Jack replied. "They're corrupt, but they aren't idiots. I let them know I had a second set of mining reports. If you find Brewster, tell him to contact me and to watch his back."

"Will do. I'll put another man on the assignment," Ed said. "Be careful yourself."

"Get as much as you can. Call me. I'll be at the paper late. Thanks, Ed," said Jack, hanging up.

He tapped a key on his desktop computer, opened the file he had slugged "GrangerCorruptPhosSpillFolo," and the computer screen flashed.

As was his habit, Jack typed a proposed headline—one the copy desk was sure to change to fit the column size. He typed his byline and began writing the lead.

GRANGER STATION PHOSPHATE DUMPING CONTINUES; COMPANY PLANS TO SPEND $1 MILLION ON CONTAINMENT WALLS TO AVERT DIKE FAILURE

BY JACK KENDALL
HERALD-TRIBUNE INVESTIGATIVE REPORTER

Two days after dumping 40 million gallons of polluted wastewater into Terra Ceia Bay, Granger Station Manager Pierre Grousland said Thursday the phosphate company plans to discharge another 60 million gallons or more of toxic wastewater over the next several days to avert a possible worse catastrophe.

Grousland said the 250-million-gallon gypsum stack is on the verge of collapse because the containment walls have weakened from heavy rain and wind over the past month.

He also announced that Granger Phosphate Co., the Bartow-based company that owns Granger, would invest $1 million to shore up the containment walls. He did not set a completion timetable or a date for the repairs to begin.

Under its state permit, Granger can discharge up to 2 million gallons per day, 10% of its daily water use. The company has asked the state Department of Environmental Protection to increase the amount to 10 million gallons per day for the next two weeks.

Commissioner Fred Fance said the Manatee County Commission plans to hold a hearing on Monday to discuss the Granger Station spill and the county's options to hold Granger accountable.

Fance, who has criticized Granger for failing to invest sufficient money over the past three years to improve the plant's safety, said he would ask county, state, and company officials to testify about the spill and explain the impact of the discharges into Terra Ceia.

"We need to prevent more harmful discharges and to find out why this large discharge happened," Fance said. "Our inspections show that the containment walls are in bad condition. Why weren't they fixed before? I hope we can get some answers."

Jack's story went on for another 15 inches. It contained quotes from Grousland, Steve Tracy, and Gloria Barton about the weekly discharges. He also included a few quotes from the neighbors and the boat captains.

He wandered over to Wiseman's desk.

"Rick, I just sent you a news story about Granger. It isn't the investigative piece that I'll send you later. I'll start back writing that in a few minutes," Jack said. "You can decide after you see both stories."

"I'm leaning toward holding it, but I want to see what you come up with first and hear what Granger's lawyer says to Peter Gantz. By the way, you should know that Mr. Lindsay told our lawyer and me to give all possible deference to whatever you write about Granger," Rick said.

"Gantz is a good First Amendment lawyer, fair, and Mr. Lindsay will be on my side," Jack said.

"Mr. Lindsay was pretty clear. He said he won't be threatened by a company that pollutes our air, water, and land to the degree it does," Rick continued. "I never heard him say that before about a story. Go ahead and work on it, and we can talk later."

Jack walked back to his desk with a big smile. He knew exactly how he would write the exposé.

He glanced over at Bobbie, who was watching the exchange, and gave her a wink and a thumbs-up. She smiled and went back to her story.

Jack finished his exposé two hours later and sent it to Rick. Thirty minutes later, the editor walked over.

"Jack, this is a great story. You provide a lot of background about the lack of containment wall maintenance and the environmental damage to the bay," Wiseman said. "Leading off with Grousland telling Cross and Decker to fake the spill and admitting why it was necessary to lower the wastewater level in the containment pond perfectly describes what happened. But the comments about paying off the state inspector to look the other way...wow, that's amazing."

He continued. "Gantz agrees the tape recording is sufficient proof and doesn't think we need, at this time, the name of the person, your James Brewster, who provided it. However, we need to state that the anonymous source who recorded it is an employee."

Jack grimaced at naming the source as an employee. "Brewster told me he can't be named as an employee. He agreed to be referred to as a 'knowledgeable source,'" Jack said. "He's scared and wants to stay on the job to get more evidence and do what he can to keep the leaks from worsening."

"Well, I can't use the quotes Brewster gave you unless he goes on the record. There's too much speculation and opinion about why he thinks Granger didn't do the repairs," Rick replied.

"Did you talk with Mr. Lindsay about this? I'm sure he's fine with running the story with my assurances about James Brewster," Jack said.

"I talked with Mr. Lindsay and our lawyer on the phone. They read the story and love it. David wanted to run the story, but Gantz agreed with me that we should wait until next week, after the commission hearing."

"I'd like to run Brewster's quotes, but we don't need them. Why hold it if the tape recording proves everything I wrote and Mr. Lindsay wants to run it?"

"Couple reasons. We need to talk more with the state about the reports and the alleged payoffs," Rick said. "Just a little more, give Miniver another chance to explain. Talk with his boss, Garvey.

"I also want to see what the County Commission does on Monday. They could call for an investigation into Granger, which would give us another reason to run the story," Rick said.

"So, holding the story isn't because we've been threatened with a lawsuit?" Jack asked.

"Not directly, but Gantz wants to cover all the bases first, and I agree with him."

"But I've allowed everybody to comment—Grousland, Miniver, and Garvey. They know what's in the story, and Granger is bluffing about the lawsuit. They don't want to defend Grousland and the other two. We've got them stone cold on the tape recording," Jack pleaded.

"Just a few more days," Rick said.

Jack's face flushed red. "Do you know what that means to Brewster? He's risking everything, Rick. His job, his safety—hell, maybe even his life—for this story."

Rick sighed. "Jack, I understand your passion for this story and the risk your source is taking, but we've got to be bulletproof when we go to print."

Jack shook his head, exhaling sharply, his anger tempered by disappointment. "I hope you're right, Rick. Because if you're not, we'll have more than just a missed deadline to regret."

He took a moment to compose himself further. "Is there nothing more I can say?" asked Jack.

"No," said Rick. "By the way, Mr. Lindsay said you did a great job."

Jack nodded. He had half a mind to look for Mr. Lindsay and plead his case directly to the publisher, who could overrule Wiseman and Gantz.

Without further words, Jack turned and walked quickly out of the newsroom. He hadn't heard from Ed and needed to find Brewster to explain. He couldn't let another delay cost them his brave inside source.

Chapter 20:
Finding Brewster

8 p.m., Thursday, July 15, 1982

Jack drove over to Ed's detective agency's office. There was a single light shining inside. He walked up to the door, turned the knob, and walked inside.

Ed sat behind his desk, a manila folder in front of him, his expression grim. "I made some phone calls and did as much as I could over the last three hours," he said, gesturing for Jack to sit. "The bottom line is James Brewster didn't exist before 1976. I can't find anything on him other than his phone number and address."

"I didn't give you much time. You have his number?" Jack asked.

"I called. No answer, so I took a ride over to his house," Ed said. "He's not home, and no one in the neighborhood has seen him for several days. It's like he vanished."

Jack's stomach sank. He leaned forward, his voice tight. "Vanished? What does that mean? He had a job. He had a life."

Ed sighed. "I didn't go to Granger. He's either hiding or

someone made him disappear. But I did find something else—two of his co-workers, Daniel Rumsfeld and Manny Hernandez. You gave me their names. I know where they live."

"Do you have their phone numbers?"

Ed tapped the folder. "Yes. Rumsfeld worked directly with the holding ponds. He'd have firsthand knowledge of the leaks and the toxicity levels. Hernandez is a night maintenance supervisor responsible for monitoring the gypstacks. If anyone saw something unusual Monday night, it'd be him."

Jack nodded. "Hernandez left me two messages and wants to talk. Can you go to his house and gather as much information as you can? He has photos of the Granger employees with the backhoe. Ask him if he knows where Brewster is. I've got to talk with him. I should go home in case he calls."

"Sure, I'll go to Hernandez's house immediately," Ed said. "Sorry, I couldn't get more on Brewster. My sources weren't as helpful this time."

"We need to keep trying. I should have pressed him for all these answers at JR's. I was so focused on getting the lowdown on Granger," Jack replied.

"You did what you could. I'll get what I can from Hernandez and try my federal sources tomorrow about Brewster."

"Good. Oh, give me Rumsfeld's phone number. I'll try to call him at home," Jack said. "Thanks. Call me later to let me know what happens with Hernandez."

"Right, talk later," Ed said.

A nagging unease settled in as Jack left the office and climbed back into his GT. If Brewster had vanished, Rumsfeld and Hernandez might be his only chance to uncover the truth. But the more he thought about it, the clearer it became: someone didn't want this story coming out.

And they were willing to silence anyone who stood in their way.

Chapter 21:
Daniel Rumsfeld

9 p.m., Thursday, July 15, 1982

"Daniel, this is Jack Kendall. Please don't hang up. I need to discuss James," Jack said, his voice filled with apprehension and worry.

"Mr. Kendall? James told me to talk with you, but I wasn't sure how to do that with a reporter," Daniel replied.

"It's okay. How is he? How are you?" Jack asked.

"I'm okay, but I'm not sure about James. I talked with him today, and he's very distressed. He wants you to know he's upset that you haven't exposed what the managers are doing. He said you promised him."

Jack took a deep breath. He had his answer about Brewster's reaction. "What did James say?"

"He's under extreme pressure to cover up what they've been doing here," Rumsfeld said. "He told me that if the newspaper doesn't run what he told you, Grousland might do something to stop him."

Jack took a deep breath and said, "He feels threatened, which is what I was worried about. Granger has threatened us with a lawsuit, and that's why we haven't published the story. The editor wants to wait a few days to see if he goes on the record. Can you let him know that?"

"I'm not sure."

"Is there a way I can talk with him?" Jack asked, feeling the urgency to press Daniel. "I must explain what happened and ask him to go on the record again. That will expose what Granger is doing. If he goes on the record, the police can protect him."

"I don't know where he is. I haven't seen him since Wednesday. Mr. Brewster hasn't been going home after work," Rumsfeld said.

"Hold on. You haven't been to work?"

"No, Grousland sent me and some other technicians home on Thursday. He told us not to talk to anyone. We all worked closely with James. He has a crew from Bartow here. I'm not sure what they're doing," Daniel explained. "I don't know whether I'm laid off or fired."

"Is James at work? Could you go there and ask him to call me?" Jack asked.

"No, I want to stay away from there," Daniel said. "He told me to be careful because what Granger is doing now is criminal."

"I thought as much," Jack said. "Have you tried to call him?"

"He called me earlier. I tried to call him back a little while ago, but there was no answer."

"Do you know where he lives?"

"Yes, but he isn't home and doesn't want people to know where he lives. I can only give you his phone number."

"We found his address, and an associate dropped by his house this afternoon. He wasn't there. Do you know where he's staying?"

"I don't know where he might be. Sorry. He's very private. Besides, there's something weird going on at Granger."

"Let me ask you about the spill," said Jack. "Do you know firsthand if Grousland did anything illegal to cause the discharges?"

"I can tell you, just on background, no names," Rumsfeld replied. "Mr. Brewster said that would be okay."

"Yes, just tell me," said Jack, slightly exasperated.

"I've been threatened."

"Grousland?"

"Yes. Two days ago, he told other technicians and me to keep our mouths shut and avoid Mr. Brewster. I know about leaks in the gypstack."

"Do you mind if I tape our conversation?" Jack asked.

"I don't want to be quoted in the newspaper," Rumsfeld said sternly. "I'll tell you what I know, and you keep my name out."

"What do you know about the spill, and what did Granger do?"

"Granger made the leaks much worse by digging into the containment walls with a backhoe and a small portable boring machine."

"How do you know it was Granger?"

"I saw a Granger truck drive out of the plant the morning of the spill," Rumsfeld said. "I told James. At the time, I thought they'd fixed the holes. But they were much worse when Mr. Brewster and I checked on them later."

"A maintenance supervisor, Manny Hernandez, left me a message and told me about the backhoe leaving that morning," Jack said.

"He took pictures."

"Will Manny go on the record?"

"He will," Rumsfeld said. "He needs to talk with his lawyer first. He said he'd call you today."

"He already left two messages. We are trying to contact him. Tell me more about the stack walls and Grousland's involvement," Jack asked.

"For weeks, Grousland and the managers did nothing to fix the weak stack walls, even when Mr. Brewster and I documented the leaks and brought them to their attention," Rumsfeld said. "I told you I saw a Granger truck leave the property towing a backhoe."

"That was early Tuesday morning?" Jack asked.

"Yes, Manny told me the night before he saw the backhoe and some other machine tear open up the two fissures that began the slow leak the day before," Rumsfeld recounted.

"You can confirm the backhoe was used to do that?"

"Yes, I saw it there, but Manny was the one who saw it being used and took the pictures."

Jack listened carefully. Rumsfeld had confirmed what Brewster and Hernandez told him about the cause of the spill and who was responsible.

"This is very helpful. Let anyone know they can call me day or night. You can give them my phone numbers, all right?" Jack said. "And tell James, if you talk with him again, to call me ASAP—and that he should watch his back."

"I will. Keep my name out of it," Rumsfeld insisted again.

"Don't worry. And if you ever need to talk with me, come

by the newspaper or call me at the office or at home. You got it?" Jack said.

"Yes," Daniel said.

"One more thing. Please tell James we will likely run the story on Monday after the County Commission meeting. Tell him not to worry; we'll expose everything. We need a little more time," Jack said.

"I'll keep trying to contact him," said Daniel, hanging up.

*   *   *

Jack slowly dialed the number Daniel had given him, wondering what he would say if James picked up. The phone rang several times, then went to the answering machine.

"Hello, James. Jack Kendall here. I need to talk with you immediately. Can you call me at home or work? I just spoke with Daniel Rumsfeld. He confirmed everything you told me on background. I'm still working on the story. We hope to run it soon. Be patient."

Jack paused for a second. "James, I'm worried about you. I interviewed Grousland. He denied everything, but he threatened me, and I'm worried he's threatened you too. I need you to go on the record. We can protect you. Let's talk. I hope you're safe. Here is my home number again in case it's at night..."

Chapter 22:
Long Week Nearly Over

7 a.m., Friday, July 16, 1982

Jack walked outside the following day to pick up the paper. He thought about Brewster and the constant stream of phosphate wastewater slime and sludge pouring into Terra Ceia. It must have reached 50 million gallons by now; another 50 million were on the way unless the county could stop it.

The gravity of the situation weighed heavily on him.

He glanced at the headline, "*Granger Station Phosphate Dumping Continues.*" Usually, he was happy to see a headline on his story. This time, it made him feel hollow. It was a quickly written substitute story on the spill and Granger repairing the giant earthen berm.

Another headline caught his eye: "*Hurricane Amos Likely*

to Strike Southwest Florida." With everything going on with Granger, he hadn't thought much about Amos. It had rapidly intensified over the last 24 hours to winds of over 100 mph.

He thought back to Brewster. Given his warnings about Granger's weak gypstack walls, what would he say about Hurricane Amos? He needed to find and talk to the engineer for several reasons, but he knew James was upset that he had not written the exposé on Granger.

Rumsfeld had told him last night about how disappointed Brewster was with Jack's coverage. This was the second time Jack had interviewed him and had not used anything from the interview in a published story.

But Jack also wanted to expose the corruption at Granger Station—the bribes, the lack of maintenance and safety, and Granger's real reasons for the phosphate slime dump. He had to explain to Brewster again that the *Herald-Tribune* had to triple-check the facts and ensure the exposé was accurate before publishing it.

Jack knew how much James wanted to get the truth out to the public, and he had his own anxiety about possible retaliation from his employers.

He needed the engineer to go on the record.

Maybe Rumsfeld had contacted Brewster, or maybe James would have seen the article and called him. Jack hoped so, but it was Friday, and the engineer was most likely at work.

The phone rang as Jack was mulling over everything at the kitchen table.

"Jack, it's Ed. I had a long talk with Manny Hernandez last night. He doesn't know where James Brewster is, but he did give me copies of the pictures Hernandez took of the Granger employees ripping apart the phosphate walls."

"I was wondering how that went," Jack said.

"It was late by the time I met with him, and I had to go to the Bradenton Police Department," Ed said.

"The BPD? Why?" Jack asked.

"He was so scared about the whole thing. He wanted to give copies to me and the police simultaneously," Ed explained.

"He told the story to the police? Who?"

"Sergeant Jones. Do you know him? He took the photos and a statement."

"I don't know Jones. Did Hernandez tell you everything?"

"I have his statement, the photos, and more, but he didn't know where Brewster went. Hernandez told me Grousland was angry with him and told him not to talk to the press and to go home. That was Thursday afternoon, so he packed up and left. He has relatives in Tampa. I have a number to reach him at."

"What do the photos show?" Jack asked.

"We'll have to blow them up because they were taken from a distance, but you can tell what they are doing: ripping apart the walls," Ed replied.

"How many photos?"

"Ten. He has them destroying the wall, and he took a picture of the truck with the backhoe leaving the plant."

"Ten? Are you kidding me? That's perfect!" Jack exclaimed.

"That's not all. Jack, one of the photos has a license plate," Ed said. "BPD was very interested in that, and several others where you can see the workers."

Jack's face lit up as Ed retold the story. "Excellent work, Ed. Gold stars for you. Can you get copies made today? Keep one set and bring one down to the paper?"

"Right-o. I'll be down mid-morning," Ed said.

"Brilliant. See you then," Jack said as he hung up with a big smile.

He leaned back in his chair, exhaling deeply, satisfied.

For the first time in days, he felt like they were finally gaining the upper hand. The evidence wasn't just strong—it was bulletproof. And Jack couldn't wait to see how Granger tried to squirm their way out of this one.

*　*　*

Jack walked triumphantly into the newsroom at 8 a.m. He had two confirmed sources backing up James Brewster and photographs on the way that would prove Granger's direct involvement in the industrial sabotage. He could call it that now.

Rick Wiseman wasn't in yet, so he sat at his desk and looked around. Bobbie wasn't there either, so he started working on his Sunday story about the phosphate spill's impact on the Granger neighborhood and Terra Ceia Bay.

At about 9 a.m., Rick came into the newsroom. Jack walked over to talk with him.

"Rick, I've got more ammunition for my story. With what I've got, I don't see why we can't run it Saturday, even this afternoon," Jack said.

Rick stared at Jack, bracing for another debate.

"I've got two Granger sources that confirmed everything James Brewster told us. One witnessed Granger employees destroying the gypstack walls with a backhoe," Jack said happily. "But the coup de grâce is we have photographs of it all."

"Will any of them go on the record?" Rick asked.

"No, but they're two sources confirming Brewster's info," Jack said.

"I've got some bad news. Granger filed a temporary restraining order last night on any coverage that accuses them of what you told Grousland. Gantz said we have a hearing first thing Monday."

"What the fuck?" Jack said, using a rare epithet for him. "You've got to be kidding me!"

"No. Gantz thinks we can beat it, but he doesn't think we should publish anything until next week, no matter what you have," Rick replied.

"But one of my sources provided photos and a statement to the Bradenton Police Department!" Jack protested. "Can't we write about that?"

"Who did that? Another one of your anonymous sources?" Rick asked.

"Yes, he's anonymous, but I believe BPD will investigate."

"Why don't you call Chief West and find out what they're doing?" Rick suggested. "In the meantime, do you have the Sunday story finished?"

"Oh my God, you're asking about that now? Yes, it's done. I'll send it over to you in 30 minutes," Jack replied, shaking his head in disbelief.

Just then, Bobbie approached Rick and Jack.

"Jack, can I talk to you for a minute? It's important," Bobbie said.

Jack looked at her and then back at Rick. He understood she was trying to keep him from saying too much in the heat of the moment.

"Sure, Bobbie, let's get some coffee," Jack said.

The two reporters walked away, Bobbie gently holding

Jack's arm for support. His hands trembled, his face tight with unspoken tension. He knew the story had to be published—not just for Brewster's sake, but to safeguard Terra Ceia and its fragile future.

*　*　*

An hour later, after Jack and Bobbie had coffee and enjoyed a quiet walk, they returned to the newspaper office.

"Thanks for the company. You always know how to calm me down," Jack said.

"You were pretty worked up," Bobbie replied. "Getting this news out there for James Brewster and everyone else is important, but just a few days won't matter in the long run." She smiled reassuringly and squeezed Jack's hand.

He nodded. "I've got to make a few calls to take care of things Rick wanted done in the Granger story."

"I'll see you for lunch, maybe?" she asked with a smile.

"Sure, let's do that," he said.

The first call was to Angus Miniver. He dialed the number, and Miniver's secretary answered.

"May I speak with Mr. Miniver? This is Jack Kendall with the *Sarasota Herald-Tribune*."

"I'm sorry, Mr. Miniver isn't in. Can I take a message?" she said.

"Please tell Angus I need him to comment on my Granger story."

"I'm sorry, is that the message?" she repeated.

"Tell Angus this, word for word. I have several sources, including a tape recording of Pierre Grousland saying you took bribes to ignore problems at Granger Station. I'm writing a story quoting these sources," Jack said slowly. "He knows the rest."

"Oh, my," she said, shocked.

"Yes. Please relay that to Angus immediately. I'm at my office," said Jack.

The second call was to Miniver's boss, George Garvey, who was also out of the office.

Jack left the following message: "Did you locate the letter James Brewster claimed he sent to you via certified mail about the fake reports from Granger? What will you do? Do you know Miniver has been accused of taking bribes from Granger to look the other way?"

He told both assistants he was on deadline and asked them to call his office before 6 p.m. He left his office and home number.

It was almost lunchtime. He had time to call Chief West before going to lunch with Bobbie.

"Charlie, my brother, Ed, came into the station last night with a Granger employee who gave Sergeant Jones a statement about the phosphate spill and some photographs. Do you know anything about this?" Jack inquired.

"I heard about it this morning. What do you need?" Chief West asked.

"Have you opened an investigation?"

"This is more a county and state environmental issue. We contacted Steve Tracy and the county administrator about it and are waiting to hear back. I'm not sure what we can do at this point."

"I understand. Thanks, Charlie. Will be in touch," said Jack, hanging up.

Just then, Bobbie came over. "Ready for lunch? I'd like to

go to the Main Bar if it's okay with you," she said.

"Just one minute," Jack replied as he dialed Steve Tracy. Another secretary picked up.

"Hi, Gina," he said. "Can I speak with Steve? Oh, he's out at Granger? Is anything going on? Okay, have him call me when he returns. Thanks."

Hanging up, Jack turned to Bobbie. "Okay, let's go. You hungry?"

"Sure," she replied with a smile.

*　*　*

Jack worked on his story all afternoon while waiting for Miniver and Garvey to return his calls. They'd likely heard that Granger had a restraining order and decided not to call back based on their lawyers' advice.

Either way, it didn't matter. Brewster didn't call, and Jack could do nothing more than write another story to advance the Monday Manatee County Commission hearing on the Granger Station spill.

An hour later, at about 5 p.m., Jack turned in all his stories and drove home. Despite the week's circumstances, he was throwing a party and didn't want to be late.

Chapter 23:
Troubling News

Friday evening, July 16, 1982

Jack wasn't sure that having a party was the best idea, given everything swirling around him, but he needed to relax for a few hours. He had done everything he could to find Brewster and report on the phosphate spill. Ed agreed to continue the search over the weekend.

He had invited Bobbie, Tom Justice, and his wife, Susan, for a few hours of relaxation. They hadn't done that in several weeks.

As they enjoyed good food and conversation, Hurricane Amos came up. The storm was located near Cuba, and forecasters predicted it would intensify as it moved north into the Gulf of Mexico.

"Is it going to hit or not?" Tom asked. "I've got five bucks saying it misses us by 100 miles."

"I should take that bet because the National Weather Service disagrees with you, but I hope you're right," Jack said.

"If we're going to get hit by this storm, can I please get a drink first?" Susan asked.

"I'll take one, too. One of your specialties, Tom?" asked Bobbie.

While Tom mixed four Mai Tais, Jack took the opportunity to explain to Susan one of the joys of playing pool: how to make a bank shot along the rail without scratching the cue ball.

"See, the trick is to clip the side rail first softly, then the ball, hard enough to make good contact but soft enough not to bounce it away from the hole," said Jack, who took aim and proceeded to drop the six ball. The cue ball trickled in behind and fell into the pocket.

Bobbie broke out laughing. "Jack, next time, try a little less difficult shot, like maybe how to break a rack of balls without scratching?"

"Hilarious, Bobbie. I promise you, Susan, I can make that shot nine out of 10 times!" Jack crowed, somewhat embarrassed at his attempt to show off.

"Jack, maybe you need a double shot of Jack Daniel's? Might improve your eyesight and reflexes!" Tom quipped, enjoying Jack's shame.

"Very funny, both of you. I'll just take the Mai Tai," said Jack, walking over to his new wet bar, where Tom was mixing the drinks for his friends.

Just then, Jack's phone rang. He picked it up.

"Jack, I've got troubling news," said Ed Kendall, his tone sharp and urgent over the phone. "It's Gordon Gecht. He's back."

Jack froze, gripping the phone tighter. "What? Where?" he asked, his voice edged with disbelief.

"One of my men spotted him at the airport, getting off a flight from Miami. He couldn't follow him but managed to snap a picture," Ed said. "Gecht's in some half-ass disguise. My man immediately saw through it. He's not wearing his trademark white suit. He also grew his hair and even had a thick black mustache. What do you want me to do?"

Jack's jaw tightened. "Nothing for now. I expected him to show up eventually, just not tonight. Bobbie, Tom, and Susan are over. Can you alert the police?"

Ed's voice dropped, steely. "Already on it. I'll also have a man posted outside your house 24/7. Don't argue. Gecht is coming after you."

Bobbie overheard the last sentence. Her face went pale as she whispered, "It's him, isn't it?"

Jack nodded grimly, setting the phone down. "Yeah. Gordon Gecht."

The name hung in the air like a storm cloud. Tom, usually quick with a joke, was silent. Susan's eyes darted around nervously.

"What's he doing in Sarasota?" she asked, her voice rising.

Jack smirked bitterly, his eyes narrowing. "I'm sure he's here to apologize for murdering Becky, shooting me, and all his other sins." He stood abruptly. "Excuse me while I make a call."

Jack dialed Sarasota Police Chief Tom Bagley's office, but Lt. Jim Stevens answered instead.

"The chief's gone for the day," Stevens said. "I'll notify Bradenton, Manatee, and the FBI. Just stay safe, Jack. Let us handle this."

Jack's voice was firm. "Ed's bringing over a picture. Gecht's in disguise. The same outfit he wore in Bogotá. Catch this son of a bitch."

As Jack hung up, Tom broke the tension. "Should we leave?"

"It's up to you. That's probably the safest option," Jack said. "Ed's man will be here soon."

Tom nodded, ushering Susan toward the door. "Come on. Let's give Jack some space."

Susan hesitated. "Be careful, Jack. You and Bobbie, stay safe."

"Jack, I would usually say, 'Call me if you need me.' However, since Gordo is in town and you two are mortal enemies, feel free to call me if you'd like to go to the movies or have a meal somewhere neutral with plenty of witnesses," Tom said, maintaining a straight face. It was a poor attempt at humor.

"Helpful as always, Tom. I'll do that. See you at work on Monday," Jack said as he watched the Justices leave.

He turned to Bobbie, who looked shaken.

"What now?" she asked.

"We knew he'd show up, eventually. Tomorrow morning, we're seeing Colonel Hanks. Tonight, we lock down the house," Jack said, heading to the security control panel.

* * *

Often, usually at night, Jack Kendall found himself hearing word-for-word the dreadful phone call he'd received from the police in Bogotá on Jan. 9, 1981.

"Your wife, Becky Kendall, has been murdered. We are very sorry."

The memory haunted him. When Jack traveled to Bogotá with Bobbie to identify Becky's body, the grim trip escalated into an investigation and manhunt for Gordon Gecht.

189

Jack learned that Gecht had killed Becky and was now working for Pablo Escobar, Colombia's infamous "King of Cocaine."

Fueled by rage, Jack partnered with Detective Matias Morales and Colonel Jaime Ramírez Gómez of the Bogotá Police Department to trap Gecht. In a shootout at the warehouse where Becky was murdered, Jack was shot in the shoulder, requiring surgery and months of rehabilitation. But he had gotten partial revenge, wounding Gecht during the firefight.

Still, Jack knew the feud wasn't over, and Gecht would try again one day.

Jack left Bogotá with a promise to Morales and Gómez: he would expose the cartel's crimes.

"You'll be doing Colombia a great service by wielding the weapon of your pen," Gómez had told Jack.

Back in Sarasota, Jack channeled his anger into journalism. He wrote a series of investigative articles about the Medellín cartel's impact on Florida's cocaine trade, exposing how casual drug use in the U.S. fueled violence and corruption in Colombia.

As his cartel reporting had gained recognition, Jack started writing about environmental issues and the healthcare industry.

But even as he focused on his career, Jack's vigilance never wavered. He'd prepared for the day Gecht would return.

Chapter 24:
Dressed to Kill

10 a.m., Saturday, July 17, 1982

The next morning, Jack drove Bobbie to the Sarasota Jarheads Shooting Range, where his late father had first brought him when he was only eight. He had already learned to shoot a .22-caliber rifle at Camp Arrowhead in North Carolina, but his WWII Marine father wanted him to learn from the best.

He also needed to talk with Col. Hanks about Gecht and brush up on his own shooting skills.

Jack and Bobbie stepped inside, greeted by shots echoing through the air from the range in the back.

Marine Corps Lt. Col. John Hanks greeted them with a hearty smile. "Jack, how are you? I'm glad you could come in for some practice. Been a few weeks."

"Hi, Colonel. Yes, we've been busy with the Granger Station phosphate spill," Jack said, shaking his head.

"I read about it. That's nasty business. Hope you get to the bottom of it," said the stocky colonel, a Korean war veteran, with a steely gaze.

"Remember what I told you last year? What I feared might happen?" Jack said, his face turning serious.

"You mean...Gecht? So that's why you're here. That SOB who killed Becky returned after all this time?" asked Col. Hanks.

"One of Ed's men saw him at the airport in disguise," Jack replied. "I want to be ready for him."

Col. Hanks nodded. "Preparation is half the battle, but I'm sorry to hear he's back. If you need help, you can call me day or night." He considered Jack to be like a son.

After moving to Sarasota in 1960, Hanks opened Jarheads, a gun shop and shooting range for veterans. He soon met Ken Kendall, Jack's father, at VFW Post 3233.

When Jack returned from Bogotá and completed his shoulder rehabilitation, he began earnestly training with Col. Hanks. Jack knew basic shooting techniques and rifle safety rules, but after the shootout with Gecht at the warehouse, he wanted to learn more.

While Jack tried to keep firearm training a secret, Bobbie soon found out and wanted to take lessons with him. Initially, she was scared of holding guns, much less firing them, but eventually, she became comfortable and quite good at target practice.

"You and Bobbie have been doing very well with your firearm and safety training," Col. Hanks said. "I'm not sure what else I can teach you at the range, other than reminding you to be vigilant."

"Yes, and, as you always say, 'Shooting a target at a range is quite different from shooting an enemy in real life,'" Jack said, repeating one of the colonel's favorite sayings.

Jack understood this distinction well, based on his recent experience. He'd never told anyone, including Col. Hanks, about killing one of Escobar's hitmen, only that he had wounded Gecht in self-defense.

"I know you won't answer this, but how do you deal with the aftermath of killing someone in combat?" Jack asked.

"It's something we don't usually talk about," the colonel replied softly. "Although your father and I talked about what we did in the heat of battle. We understood each other because we both fought at close range and watched men die within arm's reach."

Jack studied Col. Hanks carefully. "My mother told me once about a night attack the Japanese made on his company in Bougainville, but he never said anything to me."

"No, he wouldn't have. I know what you are talking about. There was hand-to-hand combat that night, and his best friend was killed beside him," Col. Hanks recalled with an icy stare. "I can tell you this. When the enemy is shooting at you, trying to kill you, it changes your thinking. It's not like you want to kill that enemy; it's more like you want to save your own life or the lives of your brother soldiers—your friends—so you fire your weapon to kill."

"When you're trained, it's automatic. It's kill or be killed, right?" Jack asked.

"Let me give you some advice. Stay cool, and if you point a gun at Gecht or someone who's trying to kill you, you need to pull that trigger. You will only get one chance because he will shoot you without thinking twice," Col. Hanks said.

Jack knowingly nodded. As they discussed Gecht and self-defense, Jack and Col. Hanks noticed Bobbie was becoming increasingly nervous and agitated.

"Now, I'm sure you're ready to start practice. You have your weapons in their cases. Do you need any cartridges?" Col. Hanks asked.

"I need two boxes of rounds for our Berettas and one for the Walther P99," Jack said.

"No problem," the Colonel replied. "Let's examine the weapons you brought, register you, and supply you, and then you can go to the handgun range."

Jack opened the gun cases, and Col. Hanks carefully inspected each pistol.

"It doesn't look like you've used these since the last time you were here," he said.

"No, I've been busy with the Granger story. They've been in the cases and locked in my gun vault at home," Jack replied.

"Looks good. Follow me to stall four," said the colonel, handing them ear protection and safety glasses. "Remember, safety first. Always treat the firearm as loaded, and keep it pointed safely away from yourselves and others."

"Are you coming with us?" Jack asked in surprise.

"Yes. I want you prepared mentally and physically if you have to face Gecht," Col. Hanks said.

Jack and Bobbie picked up their gun cases and the ammunition boxes and followed the colonel. As they entered the bustling range, the scent of gunpowder filled the air.

Col. Hanks reminded Jack and Bobbie of the rules, stressing the importance of following standard routines for general safety.

"You should always start with slow, controlled shots. Focus on your breathing, and squeeze that trigger gently. Go ahead and load," Col. Hanks advised, watching as they took their positions. He nodded in approval as they loaded their magazines.

"You ready?" Jack asked Bobbie.

"As I'll ever be," she said, taking a deep breath.

As they were taught, Jack and Bobbie took their stances, Berettas in hand.

Col. Hanks observed and offered guidance on grip and posture. "Steady, breathe, and squeeze," he whispered as they aimed at their targets.

BANG, BANG, BANG! Jack took three quick shots with the Beretta, hitting the bullseye twice.

Both Jack and Bobbie liked the Beretta. It was a lightweight weapon with low recoil, a soft trigger, and was easy to hold and fire. Jack's Walther P99, with its .32-caliber rounds, had more stopping power for a pocket gun. Still, Jack preferred the Beretta, and Bobbie liked how it fit her smaller hand and kicked less when she fired it.

Jack noticed Bobbie hadn't fired. "Do you need any help?" he asked.

"No, go ahead and keep shooting. I wanted to see how you did first. You know me; it always takes me more time to get ready," Bobbie said.

She aimed and fired three shots, hitting near the bullseye.

"Good. Now, steady your aim and control your breath," Col. Hanks told Bobbie as she took her position again.

As they practiced shooting at paper targets, the steady pop of gunfire and the clink of spent casings hitting the ground created a lively atmosphere. Jack and Bobbie's accuracy improved as they continued to shoot, a testament to their natural aptitude and Col. Hank's training.

"You're both doing wonderfully. Please continue at your own pace. I'm going back into the shop. Have fun. Let me know when you're finished," the colonel said.

"I'm going to shoot several rounds from different angles. Go ahead and train the way he taught you," said Jack.

Jack fired about 30 rounds with his Beretta and another 20 with his Walther. Bobbie fired about 30 shots, and then she was done.

"Jack, I'm returning to the shop to talk with Col. Hanks. I will wait for you," Bobbie said. "Take your time."

She still had mixed feelings about shooting. Even though she was a police reporter and visited crime scenes regularly, the sound of the gunshots, the smell of the powder, and the thought of people getting shot and killed all made her sad. But she wanted to train with Jack and support him, especially now that Gordon Gecht was back in town. She also knew that if Jack was in trouble, she could handle a gun to help him.

"Sure, I'm almost done here," Jack said.

"Okay, be careful," she said, putting away her Beretta and walking out.

Five minutes later, Col. Hanks returned. "How are you doing?" he asked.

"Haven't missed a beat. Colonel, I can't thank you enough for this. I remember coming out here with my dad, and you both taught me," Jack replied. "This always feels different without Dad, but I'm glad you're still here, teaching me."

"Ken would want me to do what I can. Plus, it's not often I get to associate with a big-time writer at the *Herald-Tribune*," the colonel said with a smile.

"Very funny."

Col. Hanks inspected the target. "Well done, Jack. Your proficiency is constantly improving. You would've been a solid jarhead, like your father."

"I almost was. You know that story about how I wanted to join," Jack said.

"Yes, you told your father, and he shipped you off to UF the next week," Col. Hanks said with a laugh.

"To be honest, Colonel, I'm doing this to protect Bobbie and get revenge for Becky," Jack said. "I know how that sounds, but it's the truth."

"I understand. But remember: with great power comes great responsibility."

"What do you mean?" Jack asked. He sensed the colonel had something on his mind.

"Bobbie told me she's worried Gecht is here to settle some grudge with you. I don't know the details, but are you sure you want to involve her?"

"She insisted on coming here with me," Jack said, setting his Beretta down after emptying his last clip. "I will protect her. I have a plan and two safe rooms if he comes for us at the house."

"Your new house has all the modern security features money can buy—burglar alarms, door and window sensors, a closed-circuit TV system with motion detectors covering your property," Col. Hanks said. "I was very impressed when you asked me to evaluate it."

"And I thought you were only impressed with my weapons locker," Jack said with a smile.

"I didn't tell you, but the whole setup worried me too," he said. "You've made excellent friendships with Chief Bagley, Lt. Stevens, and many policemen and detectives in Sarasota and Manatee, but can you count on them for 24/7 protection?"

"Yes. Besides the cops, the expensive house, and the security upgrades, don't forget the two million I inherited from Becky.

I invested $50,000 into Ed's detective agency," Jack said. "He's hired several more detectives who help me when I need them."

"Do they understand Gecht's capabilities? He's ruthless and, I imagine, has gained experience in killing down in Colombia with Escobar and his gang."

"You're right. Ed and the others have taken courses and training in investigating murder-for-hire assassins, but how to protect someone from one, I suppose, is something else."

"I've told you this many times: anytime you feel danger, call me," Col. Hanks insisted. "You've got friends here who will be at your side on a minute's notice."

Jack smiled. He knew the colonel meant what he said.

"If ever I need help, I know who to call. Thanks, John," Jack replied.

The two men shook hands warmly.

"Now I'd better go check on Bobbie. She's probably been interviewing all your customers," Jack said with a chuckle.

"She knows them all by now," Col. Hanks said, patting Jack on the back. "Let's go save them." The two friends walked out to the shop area.

After Jack and Bobbie thanked the colonel for his hospitality, they left the gun range, feeling more confident in their shooting skills. They were also haunted by a growing nervousness about what was likely to come.

But Jack also remembered what Col. Hanks always said about staying vigilant. "Keep practicing, stay aware of your surroundings, and trust your instincts. Your training and preparation will be crucial if it comes to it."

The drive home was quiet as Jack also considered what the colonel had said about involving Bobbie in his home defense. Should he tell her to stay away from his house until

Gecht was eliminated? Or was it safer for her to be close to him, just in case Gecht got cute and targeted her for some twisted reason?

Bobbie could feel Jack's anxiety. She thought about staying away from him but chose to stay close in case Gecht attacked.

The uncertainty gnawed at them as they approached home, knowing either choice carried significant risks.

Jack was confident Gordon Gecht would eventually return, but he was surprised it had taken almost 18 months. He felt ready for Gecht's return and, honestly, was glad Gecht was back so he could settle the score for Becky's death. He believed Bobbie could handle herself. His main concern was figuring out how to make Gecht's death look like self-defense.

Chapter 25:
The Hitman Cometh

Friday night, July 16, 1982

Gordon Gecht got off the airplane from Bogotá with a pocketful of money and an address. It was time to settle his grudge with Jack Kendall.

It was late afternoon when Gecht walked through the Sarasota-Bradenton Airport, trying not to be noticed. He knew he had an arrest warrant from his days as a drug dealer working for the late Robert Mackey at the High Seas Restaurant.

He had spent the past year in Colombia, working as an enforcer and hitman for Medellín cocaine drug lord Pablo Escobar, who recognized and rewarded Gecht's particular skills in intimidation, murder, and organization. Escobar had helped Gecht evade arrest by Colombian police after he murdered Becky and Michelle and shot Jack Kendall, nearly killing him when he arrived to investigate the murders.

Besides the occasional hits and threats to "business" associates, Escobar assigned Gecht a variety of tasks, including traveling to Bolivia, Peru, and Ecuador to help manage and enforce Medellín's multi-country cocaine distribution network to the United States.

But Gecht's ultimate plan was to return to the United States to take care of his unfinished business: killing Jack Kendall.

When the time was right, nearly two years after he escaped drug trafficking charges in Florida and 18 months after recovering from his gunshot wound, Gecht lined up a murder-for-hire job in Sarasota with the help of Escobar, who also wanted Kendall silenced.

While the $25,000 payment plus expenses was the standard fee, it wasn't the only reason Gecht took the job. He would have nearly done it for free when he learned his old nemesis, Jack Kendall, would likely receive the secret documents.

Walking outside to the cab stand, Gecht felt the breeze picking up. He looked at the darkening sky and clouds moving quickly from west to east. He'd heard about Hurricane Amos and hoped to finish his job before the storm hit.

At the cab stand, he read the address to the driver and headed to the Bali Hi Motel to meet Pierre Grousland, his employer, about the job.

As the cab sped from the airport south on U.S. 41 to Sarasota, Gecht's mind raced with plans and contingencies. He knew that this job, while lucrative, was also his ticket to settling old scores. It was also possible he could get some, if not all, of Robert Mackey's drug money that Kendall received from his late wife.

The Bali Hi Motel was a run-down establishment off 5th St. and the Tamiami Trail, a relic from another era. Its neon sign flickered, and the paint was peeling from its walls.

Gecht checked in under a fake name on a passport and went to the room specified by Grousland. Inside, the air was thick with the smell of mildew and cheap cleaning products.

Pierre Grousland was already waiting, seated at a small table with a bottle of whiskey and two glasses.

Grousland motioned for Gecht to sit and poured him a drink.

"You got here without any trouble?" Grousland asked, sliding the glass across the table.

"No issues," Gecht replied, taking a sip. "Let's talk about the job."

Grousland nodded, pulling out a file from a battered briefcase. "My chief mining engineer has been a problem for Granger. He's got documents that could implicate the company in fraud, bribery, and a phosphate spill. Your job is simple: eliminate him and recover the documents."

"I can see why you need my services. Got yourself in a little mess, eh?" said Gecht.

Grousland didn't react. "Take a look at this."

Gecht flipped through the file, examining James Brewster's picture closely and noting the details about his routine and the location of his apartment.

"What about Kendall?" Gecht asked. "Does he have the documents?"

Grousland leaned back, a slight smile playing on his lips. He knew Gecht's history with Kendall.

"Kendall is causing an issue. As far as I know, Brewster has the documents. Kendall has been getting information about the discharge from somebody within the company. I'm certain it's Brewster, but it could also be other people," Grousland said.

"But you just want Brewster eliminated?

"For now."

"And Kendall has been writing about it?"

"Yes, and I want to make sure he doesn't get any documents from Brewster that he can use to expose us."

"I understand. Kendall has a history of being a pain in the ass," Gecht said. "He's been writing about El Patrón and Medellín."

"You know, finding you was a blessing," Grousland mused.

"How is that?" Gecht asked.

"I got a call a few weeks ago, clear out of the blue, asking me if I needed anything taken care of," Grousland said. "I didn't understand at first, but then one of your associates paid me a visit and explained what I'd get for a small investment."

"I was told how and why El Patrón sent me," Gecht replied.

"I was offered a package deal for Kendall and Brewster," Grousland said. "You know about that?"

"The offer still stands."

Grousland took a sip of his whiskey and stood up. "You know Kendall, he won't stop asking me questions about things he has no business asking. We have filed a lawsuit against his newspaper and got them to stop for now, but I'm sure that won't be enough."

"Just give me the word, and I'll eliminate Kendall—with pleasure," Gecht said.

"Not right now. I know you want to kill him," said Grousland, taking another swig of whiskey.

Gecht nodded, his mind already formulating a plan. He

finished his drink and stood up. "I'll take care of whatever you want."

It was clear Grousland didn't know, but Escobar also sent him to kill Kendall to stop the journalist from writing about the Medellín cartel's operations in America. The job suited him fine.

Grousland eyed Gecht, a mixture of concern and curiosity crossing his face. He knew Gecht was capable, but an edge to his determination made the phosphate plant manager uneasy.

As he left the room, Gecht felt a familiar surge of adrenaline. He was skilled at taking control and making things happen. The hunt was on, and he was ready to finish what he had started years ago.

Chapter 26:
Bone Valley Murder No. 1

2 p.m., Saturday, July 17, 1982

Jack was eating lunch at his house with Bobbie after their practice session with Col. Hanks. They were talking about Hurricane Amos and how to prepare when the phone rang.

"Jack, I've heard something you're not going to like from my friend in the police department," said Ed Kendall.

"What is it?"

"James Brewster has been murdered. Happened at his Bradenton home earlier this morning."

Jack was stunned, his mouth dropping open. "Are you sure?" he finally asked a few moments later, his voice cracking.

"Lt. Duffy was at the scene all morning," Ed said.

"I'm going to call Chief West. Stand by. I'll call you back," Jack said.

As he hung up, Bobbie interrupted, her voice filled with concern. "Jack, what happened? What's going on?"

"Someone killed James Brewster. I've got to call West to confirm," he replied solemnly, trying to contain his anger.

He slowly dialed the direct line to Chief West's office. It rang three times before the chief picked it up.

"West here."

"Chief, this is Jack Kendall. A source told me James Brewster has been murdered. Is it true?" Jack demanded.

"We haven't released a statement yet. But, yes, it's true. We're investigating," West acknowledged.

"Are you sure it was James Brewster?" Jack asked, hoping there was some mix-up.

"Yes, a man identified as James Brewster was found shot to death in his car early this morning."

Upon hearing Brewster's name confirmed, Jack's body slumped several inches. He closed his eyes and shook his head back and forth.

"It can't be," he muttered in disbelief. "Chief, I knew him. He was my anonymous source in the Granger pollution story. I have been trying to get him on the record with what he knows. It was Gecht. Gordon Gecht."

"Who? What do you know?" West asked.

Jack realized he'd said too much.

"Jack, come to the station. I can give you the report, and you can talk with the investigating detective. You know something," West said.

"Bobbie's here. I want her to handle this. He was my source," said Jack somberly.

"All right. I'll tell Detective Duffy to expect her. He's here for the next hour or so, but I still would like you to come in and tell us what you know about Brewster and this Gordon Gecht," West said.

"You know, Gecht, Charlie. He was the asshole involved with the High Seas cocaine bust in Sarasota 18 months ago. He killed Becky and shot me."

"Oh, yes. Gordon Gecht. So, you think Gecht came back to kill Brewster? I'll let Duffy know. Are you coming in?"

"Charlie, I'm not sure what more I can say. I want to help, but I need to talk with my editor and my attorney first," said Jack, who had calmed down slightly but was still trembling with anger.

"Of course. All we know is he was the chief engineer at the fertilizer plant," West said.

"I can tell you a little of what I know about him, which isn't much. We've learned he has a mysterious past," said Jack, pausing. "Does Duffy know about his past?"

"Yes, a little. Have Bobbie come in and get the report. She can talk with him. When can you come in?" West asked.

"Maybe two hours," said Jack, straightening up.

"Good," replied West. "We need what you know."

"Before you go, what else can you say about the murder?" asked Jack, the shock wearing off.

"Strange thing. The victim had a driver's license under the name James Brewster, but a few things didn't add up, so we don't think that was his real name. We're looking into it."

"Not his real name? Hmm, now that makes sense," said Jack, remembering what Ed had reported about Brewster being a ghost before 1976.

"What makes sense?" West asked.

"Long story, but I couldn't get much on Brewster's past," Jack said. "Will you tell me what you find about him?"

"Possibly. We'll access his records, and we're interviewing everyone at the plant, going through Brewster's office desk and his home for clues."

"Any suspects? Witnesses to the murder?"

"None that I know of, but we can't get into that anyway. Just come in," West insisted.

"Be up there soon. Thanks, Charlie," Jack said as he clicked the phone off.

Bobbie stood beside Jack in the kitchen, listening intently. "Jack, are you all right?"

"I don't know. I can't talk about it now. We need to do the story. Can you get down to Manatee and talk with Duffy?" asked Jack.

"Of course, I'll leave right now. But I need to know you're okay," Bobbie said.

"Let's talk later. I've got to call Ed, and then Wiseman and Gantz."

"All right. I'll see you at the station."

"Or at the paper."

Before she left, Bobbie reached over and squeezed Jack's hand. "It'll be all right," she said.

He nodded as she left, then sat down on a kitchen chair. It suddenly hit him. Was he to blame for James's death? He slowly dialed Ed's number.

"You were right. Brewster, or whatever his name is, has been murdered," Jack said sorrowfully.

"Brewster wasn't his real name?" Ed asked.

"That's what Chief West said. I know you've tried your sources at the Sarasota Police Department. Try Manatee. They must know something more about Brewster."

"I'll try."

"Even though he's dead, I still need to use him in my story and confirm his real name. Why did he change it? And whatever else you can find out about him."

"Let me check."

It was Saturday afternoon, and with the deadline closing in, Jack knew Ed wouldn't wait for anything official. Ed would check with Manatee County, but first he'd call his old high school friend, who they both knew at the Sarasota Police Department, and work the story through unofficial channels, because that was often the only way to get answers in time.

While Jack waited for Ed to call back, he paced around the house. Now that he'd had a minute to think, multiple thoughts flooded his mind.

Why would a corrupt phosphate company kill a whistleblower? The motive must be more than to keep one guy quiet. And why was James using a fake name? For what purpose? Could he be an undercover federal agent? He doubted it, but killing Brewster to cover up a phosphate slime spill didn't make sense. *There must be more.*

Jack thought of Gordon Gecht. It wasn't a coincidence that he'd arrived in Sarasota yesterday and that someone was murdered today.

If Gecht had been the culprit, he likely wouldn't have returned to Sarasota to kill only Brewster. *He's coming for me.* He had already tried twice.

He recalled the first incident. During the summer of 1980, he was searching for Becky, who was missing, at Robert Mackey's house in Siesta Key. The second took place in Bogotá, when he was investigating clues related to Becky's murder.

Now, he expected Gecht would make a third attempt to kill him—and possibly Bobbie as well—because Jack had shot him and was also looking into Granger, his new employer.

Sensing danger, Jack went upstairs to his bedroom, opened his nightstand, and unlocked his Beretta's case. He loaded a magazine, then returned downstairs. Ten minutes later, the phone rang.

It was Ed. "Jack, I confirmed it. The cops discovered that 1976 was the year David Kane legally changed his name to James Brewster."

"Who is David Kane?" asked Jack, his tone a mix of curiosity and confusion.

"We know some things about David Kane," Ed continued. "He was born in Bartow. He graduated from Polk High and the University of Central Florida, and—listen to this—he attended USF medical school. He was a goddam medical doctor!"

"An M.D.? You got all this in 10 minutes?" Jack asked.

"Manatee briefed Sarasota, and I got it from my source there. They don't know why Kane changed his name, but he has no police record. We should know more in a couple of days."

"I had no idea. I didn't ask Brewster much about his background other than his age, birthplace, degree, and college."

"No one did much of a background check because his engineering license and other documents said he was James Brewster."

"I never thought to grill him on his background. I should have given you more clues to check on, but he must have changed his name for a reason. Can you find out?" asked Jack.

"I'll let you know when we get more," Ed said.

"Thanks," Jack replied.

It was time to call Wiseman.

"Rick. I just talked with Chief West. My source, James Brewster, has been murdered," Jack said bluntly.

"Murdered? What happened?" Wiseman asked.

"He was shot outside his house early this morning."

There was a pause on the other end. Wiseman's usually steady and reassuring voice now carried an edge of concern. "Jack, we need to be careful. Do you have any idea who's behind this?"

Jack clenched his fist. "I have my suspicions, but no proof. Brewster mentioned he had more documents and more evidence. We can blow this thing wide open if we can find them."

"What are you going to do?"

"I have an idea. I need to make a few calls, but what about running the story Monday morning?"

"We still have that temporary restraining order and the hearing on Monday. I'm going to call Gantz and brief him. You and Bobbie work this murder story, and we'll see where it goes," Wiseman instructed. "But first, you need to protect yourself. Whoever did this won't hesitate to come after anyone standing in their way."

"I've got it covered. Don't worry," Jack said. "Listen, Chief West wants me to come over and talk with the detective. Do I have your permission to tell them what I know about Brewster?"

"You'd better call Gantz. Got his number?"

"Yes, I have it," Jack said. "There's another thing. It seems that, in 1976, David Kane legally changed his name to James Brewster. We aren't sure why, but David Kane was born in Bartow and has no police record. I need to put that in the story."

"Glad you uncovered that. Let Peter know," Rick said.

"I'll talk with you later," Jack said.

Jack dialed Peter Gantz's home number.

"Hi, Jack. What's up?" the lawyer asked.

Jack briefed him about what he knew about Brewster's murder and name change.

"First, if Brewster, or Kane, has no police record, all we need to do is state that his name was previously David Kane," Gantz said. "Second, it's okay to let the police know you met with Brewster. Just tell them what he told you based on your reporting. You don't need to say anything he told you that you didn't use in a story at this time. I have to research this a little more."

"I have to talk with the detective pretty soon."

"I can meet you there in one hour."

"Is it okay to tell the police that Brewster felt the company was watching him? He was very paranoid about what he was doing."

"Besides what he told you, what was he doing?"

"I'm not sure, but he gave me some documents showing the forged reports to the state, and he gave me the recording he made of the three executives," Jack said. "He told me to ensure the police get these documents and the recording."

"That could embarrass Granger, but it's a stretch to think they would murder him over that," Gantz said.

"The executives admit they bribed the state inspector and discussed committing other felonies," Jack explained. "Brewster wanted Granger investigated by the police."

"I haven't listened to that tape, just what you put in the story," Gantz said. "We need to be careful we aren't withholding evidence, but Brewster is dead."

"Peter, Brewster told me he was going to get me some more confidential documents that proved Granger was covering up how bad the pond walls were, and more evidence—*proof*—they bribed the inspector."

"All this could be a motive for murder," Gantz suggested. "You'd better tell the police this as well. Brewster, or Kane, doesn't need protecting any longer."

Chapter 27:
Brewster Murder Investigation

10 a.m., Saturday, July 17, 1982

Detective Patrick Duffy spent the morning carefully piecing together clues at the scene of James Brewster's murder. The victim's body was slumped in the driver's seat of his car. He had been shot twice—once in the right arm, likely as he fled, and once in the head, the fatal blow. The headshot suggested a professional hit; death would have been instantaneous.

Officers noted clear signs of a break-in inside the house. The back door had been jimmied open, and the interior was ransacked as if someone had been searching for something.

Crime scene investigators dusted for fingerprints, their brushes working methodically across surfaces, while Duffy examined the kitchen.

Blood spatters on the tile floor, and a tipped-over coffee mug caught his attention. Looking closely at the scene, he concluded the attack had likely started there. Brewster had probably been making coffee when his assailant surprised him.

Duffy went back outside as the police photographer finished taking pictures of Brewster's body. He found bruises on his knuckles and a cut on his lip. He made several other notes and called Sheriff West.

"Sir, Duffy here. I have a theory on how Brewster was killed. It was early morning, and the victim was in the kitchen making coffee.

"Our perpetrator, a professional killer, in my opinion, picked the back door lock to gain entry. He surprised Brewster, but our victim fought back.

"My guess is he ran out of the house where he was shot in the arm. He made it to the car, where the perpetrator killed him with a headshot," Duffy explained.

"Any signs as to why Brewster was killed?" Chief West asked.

"I believe the killer was looking for something in the house. He didn't kill Brewster right away. He must've talked with him before the fight," Duffy replied. "The suspect could've been asking the victim for whatever he sought."

"I think you're on to something. Jack Kendall from the *Herald-Tribune* might be able to assist us with that. James Brewster worked at the Granger Station phosphate plant. Kendall knows him and possibly what the killer was after. I asked him to come in and talk with you this afternoon," Chief West said.

"Roger. I'm almost done at the crime scene. I'll be in shortly," Duffy said.

Chapter 28:
Gecht's New Assignment

Saturday, July 17, 1982

Gordon Gecht wasn't happy. He had only completed half of his assignment. Although he had killed Brewster, he had done so sloppily, and he had failed to find the documents Grousland wanted.

He did find a clue: a name and a phone number in Brewster's wallet.

"Pierre, he's been eliminated," Gecht said over the phone.

"Good," Grousland said.

"I couldn't find your papers. Brewster might have already given them to Kendall," Gecht continued. "If he didn't, I have a lead where they might be. Do you know anything about a girl named Elizabeth?"

"I always thought Brewster had a sister, but I don't know anything about her," Grousland replied.

"What do you want me to do?" Gecht asked. "Should I go after Kendall and see if he has the documents, then terminate him? Or find the sister?"

"I don't want Kendall killed now. If he has them, the documents are probably in the newspaper office, and it's too risky to search," Grousland said. "Besides, newspapers have security inside and out."

"That doesn't bother me," Gecht growled.

"We have to be careful right now," Grousland said. "Killing a reporter writing about us has to be a last resort."

"So, what's the next move?"

"You must track down the sister. This time, be more patient. Recover the documents before eliminating her."

"The same arrangement?"

"Ten thousand for her, plus another $15,000 for getting us the documents."

"More for the documents? I never had this arrangement before," Gecht said.

"The documents are critical," Grousland insisted.

"It might take a day or two, but I'll get the girl—and your documents," said Gecht, hanging up the phone.

Chapter 29

Brewster Murder Aftermath

1 p.m., Sunday, July 18, 1982

Jack and Bobbie were in the living room, watching a weather report about Hurricane Amos intensifying as it entered the Gulf of Mexico west of Cuba.

"This tropical cyclone is expected to closely follow Florida's west coast, remaining about 100 miles offshore as it intensifies over the next two days. Sustained winds arc 100 miles per hour, with gusts reaching 120 miles per hour. However, this is just the beginning," said meteorologist Bryan Norcross, standing before a large screen displaying the storm's path.

The graphic behind him shifted. "As you can see, our projected path currently calls for Amos to land as a Category 5 hurricane with sustained winds nearing 190 miles per hour just south of Tampa Bay into the Sarasota-Bradenton area. Everyone from Venice to Tampa should prepare for a catastrophic storm surge and landfall. It will be like an EF5 tornado 20 miles wide. I'll have hourly updates on this historic storm. This is Bryan Norcross, signing off."

Jack and Bobbie were starting to understand how destructive the hurricane would be when the phone rang.

"Hello?" Jack asked, still mesmerized by the weather report.

"Jack, this is Fred Fance. Sorry to bother you at home," said the commissioner.

"Are you watching the news?" said Jack.

"About the hurricane?" Fred asked. "Yes, that's another issue we must address on Monday."

"It's going to be a Category 5, and it's coming straight for us!" exclaimed Jack in disbelief.

"I know, but I'm calling about the board meeting on Monday."

"What about it?"

"You probably haven't heard this yet, but James Brewster was going to testify," said the commissioner.

"He what? In public?" Jack asked, taken aback. "No, I didn't know anything about that. I don't understand. He didn't want to be identified in my story."

"He came to see me on Friday afternoon and told me everything about Granger Station. He said he gave you the same information for a story, and you hadn't done anything with it," Fance recounted. "He read about the scheduled meeting and wanted us to do something about the spill and the corruption at Granger."

"That's true. I wrote a story, but my editor decided to hold it for a couple of days. I was asked to verify more facts and gather corroborating information before we published it. Then, Granger filed a motion for a temporary restraining order to delay its release. We have a hearing Monday morning, about the same time as your meeting," Jack explained.

"I talked with him on Friday afternoon. He was frustrated and wanted to get the information he had on the public record," Fance said. "I also sensed he was terrified. He didn't exactly say why, but I gathered his employer was on to him about talking with you and that he'd sent letters to the state."

"Yesterday, I told Detective Duffy everything I knew about Brewster and Granger," Jack said. "I thought James was worried, but I last saw him on Wednesday. I'd been trying to talk with him since then."

"I wish I knew how serious the situation was. I would've gotten Mr. Brewster police protection," said Fance, frustrated.

"I was worried he might be in danger," Jack said. "Have you talked with Chief West or Detective Duffy about this?"

"Yes, I was down at the station yesterday. I saw Bobbie's story this morning and thought I'd better call you just in case you were doing something more for Monday."

"I'm still waiting for my editor to let me know if we'll run the Granger corruption story now that Brewster's dead."

"Wouldn't that violate the court order?"

"We're talking with our lawyer about it, but Fred, I don't care if it violates the U.S. Constitution! Brewster is dead, and he was my star source, and I'm ticked off."

"What do you need from me?"

"The whole situation has changed now," Jack said. "Tell me about the meeting."

"Well, I was planning to open the meeting with a report from Steve Tracy about the timeline of the spill and the reasons behind it. Then I was going to discuss the environmental damage to the land, air, and water," Fance replied.

"That aligns with my story," Jack said. "It's another reason we should run the article Monday morning."

"I hope you do. After that, I intended to give the Granger representatives a chance to share their perspective," Fance continued. "I invited Pierre Grousland, and he mentioned that one of their attorneys would be present. They'll explain what went wrong and what measures are being taken to address it.

"After Tracy and the commissioners questioned them about their account, I was going to call James Brewster as a surprise witness."

"Did James tell you what he planned on saying?"

"Yes. He wanted to talk about how Grousland and Cross falsified his reports to the state DEP, how he tried to alert the state to the fraud, and how neglect and deliberate sabotage of the gypstack weakened the walls and caused the spill.

"Then, we were going to play the tape recording," Fance said. "James was going to explain it all."

"That's the smoking gun!" Jack exclaimed. "I can see why James wanted to present his story at the meeting. He would've gotten maximum coverage with that approach. Print, radio, and TV would be there."

"Granger would have much explaining to do," Fance said.

Jack laughed sarcastically. "I don't understand how they could explain Grousland admitting to bribing Miniver and ordering the backhoe to dig out the walls, all while intentionally discharging 100 million gallons of toxic wastewater to maintain high production and profits for the company."

"I never thought a company in Manatee County would do such a thing," Fance said.

"And kill their employee," Jack added softly, pausing. "Wait a minute, when did you meet with Brewster and decide to add him to your agenda?"

"Friday afternoon. Why? What's wrong?" asked Fance.

Jack exhaled slowly. "Because James was killed on Saturday morning. And now it looks a hell of a lot like someone didn't want him speaking in a public meeting."

Fance's breathing hitched. "You're telling me he may have been murdered *because* I put him on that agenda?"

Jack shook his head. "I'm telling you someone was terrified of what he knew."

"My God... I put a target on his back?" Fance said, his voice trembling.

"Fred, this had to be set in motion long before your agenda. Just between us—Gordon Gecht, the man who murdered Becky and shot me, showed up in town this week. I'm convinced he's behind it. The police are already looking for him," Jack said.

Fance's lips tightened, and he looked away. "Jesus... I didn't know." He swallowed hard, the weight of it settling on his shoulders. Then he fell silent.

"It's not your fault," Jack said, trying to console the commissioner. "Keep doing your job. By the way, are you still going to hold the meeting?"

Fance took a deep breath. "No, we have to postpone the Granger testimony until the police sort things out."

"Oh, I see. You postponed the meeting," Jack repeated so that Bobbie could hear. He was disappointed.

"I don't see what else we can do. It's a regularly scheduled session, and we have other business to discuss. Tracy will give us a brief update on the spill, and we'll probably hear from the public, but I won't allow anyone to speculate on why Brewster died or who's to blame."

"I understand. Say, commissioner, can you hold the line for a minute? I want to talk with Bobbie quickly before she leaves for the Manatee sheriff's office."

"Sure, go ahead."

Jack turned to Bobbie, sitting beside him, listening to the conversation. He placed his hand over the receiver.

"I think we have another story to write for Monday," he said.

"I know. I'll check with Detective Duffy and my sources about Brewster," Bobbie said.

"Good. I'll get the quotes from Fance on Brewster's death. Also, find out if they've called in Grousland as a suspect or person of interest. Whatever theory they're working on."

Bobbie smiled. "Jack Kendall, one thing no one can say is that spending Sundays with you is boring," she said with a laugh. "I'm on it. I'll see you later at the paper."

"Right," said Jack. "See you soon."

He lifted his palm off the receiver. "Fred, sorry. You still there?"

"Still here. I want to help you as much as I can. I feel terrible about what happened to James Brewster," Fance said.

"I know how you feel. Before I ask you some questions about Brewster, do you plan on saying anything about the audio?" Jack asked.

"No, not now. I gave the police the recording and a statement about Brewster," Fance said. "How else can I help you?"

"Please give me a comment on Brewster's murder. It seems pretty clear to me it was tied to your hearing Monday and that he was planning to expose Granger's corruption."

"Let me see. First, I don't know who killed James Brewster or why. He told me how frustrated he was with Granger's management of its fertilizer plant. He also told me he was scared that managers knew he was leaking information to the press and had written letters to the state DEP about falsifying plant safety and quality reports.

"Finally, I want to state on the record that the Manatee County Commission will thoroughly investigate the phosphate spill into Terra Ceia and determine if Granger should continue to hold an operating permit in the county," Fance said. "This is apart from the murder of its chief engineer."

"Did James say anything about being scared of his employer?" Jack asked.

"He thought people were watching him and that he was in danger," Fance explained. "I just didn't think in a million years a company, phosphate or not, would do something like this."

"I knew he was scared, and he told me he was in danger," Jack said. "But I thought, at first, he meant he was in danger of losing his job. Later, he explained he needed a few more days to gather evidence. Still, I agree with you. What company would kill an employee? I didn't think anything like this would happen."

"We don't know everything about what happened, but for reasons we may never understand, Brewster was committed to exposing this corruption, and he seemed to know he was in danger," Fance said.

"He was. Listen, I have everything I need from you. Thanks, Commissioner Fance—Fred, for calling me about this and for sharing your thoughts," Jack said. "Now I've got to let my editor know what you told me."

"Jack, you're doing an outstanding job on this story. Don't blame yourself too much. Good luck," Fance said.

"Thanks," said Jack as he hung up the phone and blankly

looked at his notes.

While the shock over Brewster's death had passed, he felt a heavy weight settle in his chest. Guilt gnawed at him for not trying harder to contact Brewster the past few days. All the while, James had been on his own, scared, and then killed in front of his house that Saturday morning.

Still, he and Bobbie were also in danger with Gecht on the loose. He set aside his emotions for a moment and called Wiseman.

"Rick, it's Jack. Brewster was supposed to testify at Monday's County Commission hearing on Granger. Fance knows everything, and with Brewster dead, the hearing's postponed. This can't be a coincidence," Jack said.

"That's a significant development," Wiseman replied. "What's the plan?"

"Bobbie is on the cop side for updates, and I'm getting quotes from Fance for the story," Jack explained.

"I know what you want—to run the story. But we still have the problem of Granger's temporary restraining order, and we need to find a way around it."

"Have you spoken with Gantz?"

"Not yet."

"I didn't bring it up when I talked with him, but see if he can talk with the judge today about reversing himself. Show him my story. Tell him that with Brewster dead before he was to testify, the public has the right to know about the spill," Jack suggested. "If we can demonstrate that the information is in the public interest, we might get the order lifted."

"Good idea. I'll call him now," Rick said.

"Thanks."

"Listen, I've changed my mind about the story. If we get

the order lifted, I favor packaging it for A1 with sidebars on your hearing and Bobbie's updates. I hope the police have new leads."

"She knows, and she's working on it."

"I need you to hurry down to the newspaper office. I'll call Gantz and inform Mr. Lindsay about the changes and that we'll be working overtime today."

"Sounds like a plan. I'll see you soon," Jack replied as he hung up the phone.

Jack hoped Gantz could persuade the judge to allow his exposé to be published, finally, but he was still angry that it had cost Brewster his life. He wouldn't rest until the truth was revealed and those responsible were held accountable. Brewster deserved it, and Jack was determined to see it through.

He drove his GT through the nearly deserted streets in silence. He didn't even turn on the radio to hear the latest update on Hurricane Amos, although the destruction that storm was about to unleash lingered in the back of his mind.

Chapter 30:
Nervous Eyewitness

2 p.m., Sunday, July 18, 1982

Jack parked his GT, walked quickly to the front door, and used his keycard to enter the empty *Herald-Tribune* front lobby. He nodded at the weekend security guard, an off-duty Sarasota city cop sitting in a chair, apparently taking a break.

"Quiet today, Frank?" Jack asked, stopping for a short chat.

"Same ol'," the middle-aged officer replied.

"Has anybody told you to be on special alert?" Jack asked.

The burly guard stood up. "No, should I be?"

"Just keep an eye out for anything unusual. The engineer at Granger Station, whom I talked with about the phosphate spill, was murdered early Saturday morning," Jack said.

"Right, I read Bobbie Jackson's story. He was killed at his house in Bradenton," Frank said. "Who was this guy to you?"

"He was an anonymous source about the corruption at the plant. It's pretty clear to me, Granger did it."

"Jack, why do you think the murderer will come here?"

"If Granger did kill James Brewster, it must have been to silence him about the spill. He could come here to get the documents Brewster gave me. He probably doesn't know we gave the originals and the audio to the police."

"Do you know who killed Brewster? Do they have a description?"

"Not exactly, but if you see a man, maybe 6 feet, long black hair, thick black mustache, anywhere on the property, call your police friends because he's armed and dangerous," Jack said.

Frank firmly nodded. "Got it," he replied, his voice steady and serious. He shifted his stance, subtly adjusting his grip on his holstered weapon. "I'll keep an eye out. You stay safe, Jack. If this guy shows up, we'll handle it."

Jack walked to the elevator and punched the fifth floor for the newsroom. He walked into the darkened room and switched on the lights. Wiseman wasn't in yet. The copy desk would be in by 4 p.m. He went to his desk, turned on his computer, and pulled up his Granger story.

He wrote a new lead, indicating Brewster had been murdered on Saturday. Bobbie would write an updated second-day story on the investigation.

Jack read through the piece line by line, tweaking it to make it clear that James Brewster, now deceased, was his source and that he'd legally changed his name from David Kane in 1976.

As he was working, the phone rang. It was Frank from downstairs.

"Jack, I've got a young man named Daniel Rumsfeld. He

says he works at Granger and wants to talk with you about James Brewster."

"Did he show you an ID? I've talked with him, but I've never met him," said Jack, suddenly wondering if it might be a ruse by Gordon Gecht to draw him out.

"Yes, why don't you come down?" Frank asked.

"I'll be right there," Jack replied.

To be safe, Jack hurried down the five flights of stairs, cautiously opening the first-floor door. Moving silently, he positioned himself for a clear view of the security desk by the front entrance. He was relieved to see Frank conversing with a young man, not the killer, Gecht.

Walking toward the two, Jack sized up Daniel Rumsfeld. While taller than average at about 5'10 "and 180 pounds, Daniel was still much shorter than Jack. He was dressed casually and looked relieved when he saw the reporter approaching.

"I recognize you from your newspaper picture," Daniel said. "You told me to come see you any time."

"Daniel, how are you? Do you have more information than what you gave me Thursday night?" Jack asked.

Rumsfeld seemed nervous and said nothing.

"I take it you heard about James Brewster?" Jack asked sympathetically.

Daniel looked down. "Yes. I saw something that scared me yesterday. It's bothered me all night."

"It's all right. Let's go upstairs and sit at my desk," Jack said.

They rode up the elevator in silence. Jack scrutinized Rumsfeld, who seemed fidgety and nervous. It was clear the young technician was frightened. Jack led Rumsfeld to his desk.

"Have a seat," Jack said.

"Saturday morning, I rode my bike to Mr. Brewster's house

to talk about Grousland's warning that I keep quiet. I told you about that Thursday," said Daniel breathlessly.

"Take a deep breath," Jack encouraged, understanding what Daniel was getting at.

"As I turned the corner, I saw the man!" Daniel exclaimed.

"You saw Gecht?" Jack asked excitedly.

"I saw the man who murdered James," Daniel blurted out in a panic.

"Can you identify him?"

"I'm pretty sure I can," Daniel said. "I was down the street a bit, but I saw him. He had a strange outfit on. He dragged Mr. Brewster out of the house, along the ground, and put him into his car. It was horrible."

"Did he see you?"

"No. I made sure. When I saw him, I dropped down onto the sidewalk. I watched as long as I could and then turned around and rode as fast as possible to the nearest store, where I hid for the next hour."

"Daniel, you have to tell the police all this. You witnessed a murder."

"I didn't want to go to the police because of what Mr. Grousland told me," Rumsfeld said. "I'm sure he had James killed."

"So, you came here to tell me all this off the record?" Jack asked.

"If something happens to me, you'll know the story," Daniel said.

"Can you describe this man?"

"Yes, he had long black hair in a ponytail and a black mustache. A little taller than me and much shorter than you."

Gordon Gecht. Jack knew it was him from the black

mustache. It matched the description of Gecht's disguise in the airport photograph.

"I'm scared this man might come after me, and I don't want to return to work even if they call me back next week," Daniel said.

"I'm glad you came to me. I know this man, and he's extremely dangerous. We need to call Lt. Stevens now," Jack said.

"Who is Stevens?"

"He's in charge of detectives. He can send over a squad car to take you in for a statement and protect you."

"I have to do this?" said Daniel, his voice shaking.

"Daniel, you don't have to go public with your story, but you must tell Lt. Stevens what you saw and who killed James," Jack said firmly. "Catching him will also protect you in case he sees you."

"I'm scared, but I'll do anything to help you and the police find this man. James was my mentor—and my friend," Daniel said.

Just then, Wiseman and Gantz entered the newsroom.

"Over here, I want to introduce you to one of my anonymous sources," Jack said. "He just told me he saw Gecht murder Brewster. Peter, this should help lift the restraining order with the judge."

Chapter 31: Elizabeth's Sorrow

Sunday morning, July 18, 1982

Elizabeth checked her answering machine, noticing that James hadn't returned several calls from the night before. She wondered what he was doing. He always made a point of letting her know where he would be; he should have been home by now.

Concerned, she quickly got dressed and drove over to his house. As she turned the corner, her heart sank at the sight of two police cars parked outside.

"Why are the police here?" she thought, pulling over to the side of the street. Her hands began to tremble, and tears filled her eyes. Was her brother—the person she leaned on most, her reason to live—dead? It felt like the only explanation for his silence and the police presence.

Stunned by the thought, Elizabeth parked her car, got out, and started walking toward the house.

Elizabeth slowly walked along the sidewalk toward her brother's house. Each step felt painful, and she was breathless and weighed down.

When she reached the driveway, she paused. James's car was parked there with the driver's side door wide open. She stared at it in disbelief.

"Ma'am, may I help you?" asked the officer standing by the car.

Elizabeth remained silent.

"Are you a neighbor? Did you see anything yesterday morning?"

She finally managed to say, "No. What's going on? Why is the door open?"

"There was a murder yesterday. If you know anything about it, please let me know."

"Who did this?" she asked.

"It's under investigation. Please go home. You'll be safe."

"Safe?"

Elizabeth looked at the officer in bewilderment, then turned and walked away. She knew what she had to do. She had no choice. There was nothing left for her to do except what she'd wanted to do from the beginning.

James was gone, her parents were gone, and she was left alone to complete the job—her own way.

Elizabeth got into her car and drove to her apartment. Even though James's death was devastating, she set aside her emotions. She had things to do.

She often drove to her hometown of Bartow to see her parents' house and lay flowers on their graves. When she was near them, she could feel their presence. She could talk with them anywhere, but their voices sounded stronger at her old house or by their grave.

This trip was different. James had told her where CFO Harold Maynard's office was in the Granger building. Once there, she could easily find where he kept his most secretive documents.

A few days earlier, James finally permitted her to search Grousland's house. She disguised herself, broke into the manager's home, and found incriminating documents revealing corruption, payoffs, and a complete conspiracy at Granger Station. Like the other documents James had given her, she'd put them in her safe deposit box at her bank.

As she'd read the papers, however, references hinted that even more incriminating documents existed at the corporate office in Bartow. One paper cited another co-conspirator, CFO Harold Maynard.

She wanted those documents because she thought they could provide evidence that Granger ordered her brother's assassination. So Elizabeth got on I-75 and headed north to Bartow for the 80-mile trip.

About halfway there, Elizabeth noticed a black car behind her, slowing and speeding up to keep pace. She guessed it could be a Granger spy. It didn't bother her. Once she got into Bartow, she knew a few shortcuts to the Granger corporate office, and she could use those to lose the driver.

As she approached the first stoplight in the city, she slowed to allow it to turn yellow. Then, when it turned red, she gunned the engine and turned left into oncoming traffic. It was a risky move, but when she looked back, the black car was stuck.

On the next street, she turned and hid behind a building.

She waited for the black car to pass, then doubled past the same traffic light she had run and headed in the opposite direction.

Ten minutes later, she was at Granger corporate headquarters. She drove past slowly, looking for security outside. There was none, just as James had told her. *Cheap, arrogant bastards*, she thought. *They don't even guard their building.*

She parked on a quiet street two blocks from the main road, just in case the man following her guessed she was going to Granger.

Stopping the car, she opened her second suitcase and pulled out the housekeeper's outfit she had stolen from the hospital where she worked. She put on a blonde wig and applied some cheap lipstick and makeup.

Once in disguise, Elizabeth drove to the next street, where she stopped the car again, got out, and walked to Granger's offices carrying a dark-colored backpack.

She knew how to get in a side door. Once inside, she found the maintenance room and commandeered the pushcart with the housekeeper's mop, pail, and cleaning liquid to complete her disguise.

Maynard's office was in the executive office suite area down the hall. She pushed the cart slowly but deliberately.

When she reached his door, she tried the knob but found it locked. She opened her backpack and pulled out two bobby pins, ready to pick the lock. She had practiced this technique repeatedly and was now quite skilled at it.

Inserting the bobby pins, she twisted them until she heard a click, then turned the knob. She pushed the door open and went directly to the tall filing cabinet behind the CFO's desk.

She pulled on the handle of the top drawer, but it was locked as well. A smile crossed her face as she quickly picked that lock too. Once the drawer was open, she rifled through the files until she spotted the words "GS Confidential."

After reviewing the contents, she selected two papers outlining the company's strategy to maximize profits by reducing maintenance costs. A third document, dated the week prior, authorized $200,000 for "expenses related to Granger Station security." She assumed that amount was the price of James's life. Closing her eyes for a moment, grief washed over her, but there was no time for that—only revenge.

She hurriedly tucked the papers into her backpack, closed the drawer, locked the door behind her, and left the office. Five minutes later, she was in her car, none the wiser.

As she started the engine, Elizabeth thought about the day before, when her brother had been murdered. She knew she was nearing the end, with only four small things left to do.

Chapter 32:
Granger Executives Sought

Monday morning, July 19, 1982

Jack's article about corruption and the cover-up at Granger Station, as well as a follow-up of Brewster's murder, was featured on the front page of the *Herald-Tribune*. Gantz successfully petitioned the judge to lift the restraining order until a hearing later in the week. The legal team reviewed the situation carefully early Sunday evening, and Mr. Lindsay approved it.

It had a different headline and lead paragraph now because Brewster's murder seemed linked to his scheduled public testimony Monday morning. Even though the story had been withheld since Friday, Jack felt the updated version gave a fuller picture of what happened at Granger Station and explained why Brewster was killed.

Jack's 3,000-word story with charts and photographs created quite a buzz in the region. For the first time, the public learned the truth about the grimy underbelly of the phosphate industry, at least how one company abused the public's trust for higher profits.

By the afternoon, the police departments in Manatee and Sarasota counties began searching for three new persons of interest: Pierre Grousland, Herbert Cross, and Louis Decker.

* * *

Immediately after reading Jack's Monday morning story at 6 a.m., Grousland phoned Granger CFO Harold Maynard, the corporate executive involved in the conspiracy to kill Brewster and boost Granger's profits, to give him the bad news.

On the other end of the line, Maynard acted calm. "I'll send a temporary manager, Jeffrey Risser, to oversee operations at the plant," he calmly instructed. "You, Cross, and Decker must lie low for a while. Disappear."

Grousland's heart raced as Maynard assured him they had taken additional measures to protect the company from the mounting allegations.

"If the press starts digging into this," Maynard continued, "we'll simply tell them you're all on administrative leave. We need to get ahead of this situation. In the meantime, we'll initiate a fake investigation into the *Herald-Tribune*'s claims to buy us some time. Now, get lost. Goodbye."

After discussing the situation with Maynard, Grousland

felt a mix of anxiety and urgency. He quickly called Cross and Decker and instructed them to drive to Sarasota County immediately.

"Book into small hotels. Don't even tell me where you're going—do it," he ordered, his voice taut with the weight of their situation.

He knew where he would stay in Sarasota. A small motel off U.S. 41 called the Bali Hi.

* * *

After hanging up with Grousland, Maynard's jaw tightened as he dialed the number for Dick Button, Granger's general counsel.

"Dick, it's Maynard," he said, pacing the length of his office. "We have a disaster brewing at Granger Station. I must know how to shield the company from these idiots without admitting guilt. How do we publicly distance ourselves from this mess?"

There was a long pause on the line. Finally, Button's voice came through, calm but laced with urgency.

"We gotta put out a statement, and it's gotta be solid," Button said in his New York accent. "Somethin' that owns the problem but lays blame square on the station execs. Somethin' like this: Granger Corporation condemns the reported actions at Granger Station. These decisions do not align with our values of accountability and environmental stewardship. We are launching an internal investigation to address these concerns and cooperating fully with authorities. Our priority is ensuring transparency and restoring trust with our stakeholders."

"Is that it?" Maynard asked.

"We gotta spin this like it's a betrayal of what we stand for, not some kind of systemic problem," Button continued, his accent sharp and deliberate. "The public's gotta see Granger as the victim here. We're talkin' rogue managers runnin' wild, not Granger bein' some kinda willing accomplice to all this negligence and corruption. Capisce? That's the angle we need to hammer home."

Maynard stopped pacing, the weight of Button's words sinking in. "And what about the fallout? We've already lost our temporary restraining order request, and the public seems outraged over Jack Kendall's articles," he pressed. "We'll be facing lawsuits, the EPA breathing down our necks. If this gets tied back to corporate, we're finished."

"That's why the statement's gotta be airtight," Button said firmly. "We nod to the concern, we pledge action, but we don't own up to nothin' at the corporate level. This ain't about takin' the fall; it's about redirectin' the heat. We're the problem solvers here, not the problem creators—got it?"

Maynard exhaled, his tension easing slightly. "Draft it. Make sure it's perfect. I'll need it by the end of the hour."

"It's done already," Button replied with icy efficiency. "This isn't the first time I've had to pull this company's ass outta the fire."

Chapter 33:

'Find My Documents and Kill That Girl!'

Later Monday morning, July 19, 1982

Pierre Grousland waited in his room at the Bali Hi Motel, wondering how he would escape the mess his company had put him in.

He knew it was easy to blame Bartow corporate for the overly ambitious phosphate fertilizer production schedules and the budget constraints for maintenance on the containment walls that created the need for the discharges.

But he'd taken the money they offered. His plan was simple: Follow orders until the gypsum stack was full and fertilizer prices dropped by 20%, making the plant unprofitable. Then,

Granger would shut down the plant and put it up for sale. He'd retire and move to Alabama, his home state.

Now, he was facing arrest and a lengthy jail term, possibly the death penalty, if they found out he was involved in James Brewster's death.

He wasn't going down without a fight. A knock on the door interrupted his thoughts.

Grousland looked through the hotel door's peephole. It was Gordon Gecht.

As soon as Gecht stepped into the dingy motel room, Pierre Grousland's face contorted with rage. He didn't waste a second.

"You stupid, incompetent son of a bitch!" Grousland roared, slamming his fist on a rickety table. "How hard was it, huh? Get the goddamn documents. But no! You couldn't even do that right!"

Gecht, full of rage himself, had no choice but to take it if he wanted to get paid and stay on Escobar's good side.

"I did everything to catch up with her. I even followed her to Bartow Sunday before I lost her in traffic," Gecht said, his frustration overflowing.

"What was that bitch doing in Bartow?" Grousland growled.

"I don't know, but she went there," Gecht said quickly. "Then, I searched her apartment again."

"You couldn't find anything?" Grousland asked, his voice turning whiny.

"No. The girl's smart. Either she has everything with her, or it's somewhere else."

"I don't care what you have to do. God damn it, Gecht. Find my documents and kill that girl!" Grousland shouted, frustrated.

"Why do you want those documents anyway? Kendall

already used them to write his fucking story, and he had the audio tape," Gecht said.

"No. Kendall wrote the story based on some documents Brewster stole from my office last week. But the documents I want you to get back were stolen from my house and are more sensitive," Grousland explained. "They also implicate you in his murder."

"You put that in writing?"

"They were notes that I'd planned to get rid of," said Grousland dejectedly. "You aren't the only one who screwed up."

"I didn't screw up. I'll find the girl and kill her. She must have stolen them to give to Kendall," Gecht said.

"If she did, she hasn't given them to Kendall yet," Grousland said. "Nothing in his story this morning referred to those documents."

"So, are you worried about a second story?"

"Now you've got the picture. I'll give you 24 hours to get them back. If you can't find that girl with my documents, kill Kendall and get whatever you can from his house or the newspaper," Grousland ordered.

"That's a big assignment. I need $50,000, half upfront," Gecht said.

"But you haven't even found that girl," Grousland objected.

"Half up front is the deal," Gecht said. "Just like the girl."

"All right," Grousland acquiesced. He reached under the mattress and pulled out a bag of cash. "When I left the office this morning, I took all our cash. This just about taps me out, so make sure you get that girl and the documents."

"You mean you won't have the other half when I finish the job?" Gecht asked.

"You have enough. If you get the documents and the girl, you have your money," Grousland said. "If you need to kill Kendall, I'll get the other half from Bartow."

As Gecht took the money, he said confidently, "Pierre. Don't worry. I *will* take care of Kendall. No charge to you. Either way, I'll find the girl, get your documents, and finish the job. I have an idea where she's going."

"One more thing," said Grousland, handing Gecht a piece of paper. "Take this phone number. If I'm not here, leave a message if you want to contact me. I don't know how long I'll be here."

"Right."

"Listen, Gecht, I have problems you don't know about. Just get your job done."

"With pleasure," the professional killer said as he left the room.

Chapter 34:
Hurricane Amos

Sarasota Journal
Monday afternoon edition, July 19, 1982

DISASTER LOOMS: GYPSTACK CRISIS UNFOLDS AMID HURRICANE AMOS

BY JACK KENDALL
HERALD-TRIBUNE INVESTIGATIVE REPORTER

As Hurricane Amos barrels toward Southwest Florida as a Category 5 storm, a brewing environmental crisis threatens to compound the devastation.

Local officials decided to release millions of gallons of toxic wastewater into Tampa Bay to prevent an even greater disaster at Granger Station, a phosphate plant in Manatee County.

On Sunday, Granger Station's state-appointed emergency manager, Stuart Locker, called Manatee Commission Chair Bev Gargies with an urgent plea.

The plant's towering gypsum stack—a mountain of radioactive waste left behind by phosphate processing—was on the verge of collapse. Containing more than 150 million gallons of wastewater and an additional five million gallons in nearby holding ponds, the stack's structural integrity was no match for the relentless rainfall and surging winds forecasted from Amos.

"We have to alleviate pressure on the walls to prevent a total collapse," Locker told Gargies. "If the stack fails, the neighborhood and the bay will be inundated with toxic sludge."

Recognizing the gravity of the situation, Gargies approved the discharge of 100 million gallons of wastewater into Terra Ceia Bay.

"There really wasn't a choice," Gargies said during an emergency press briefing. "This is about protecting lives and trying to contain the damage. But make no mistake, the environmental impact will be severe."

At 10:52 a.m., the Manatee County Commission authorized the wastewater release and a voluntary evacuation of the Granger Station neighborhood. Hours later, Governor Bob Graham issued a mandatory evacuation order for nearly one million people across Manatee, Hillsborough, Pinellas, and Pasco counties.

Environmental experts warn that the discharged wastewater contains a cocktail of hazardous materials, including radium-226—a radioactive substance with a half-life of 1,600 years—and heavy metals such as lead, mercury, and thallium.

"Granger's wastewater is some of the most toxic I've encountered in my 40 years working with phosphate facilities," said Locker. "Even with the release, we can't guarantee the stack walls won't fail."

Piney Point and the Riverview phosphate plant, larger facilities off Tampa Bay, are also in the storm's projected path. The two fertilizer plants contain more than 900 million gallons of phosphate-laced wastewater and slime.

Locker, who had taken over from Granger's temporary manager, Jeffrey Risser, pointed directly to the cause of the crisis.

"Granger's maintenance budget was a joke," he said. "They gambled that this day would never come. This negligence is emblematic of a more significant issue plaguing Florida's phosphate industry."

Across the state, 24 gypstacks hold nearly one billion tons of waste, much of it sitting precariously close to the Floridan aquifer, the state's primary source of drinking water.

Gov. Graham's emergency declaration included a call for action. "After Amos passes, I will ask the state legislature to hold hearings on how to address the phosphate industry's gypstack crisis," he said. "Even if these stacks aren't an immediate threat to our bays or rivers, they remain a ticking time bomb for our aquifer and our people."

The environmental toll facing Tampa Bay is staggering. The phosphate wastewater, sludge, and slime—laden with radioactive material and carcinogens—could take decades to cleanse from the ecosystem. Already battered by red tide and habitat loss, local wildlife face yet another existential threat.

"This will take years, if not generations, to recover from," said Sarasota Bay Estuary Program marine biologist Dr. Ellen Carver.

As Hurricane Amos inches closer to landfall, the people of Southwest Florida are bracing for a storm that will reshape the region. But long after the winds die down and the floodwaters recede, the scars left by this man-made disaster will linger.

For Florida, the question remains: how many more wake-up calls will it take before meaningful reform comes to the phosphate industry?

Chapter 35:
Pierre Grousland, Bone Valley Murder No. 2

Monday afternoon, July 19

Chief Tom Bagley shook his head as he read the police report on the death of the manager at Granger Station. It was the second murder related to the phosphate plant in two days.

The report stated that Pierre Grousland was found by a maid in a room at the Bali Hi Motel with his head bashed in and a bullet in his head.

Because his skin had an unusual purplish color, Detective T. Paul Terry had ordered an autopsy. The county pathologist, Dr.

Vinny B. Bah, found Grousland had thallium and phosphoric acid wastewater in his stomach.

What was striking about the death, besides the phosphoric acid in his stomach, was the thallium, a tasteless and odorless poison. Police were puzzled about the motive for the murderer to inject him with thallium. It was a slow-acting poison.

Was the killer sending a message? Both chemicals were commonly found in phosphate mining and fertilizer processing, and Grousland was the architect of the recent spill.

Dr. Bah said the head wound, caused by a hammer, and the "ingestion of thallium and phosphoric acid" in the stomach were administered after Grousland was shot in the head.

"Chief, this looks like a sadistic revenge killing to me. I've assigned Detective Terry to the case," Stevens said. "He's our most experienced investigator in serial killings. It could be the same killer, or connected in a way we don't yet understand. Even though the gunshot to the head was the cause of death, the head wound, the thallium, and phosphoric acid were just gratuitous."

"Are you coordinating with Manatee? Detective Duffy is handling the investigation into the murder of James Brewster, who also worked at the Granger plant," Bagley said.

"Yes, Detective Terry knows the background," Stevens said.

"Make the connection. Keep me posted," the chief said.

Bagley needed to have an informal chat with Jack Kendall about this death. They had a good relationship. Kendall always honored off-the-record and background discussions and had been helpful with the Brewster investigation in Manatee.

Chapter 36:
The Conspiracy Deepens

Later Monday afternoon, July 19, 1982

Staying busy did not ease Jack's overwhelming sadness over Brewster's death. He had been getting to know and to like James, the phosphate mining engineer who had become an environmental whistleblower. Jack blamed himself for not doing more to ensure the exposé on Granger Station was published that Friday morning.

Although the circumstances were different, Brewster's death reminded Jack of when, two years earlier, Charlie Tolbert had killed himself. During a hostage stakeout, Tolbert had asked Jack to interview him as a condition for releasing two teenagers. Still, it turned out that the interview was only a pretext for his suicide.

The shock and horror of witnessing Tolbert's final moments haunted Jack. Now, like Charlie Tolbert, Jack blamed himself for James Brewster's murder.

Jack buried his face in his hands. He had devoted his life to uncovering the truth and shining a light on corruption and injustice, but at what cost? The people who had trusted him and taken risks to expose the truth were paying the ultimate price.

He uncovered his hands from his face and took a deep, shuddering breath. He needed to talk to Bobbie.

Jack picked up the phone and dialed her extension. She had spent nearly three hours at the Manatee downtown police station and had just arrived at the newsroom.

"Bobbie. Can you come over for a few minutes? It's about Brewster. I have some notes for your follow-up, but I want to talk with you."

There was a pause on the other end, and Jack could hear the concern in Bobbie's voice when she replied, "I'll be there in a second."

Jack watched as she walked over from across the room. They had grown close over the past year and a half, particularly the last month. He didn't want to admit it, but he thought he might be starting to fall in love with her.

"What is it, Jack?" said Bobbie as she sat beside him in an empty chair.

"We have to nail Granger. I can't let James's death go unanswered. What do you have on the investigation?"

"I found out Manatee police are looking into Granger's illegal actions based on the documents, the audio tape, and the other evidence Brewster provided. It's still early, and I don't have much to write about other than that," she said.

"James would be happy they're opening a criminal investigation. It's what he said he wanted our story to do."

"You know the state ordered Granger to suspend phosphate fertilizer production at the plant?"

"Yes, I wrote a short story for tomorrow's paper. The state should do much more than that," he said. "At least they brought in a competent emergency manager for Granger. Stuart Locker is trusted in environmental circles."

Bobbie looked at Jack, her eyes filled with concern. "The state is finally realizing they have a problem. I hope they investigate Angus Miniver and anyone else involved in the cover-up. What else is bothering you? You're acting odd. Is it Brewster?"

Jack sighed. "Yeah, I lost another source."

Bobbie slid her chair closer and touched his shoulder. "Jack, listen to me," she said softly. "What happened to James isn't your fault."

Jack shook his head. "But if I had pushed harder to get the story out sooner, maybe James would still be alive."

Bobbie gently squeezed his shoulder. "You did as much as you could. Besides, you're not alone in this. We're a team. We'll get through this together and make sure James didn't die in vain."

Jack looked at Bobbie. He saw more than a glimmer of reassurance and hope in her clear blue eyes. He saw love. He knew she loved him. He had been resisting her. It surprised him that Bobbie's compassion and caring touched him in a way he hadn't felt before, even with Becky.

"Maybe you're right," Jack said. "We need to make sure his story is told."

Bobbie nodded, a determined look on her face. "We will

get to the bottom of this. One step at a time." She stood up and squeezed Jack's hand, then she released it.

Jack felt calmer. He always felt better after talking with Bobbie.

"Do you need my help with anything?" he asked.

"It's a police story at this point," Bobbie said. "You can help me if you want. Why don't you review the documents Charlie gave you again? Who knows, maybe you missed something. I need to get back to my story on the investigation."

"Sure, thanks again, Bobbie. Uh, wait a second...I have one more question," Jack said softly as she stood there with an eager expression. "Let's talk some more about this when you have a chance."

Bobbie smiled. "Anytime. Just let me know."

She turned, and Jack's gaze lingered—only now did he truly see her, the quiet, unhurried grace of each step revealing a beauty that caught him off guard and drew him in.

Jack shook his head and smiled. She was not only beautiful but also intelligent. He temporarily shook off those thoughts. Bobbie was right; he needed to review Brewster's documents again to determine with whom James was collaborating. He believed the note stating that the documents were in "good hands" alluded to another person, but that person's identity remained a mystery.

He had securely stored copies of Brewster's documents in a locked room at the newspaper while the originals had been submitted to the police as evidence.

Brewster had promised to get additional documents from Grousland. Was that the reason for Brewster's murder? Did he have those documents for the Monday commission meeting? If so, perhaps he entrusted them to the mysterious person.

The phone rang as Jack started to get up to go to the secure room.

"Jack, this is Chief Bagley. I've got a favor to ask. You owe me one, maybe two."

"Sure, Tom. What is it?" Jack asked.

"You probably haven't heard yet...but the manager of the Granger Station phosphate plant has been murdered."

"Pierre Grousland?" Jack exclaimed. "Does Bobbie Jackson know about it?"

"Probably not. I will withhold the police report for a few hours until we examine a few things. You can tell Bobbie to call us," Bagley said.

"Chief, what's going on? Two dead sources. First, James Brewster. Now, Grousland?" Jack said in exasperation.

"I know. This is serious, Jack," said Bagley. "We need a little help. Who would want to kill him?"

"I don't know," Jack replied. "Why do you think I would have that information?"

"You seem to know quite a bit about Granger Station and the people who work there, like Grousland and Brewster," Bagley said. "You've talked with them a lot lately. Any off-the-record information you can't print?"

Jack paused, wondering what he could tell Bagley. "I know a few things about Grousland, and I can give you my thoughts," he said. "Will this be used in the investigation?"

"Right now, no, just between us. I asked Detective Terry to call you as a formality because you've been looking into Granger Station and knew them both."

"Well, Grousland is a scumbag mining official. He's corrupt from head to toe," Jack said. "He's bribed government officials, falsified documents, and is involved in multiple conspiracies."

"I read your story," Bagley said. "But who has a motive to kill him?"

"I suspect Granger hired the murderer, Gordon Gecht. It follows that if Granger hired Gecht to murder James Brewster, which I believe they did, they could have hired Gecht to murder Grousland," Jack suggested.

"This is one of our theories," Bagley said.

"One, you have more than that?" Jack asked.

"We may have more to tell you later after we run down a few leads," Bagley said. "Stand by. Detective Terry is going to call you now, and you can ask him."

Jack set the receiver down and waited for Terry to call. Jack liked Terry. He was a rising star in the Sarasota Police Department and had solved a multiple-murder case the year before.

A few minutes later, the phone rang, and Jack picked it up.

"*Herald-Tribune*. Jack here."

"Jack, this is Detective Terry. Chief Bagley asked me to call about the Grousland case."

"Yes, how can I help?" Jack asked.

"I understand you heard about Pierre Grousland. The chief told me you think Gordon Gecht killed Pierre Grousland and James Brewster," Terry replied.

"Seems logical to me that Granger is trying to tie up loose ends to protect its business. They were caught red-handed destroying the gypstack wall and dumping all that slime phosphate into the bay. I don't have any direct evidence about the murders, just the conspiracy. Are you working with Detective Duffy in Manatee on this?"

"Yes. We also think they're linked, but that is not for publication. Chief Bagley said you are good to discuss this off the record."

"For now. We can talk about what to go on the record with you about later," Jack said. "Let's think this through together. First, Brewster. I can tell you that Brewster thought he was in danger. He implied the threat came from Granger, but it wasn't about losing his job. I didn't realize that right away. He said in so many words that he was willing to sacrifice his life to expose what Granger was doing."

"I see. You talked with Brewster. Did he tell you he was in danger from his own company?"

"He implied it. I also heard it from several employees. Grousland, his immediate boss at the plant, threatened him on the audio tape. Have you listened to it?"

"Yes, we reviewed all the documents you provided us. They're highly incriminating but not evidence of murder," Terry said.

"No. Brewster said he had more incriminating documents. I haven't seen them. Are you looking at a corporate connection?" Jack asked.

"To someone killing Brewster? Yes. We are looking at everything: his employer and the enemies he might have had."

"As I said before, the murderer, Gecht, is behind this. Did it occur to you that within a day after Gecht arrived in town, Brewster was murdered? Then Grousland? My guess is that Granger hired Gecht to kill Brewster and also murdered Grousland for the same reason. To keep him quiet."

"Gordon Gecht is the one involved in the High Seas cocaine ring in Sarasota?"

"Yes, and he fled the U.S. and is involved with the Escobar coke cartel in Colombia," said Jack, pausing. "He also killed my wife, Becky."

"Ed told me. I was sorry to hear about your wife," Terry replied. "Was Gecht the one who shot you in Bogotá last year?"

"Yes. You need to know that he's a dangerous asshole," Jack said. "If Gecht killed Grousland to eliminate a witness, he probably is also after Decker and Cross. They were on the recording as conspirators."

"Do you think they could be next?"

"Definitely. Where are those guys? My sources told me they weren't at the fertilizer plant. Did they vanish?"

"We're looking for them. We can't find a local address besides the fertilizer plant," Terry said. "I can tell you this: besides the employer, we believe there is at least one other connection, an obvious one."

"An obvious one? Tell me something I don't know," Jack said.

"I shouldn't say. But, off the record, I wonder if there is someone else who is upset that Brewster was killed, and could that have led to Grousland's murder?" Terry hypothetically asked.

"Well, if Gecht didn't kill Brewster and Grousland, I don't know who else could have done it. Wait, are you saying that the person who killed Grousland did it as revenge for Brewster's murder?"

"Possible theory. Again, off the record."

"You know something you aren't telling me. Hmm. Brewster gave me a lot of secret Granger documents, and he said he had more. I never saw them, but I have something that might help you. It's something I started thinking about right before the chief called."

"What's that?"

"In the documents James gave me, I found a handwritten

letter that said he had other, more incriminating documents in 'good hands,' suggesting he gave the originals to somebody for safekeeping," Jack explained.

"We think so too," Terry said.

"You think so? Do you think he was working with someone? Is someone helping James? Can you confirm this?" Jack asked excitedly.

"Off the record, yes."

"I always thought that. Do you have someone in mind?" Jack asked. "We looked into Brewster's background and couldn't find anything earlier than 1976. You found out more, didn't you?"

"We did, and the chief said if you want anything more about that, you should call him," Terry said. "Listen, that's all for now. I appreciate the conversation. Let me know if you find anything else. We're going to find Grousland's and Brewster's murderer."

"Before anybody else gets killed, I hope," Jack said.

"Right," said Terry as he hung up.

Jack immediately called Chief Bagley.

"Hi, Chief. I just had a good talk with Detective Terry. He's thinking the same as me and looking for Decker and Cross," said Jack. "He also hinted you might have a secret about Brewster to share."

"We found something in Brewster's past we're looking into," the chief said.

"We only found details on him after he graduated from college in 1976. You must know about Brewster further back. Does he have a fingerprint record or an FBI file?"

"I can't give you any information we got from the FBI. But I can tell you one thing—off the record, you can't print it, our usual arrangement."

"Deal. What is it?"

"Just between us...Brewster has a sister," Bagley said. "Now, I've got to go."

As the phone clicked, Jack slowly set the receiver down. "Brewster has a sister?" he said to himself, pausing. "Of course."

Chapter 37:
The Real Elizabeth Brewster

Early Tuesday morning, July 20, 1982

James had rented a small apartment in Sarasota near J.R.'s Old Packinghouse Café so that he and Elizabeth could use it as a hideaway if either of them ran into trouble. It was built as a granny unit, with a bathroom and kitchen above the garage, in a residential neighborhood. Still, it served Brewster's purposes for secrecy.

After stealing the Granger documents in Bartow, Elizabeth drove to the garage apartment. She sat on an old sofa and read through more than 50 pages of highly incriminating paperwork.

Elizabeth discovered what James suspected: extensive corruption at Granger. The documents showed regular bonuses paid to Grousland, Decker, and Cross for withholding maintenance expenses and maximizing production. They also detailed payoffs to state inspector Angus Miniver for ignoring false reports and state regulations. She also found notes describing how the company sabotaged the containment wall and paid employees for doing it.

However, the documents also referred to corruption at two other phosphate fertilizer plants that Granger owned, which nearly matched the crimes in Manatee County.

Stunned by the breadth of the corruption, Elizabeth realized it was far more than James had known. She wished he were alive to help her, but she pushed those thoughts aside, knowing she had to stay focused to avoid slipping into depression. She needed to continue her plan at all costs.

When Elizabeth and James first devised their scheme to expose corruption in the phosphate industry after their parents died in 1975, they both understood the challenges ahead and accepted that death was a possibility.

But there was one thing Elizabeth could not control: her bipolar disorder, which caused mood swings that could last days or weeks, was worsening. Even James was unaware of her darker side; the constant stress amplified her condition.

Doctors had warned her parents that she was likely to develop schizoaffective disorder in her late twenties, given her occasional abnormal thoughts. For the past seven years, Elizabeth had obsessively focused on avenging the deaths of her parents by targeting the most corrupt phosphate executives she could find.

Medication helped keep her condition under control, and

her brother's support provided stability. Their shared quest to expose the corruption in phosphate mining helped her remain focused and balanced.

Now, however, with her beloved brother gone and having stopped her medication, Elizabeth had been experiencing a manic high—what doctors termed hypomania—for the past week. She had been sleeping little and was more active than usual.

Despite her condition, she remembered how James taught her to make and stick to a plan. But she needed to act quickly before anxiety and depression returned.

Elizabeth's high intelligence gave her a creative mind. She could solve problems and create solutions through abstract reasoning. However, her low emotional intelligence limited her ability to understand people. She felt little empathy for issues outside her narrow range of interests.

When she'd killed Grousland, for example, Elizabeth believed she had achieved two objectives. First, it drew the police and media's attention to Granger Station. Second, it avenged her brother's death. She hoped that the upper management at Granger would stop discharging wastewater into Terra Ceia, viewing that pollution as akin to spitting on James Brewster's grave.

Desperately missing her brother, Elizabeth was now on her own—unrestrained by James's caution but fueled by her anger at his death.

It was nearly 6 a.m. when Elizabeth got into her car and drove to the nearby 7-Eleven. She paid 25 cents for the *Herald-Tribune* and returned home. Upon seeing the story's headline, she smiled. Everything was going according to plan. Pierre Grousland's death was just the beginning.

GRANGER STATION MANAGER KILLED IN LOCAL MOTEL ROOM

BY BOBBIE JACKSON
HERALD-TRIBUNE STAFF REPORTER

Pierre Grousland, embattled manager at Granger Station phosphate plant in Manatee County, was found shot to death Monday morning in a room at the Bali Hi Motel.

Grousland, 58, has been implicated in a conspiracy to sabotage the phosphate containment wall and illegally release 100 million gallons of highly toxic wastewater into Terra Ceia Bay.

Police officials said they have no motive or suspects for the killing. They urged the public to come forward with any information regarding the death.

Grousland was also being sought for questioning by Manatee County and Sarasota County police for the murder of James Brewster, chief engineer at the plant and a whistleblower on alleged corruption.

Herbert Cross and Louis Decker, two other Granger executives, are also being sought by police for questioning.

They were reported missing from their apartments in Ellenton, said Manatee Sheriff Charlie West.

"We are looking for these two men, and when we catch them, we have several questions about the phosphate spill last week," said West.

"I pray that anyone who sees these two men will contact us immediately. Do not take justice into your own hands. Just report their whereabouts, and we'll take it from there," West said.

Granger Station is owned by Bartow-based Granger Phosphate Co., which also owns two other mines and two fertilizer plants in Florida.

Elizabeth finished the *Herald-Tribune* article and said, "Chief West, calm yourself. I will find these two asswipes. There will be more deaths for you to investigate—and more vengeance for my dead brother."

Invigorated by the coverage of her deed, she very much wanted to immediately hunt down and kill the man or woman who'd murdered her brother. But, according to her plan, she had other things to do first.

Returning home, she sat in the kitchen and thought through her to-do list, still fighting the urge to hunt down the culprit. Her next task would be to contact Jack Kendall about the documents she had stolen from Grousland's and Maynard's offices. James's voice echoed in her mind, guiding her every move.

She grabbed her bag, glancing at the framed photo of her parents and James on the counter. As she walked outside, she began to talk to them.

"James, I did what you told me. I got the papers. I know what to do with them."

She hesitated, her voice softening. "Mom, James told me to give them to that reporter. He told me to trust Kendall. He'll do the right thing and expose the company."

Her hand trembled as she reached out to unlock the car door. "I had to kill that man, James. Tell her why I had to do it. She'd understand if she heard it from you."

Elizabeth's expression hardened, her tone resolute. "See, Mom? James knew what he was doing was dangerous. And I know what I'm doing is dangerous, but all this will save lives. You *said* it would."

She stood there, looking at the sky. "Mom, you may not have understood, but I'm doing what I was born to do: kill phosphate asswipes who made decisions that killed you and Dad. I'll stop their contamination of the environment and make you both and James proud."

Satisfied, she got in her car, drove to a nearby public phone, and inserted a dime.

"Jack Kendall, I have something for you from James. I wouldn't have to do this if you hadn't let him down. He trusted you. Now he's dead. Be on alert. More will fall at Granger Station."

Chapter 38:
Bone Valley Murders 3, 4, 5

Later Tuesday morning, July 20, 1982

Elizabeth Brewster meticulously studied the movements of Cross and Decker, who lived near each other in corporate luxury apartments in Ellenton, about five miles east of Granger Station.

Their routine was to work until after 6 p.m., go for dinner together—usually until 7 p.m.—and then go home to their apartments.

She planned to drive to Granger and look for their cars. If they weren't at work, which she doubted, as they would have disappeared after she killed Grousland, they likely would go to their apartments to hide or pack for a getaway.

Before leaving her own apartment, Elizabeth took out the

disguise she had purchased over the past several months: a blonde wig, heavy mascara, a fake scar, a fat dress, and high-heeled shoes that made her three inches taller.

She donned her disguise and quickly checked her reflection in the mirror. She smiled, hardly recognizing herself.

*　*　*

Earlier that morning, Cross and Decker nervously read Bobbie's *Herald-Tribune* story about Pierre Grousland's murder.

"I don't like it," said Decker. "Someone killed Pierre? What should we do?"

"We've got to get away from here as soon as possible," Cross said.

"Are you thinking the same thing I am?"

"That Granger is behind it? We know they took a contract for Brewster. They could easily do the same for us."

"You think Pierre told the killer where we're hiding?"

"Granger knows. I used the company card in this hotel room."

After discussing what to do, the two executives agreed to drive home to Pensacola, pick up their families, and head to Texas or even Arizona. They needed to get as far away from Florida as possible.

As they drove past Ellenton, Cross decided at the last minute to stop at their apartments to pack the rest of their belongings.

"Are you sure?" Decker asked. "It's a risk."

"It'll be okay. We'll only be a few minutes," Cross said.

The men parked and hurried inside their apartments to gather the few necessary things. They agreed to meet by their car in five minutes. The drive to Pensacola would take more than eight hours, and they didn't want to dally.

Cross entered his apartment and went straight to the bedroom. He told himself he would only take the essentials—personal things. A framed picture of his wife and kids sat on the dresser next to a small jewelry tray. He opened the closet and reached for two expensive Italian suits still wrapped in plastic.

* * *

Elizabeth was waiting for him.

For a moment, she felt nothing at all. No fear. No rage. Just a hollow calm, as if something inside her had finally gone quiet. This was the part of her mind that worked best—the part that planned, waited, and finished what others started. The grief, the voices, the years of unanswered suffering all compressed into a single, cold certainty: this had to be done.

"Welcome home, phosphate scum," Elizabeth said, her voice cold and steady, as if she were greeting a stranger instead of a man who deserved to die.

Cross froze for a split second, his body stiffening, his head turning just enough for confusion to register. But it was already too late. She pulled the trigger once. The bullet struck the back of his skull with a sickening thud, and he collapsed in a heap, his face never touching the floor.

Moving swiftly, she knelt beside him and swung the hammer with brutal force. Once. Twice. The dull, wet cracks echoed in the small room, heavy and final. Blood spattered across her gloves and the carpet, but Elizabeth didn't flinch or look away.

Although he was already dead, she pulled up his shirt and

injected a fully loaded syringe of thallium and phosphoric acid wastewater into his stomach. She watched the needle disappear beneath the skin, satisfied. Then she wiped her hands, stepped into the bathroom, and waited for her second victim.

* * *

Five minutes later, Decker stood by the car, checking his watch. Cross had said he'd only be a minute. Irritated, he decided to see what the holdup was.

"Herbert? Where are you?" he called as he entered the quiet apartment. "C'mon, we don't have a lot of time."

The silence unsettled him. He checked the kitchen, then walked toward the bedroom.

"Really, what's the problem?" he said as he stepped inside.

Cross lay sprawled on the floor. Blood soaked into the carpet from his shattered skull.

"Here's the problem. Join your friend, asswipe," Elizabeth said as she stepped from behind the bathroom door and calmly shot him once in the back of the head.

Decker fell face-first, collapsing beside Cross's motionless body.

Without hesitation, Elizabeth walked over and brought the hammer down twice on the back of his skull. The sound was familiar now. Routine. As with the other target, she injected him with thallium and phosphoric acid, pressing the plunger all the way down.

She stood there silently, looking at the two men sprawled on the floor, blood seeping outward, mixing together. Her eyes glazed over as she thought of her parents, of her brother, and of how long this reckoning had been waiting.

"For you, James," she said softly, then turned and left the apartment.

She took her time walking to her car parked around the corner. She scanned the street. No movement. No witnesses.

Elizabeth smiled.

Three down, one to go, she said to herself as she drove off toward Bartow.

* * *

On Tuesdays, Harold Maynard always visited the company's largest phosphate fertilizer plant in Polk County in the late afternoon to review the production and financial books. He was punctual and always followed his schedule. Elizabeth knew this and waited for his car by the entrance to the Mulberry plant.

She had learned that schedules were a kind of arrogance—men like Maynard believed routine made them untouchable. Predictable. Safe. That belief, she knew, was the real weakness.

At 4 p.m., Maynard turned onto the road to the plant, and Elizabeth watched him from the side of the street. At first, he was oblivious to the old Pontiac Bonneville, her late mother's car, its faded paint and dull chrome blending easily into the landscape of scrub and chain-link fencing.

But Elizabeth saw him coming, had raised her hood, and was standing by her car. She waved at him as he came closer, her posture helpless, practiced.

Maynard spotted the unusual-looking lady and, being in a good mood, decided to stop and help. "What's the problem? Engine trouble?" he asked.

"Yes, it's my fault. I should have fixed this engine when my mechanic told me about it. Something about the valves. Faulty valves?" Elizabeth said in an unusual, foreign-sounding accent. "Would you mind taking me to the nearest service station? I can get someone to help me from there."

"All right. It isn't far. Get in my car. It'll only take a few minutes," he said.

"It will probably take less than that," she said cryptically.

As Maynard walked to his car, Elizabeth followed him. She glanced up and down the road—empty, quiet, late-afternoon heat shimmering off the asphalt. The hammer rested flat against her thigh beneath the dress, steady, familiar.

For a fleeting second, she thought of her brother—how careful he had been, how he had trusted the system to do the right thing. That thought hardened her resolve. The system didn't deserve trust. It deserved consequences.

Looking around for any cars, she took out the hammer from under her dress and bashed Maynard especially hard on the back of the head. The blow landed with a hollow crack, and he collapsed forward, unconscious, crumpling like a discarded coat.

"No, I'm sorry. I don't have a car problem any longer," she said.

She noticed how quiet it became afterward, as if the world itself had exhaled. This silence felt earned. Necessary. The voices that usually crowded her thoughts receded, leaving only focus—and that frightened her less than the chaos ever had.

Luckily, Maynard was a tiny man, weighing only 140 pounds. She quickly dragged him into his car, bashed him on the head another time, and promptly injected him with thallium and phosphoric acid wastewater. Her hands did not shake. She was past that now.

This part mattered to her. The chemicals weren't just a signature—they were truth. Thallium. Phosphoric acid. They were representative of the same invisible killers that had taken her parents. If anyone ever understood what happened, she wanted the message to be unmistakable.

Elizabeth then calmly walked over to her car, closed the engine hood, got in, and drove behind a fence. It was the perfect cover. She removed her high-heeled shoes and put on more comfortable sneakers, the ritual oddly soothing.

She then walked to Maynard's car, got in, and drove it back onto the Mulberry plant property. She knew exactly where the deepest toxic wastewater holding pond was located. She had studied the maps, the flow charts, the lies.

Looking at the now-dead Maynard, she shot him in the head and then drove his car into one of the phosphoric acid-holding ponds, jumping out as it rolled down the bank.

As the car slid beneath the surface, Elizabeth felt something inside her shift—relief tangled with exhilaration. This was where he belonged, she told herself. Back in the poison he'd helped create. Reduced to waste, like everything else they had buried.

She watched as it sank to the bottom. She looked around. No one saw her.

She walked back to her car and drove home to Sarasota.

For several days, nobody could find him.

Chapter 39:
Sinister Visitors

Tuesday evening, July 20, 1982

The wind howled outside as Hurricane Amos churned toward the Sarasota-Bradenton area, still a day away but already sending fierce gusts across the barrier islands and bays. Jack was in bed upstairs as the storm battered the windows. The looming Category 5 monster with 190 mph winds and a predicted 25-foot storm surge was on everyone's mind, but for Jack, there were more immediate concerns.

The doorbell rang over the rattling outside. Bobbie stirred in the bed next to him. "Who is it?" she asked. He checked the video feed from the hidden security camera and saw a dark-haired young woman beside the security guard, Francis, with the wind blowing around them. "I'm not sure," he whispered. "Stay here, lock the door."

He pushed the button on his pager to summon Ed, signaling the need for additional backup to cover the yard.

Jack quickly put on his pants and shirt. He pressed the speakerphone in his bedroom and asked, "Francis, who's with you?"

"I'll let her introduce herself; you won't believe it," the security guard replied. Despite the 40 mph gale-force winds, the rain from the outer bands of Amos hadn't begun yet.

"My name is Elizabeth Brewster. My brother James sent me."

Jack's stomach tightened. Bobbie gasped. So, Chief Bagley was correct. James did have a sister. She could tell him about James and explain what had happened over the past few days.

"Did you leave a message on my answering machine?" Jack asked.

"Yes," Elizabeth responded.

"Hold on. I'll be there in a minute," Jack said. He turned to Bobbie. "Go into the safe room and take out your Beretta. Wait for my signal."

Through the speakerphone, Jack said, "I'm coming. By the way, on the phone, when you called, what did you say you wanted?"

"I told you I have some documents that James wanted you to have for your stories," Elizabeth said. "Let me in, and I can show you."

"Be right there."

"Make it quick. I don't like standing out here. Somebody could be following me."

Jack quickly turned for the door when Bobbie touched his arm. "Be careful. She's unpredictable."

He nodded but didn't move right away. He looked at Bobbie—saw her beautiful face filled with worry—and felt the quiet weight of how they'd arrived here. It hadn't been sudden or reckless. One long night had turned into another, grief giving way to closeness, closeness to comfort. Nothing rushed. Nothing hidden. When they finally ended up together, it felt less like crossing a line than admitting what had been there all along.

She was exactly what he needed after Becky. Bobbie had been his friend before the marriage, his confidant during it, and his anchor after it fell apart. He hadn't rushed love this time; he'd grown into it, carefully, honestly. And through all of it, she had stayed—steady, patient, choosing him even when he wasn't sure he could choose anything at all.

The wind whipped through the trees outside as Jack walked down the stairs to the foyer. The storm's growing ferocity blew inside as he opened the front door.

Elizabeth stood there, her dark, glossy hair blowing about her. She was a striking young woman, taller than James, with vibrant green eyes that seemed to hold both intensity and mystery.

"Sorry, Elizabeth," Jack said. "I have to be careful. This is Francis. He looks out for me."

"I am not here to hurt you. I want you to do what you promised James," she said.

"Come inside from the storm," Jack replied, holding the door.

She stepped inside with Francis closely following.

"What do you mean somebody could be following you?" Jack asked.

"It's just a feeling I have," she said.

"Okay, you're here. Now, tell me about yourself."

"My name is Elizabeth Brewster. James was my older brother," she said. "I've been helping him fight against phosphate mining."

Just then, the phone rang.

"Let me get this. Francis, please escort Elizabeth into the living room," said Jack as he picked up the receiver. "Hi, Ed. Elizabeth Brewster is here. Come over so Francis can go back outside and stand guard. Something is going on."

"Right," said Ed. "Five minutes."

Jack walked into the living room. Elizabeth sat on the sofa, holding a large, thick manila envelope. Now gusting on and off, the storm's wind rattled the windows.

"What can I do for you?" Jack asked.

"I'm here to help you expose Granger and whatever else you need," she said.

"I'm a little surprised. James never told me about you."

"Well, he wouldn't, would he?"

"No, I suppose not. James didn't tell me much about himself and nothing about you or your family, only about Granger Station," Jack replied. "I have many questions. I'll turn on my tape recorder if you don't mind. I recorded James."

"I don't mind," Elizabeth said. "Do you mind if I take off my jacket? I didn't expect the weather to be like this."

"It's going to get quite worse. Now, tell me why you and James did all this," Jack requested.

"It's simple. Phosphate mining is evil, and James and I want to expose how dangerous it is for people and the Earth," Elizabeth explained.

"James told me how he felt about it. Hold on," said Jack. He walked over to the stairs and shouted, "Bobbie, you can come down now!"

Bobbie walked down the stairs and entered the living room, her Beretta discreetly tucked out of sight.

"Elizabeth, meet Bobbie. She's a close friend and a fellow

reporter. She wants to help, too," said Jack.

Bobbie nodded at Elizabeth, who briefly glanced at Bobbie before returning to Jack.

"Now, before we start talking, your message on my answering machine said others at Granger will die. What happened?"

"Yes, that was me. But I don't want to talk about that. Let's talk about these documents," Elizabeth said.

"Did you kill Grousland?" Jack asked.

"I'm cleaning up phosphate scum," she said. "Now, do you want to know what I have?"

Jack didn't answer right away.

The room felt smaller, tighter, like the air had been pulled out of it. He stared at her, searching for irony, deflection—anything that would let him believe she was speaking metaphorically. He'd heard bravado before. This wasn't that. Her voice was flat, controlled. Serious.

"You're telling me this like you expect me to nod and take notes," he finally said, carefully, his reporter's instincts kicking in, warning him of danger. "I asked you a question, Elizabeth. Did you kill Grousland?"

She held his gaze. Didn't blink.

"I told you," she said. "I'm cleaning up phosphate scum."

Jack exhaled slowly, rubbing a hand across his mouth. He thought of the victims, the ones he knew of—James Brewster and Pierre Grousland—and the thin line he'd spent his career walking between exposing crimes and becoming entangled in them. He felt the line disappearing.

"For the love of Mike," he muttered. Then, he spat it out, loud and clear: "You know what you're saying puts me in the middle of this, right? I'm not your priest or your safe haven. I'm a reporter."

A corner of her mouth twitched—not quite a smile.

"That's why I'm here."

Jack's eyes dropped to the envelope in her hands—thick, overstuffed, heavy with whatever truth she thought could justify murder.

"In the big envelope?" he asked, his voice low now, wary. "Is that your proof... or your absolution?"

"It's all here. Before James died, my brother told me to trust you."

"I'm sorry James died. I lost someone very close to me not long ago. What do you have?"

"Papers that can expose what Granger has done to the environment and prove they killed James."

"You know what happened to him?"

"I know what happened. They killed James, and now they're all dead. Do you want to see these papers?" asked Elizabeth, getting frustrated.

Jack looked at Bobbie and Francis with concern. She'd just admitted to killing Grousland and possibly other Granger executives.

"Don't worry. You're safe. I'll protect you," Elizabeth said. "You learned a lot about Granger Station and what Grousland did from the recording James made, the documents he gave you, and what he told you."

"Yes, James was a passionate environmentalist," Jack said.

"He was more than that. He gave his life to show the world how evil the phosphate industry is."

"My story Monday was mostly based on what James told me and proved."

"I know. These documents implicate the whole company in a conspiracy at Granger and at two other plants."

Just then, the doorbell rang. It was Ed's unique pattern—two short and two long chimes.

"Francis, can you let Ed in and then go back outside and look around? Be careful," Jack said.

Ed walked into the living room. "What's going on?"

"Ed, meet Elizabeth Brewster, James's sister. She's here to give us more Granger documents and tell us what's going on with all the deaths," said Jack, who turned to Elizabeth. "So, these documents implicate Granger in what?"

"These memos and reports prove what James told you. How Granger polluted the bay and the land where they mine the phosphate," she said.

"What else?" Jack asked.

"It shows the plan Granger had when it bought the three plants, including where James worked, and how the company is trying to make as much money as possible by limiting maintenance, mining at full production, and then selling the plants when the price of phosphate drops. They're evil, and they must be stopped."

"You read all this in those documents?"

"Yes. We want you to report this and get Granger shut down for good."

"I'll look over these papers and do my best," Jack said. "But I need you to understand a few things. First, journalism isn't magic. I told James this. It requires confirmation. It's about getting to the truth as much as possible. If these documents are authentic—and I believe they are—did you or James steal them from Granger's offices?"

"What difference does that make? I took them from Grousland's house and the Granger office in Bartow," Elizabeth said.

"If true, I can report this, but the police will include these in the investigation, so I will have to tell them how I got them," Jack said.

"I'm sure that will be all right," she said. "They're authentic."

Bobbie interrupted. "Elizabeth, Jack asked you earlier why you're doing these things and why you killed those people."

"They killed my parents and James," Elizabeth said.

"Your parents? What do you mean?" asked Jack.

"I explain that in a paper I wrote about how and why they died. It's in the folder. In short, after they married and before James and I were born, our parents bought land and built a house on reclaimed land from a phosphate mine. Except they weren't told about the dangers of radon," Elizabeth explained. "The radioactive uranium in the phosphate ore decayed into radon gas. My parents breathed it, day after day, in their house, and over the years, they contracted cancer. They were killed by people who knew the dangers and decided that making money was more important than my parents' and other people's lives."

"Oh, I'm so sorry, Elizabeth," Bobbie said. "We'll do whatever we can to report this fully."

"You must. There is one document, handwritten by Grousland, admitting he hired someone to kill my brother," Elizabeth described without any emotion.

She handed the envelope to Jack. "The full story is in these documents. They're copies, by the way. I have the originals in a safe deposit box at my bank. I'm telling you this in case something happens to me."

Jack opened the envelope and began leafing through the papers. "These are damning. They show Granger's negligence and deliberate pollution, as well as their plans to exploit the land. Ah, here it is—the handwritten note from Grousland admitting he hired someone to kill James."

"I told you, but that's not all," Elizabeth said. "These documents tie Granger to similar operations at two other plants in Polk and Hillsborough counties. It's a pattern of corruption."

Jack set the papers down, his mind racing. The storm outside seemed to echo the storm of revelations unfolding in his living room. He glanced at Ed, who shook his head and shrugged. It was evident to Ed that she was telling the truth and that she and her brother had concealed their plans exceptionally well.

"I also want you to know that our attorney, Gale Cooper of Plant City, is preparing to file a lawsuit charging Granger with fraud and the state environmental department for negligence in not enforcing its own laws," Elizabeth said. "You can interview Mr. Cooper."

"Whoa, Elizabeth. You're telling me so many things right out of the blue," Jack said. "Why did you pick tonight—of all nights, with the hurricane outside—to see me?"

"I don't have much time. A man followed me to Bartow on Sunday. I shook him, but I think he works for Granger and is trying to get the papers I stole from Grousland," she replied.

"Excuse me, miss, does he have long black hair and a thick black mustache?" Ed said.

"Yes," Elizabeth said with a quizzical look on her face.

Ed reached into his pocket and showed her a picture of Gordon Gecht. "Is this him?"

"Yes," she said, nodding. She looked at Ed for an explanation.

"Jack, it's as I feared. Gordon Gecht has been watching you and Elizabeth. I agree with her: Granger must have hired him, and he murdered James," Ed said.

"His name is Gordon Gecht?" Elizabeth asked, her eyes narrowing with fire. "If he's the one who killed James, I have one more to kill."

"Not unless I kill him first, Elizabeth. He and I go back several years," Jack said. "He not only killed James, but he killed my wife, Becky."

Elizabeth looked at Jack without shock, only an acknowledgment of shared suffering. "I think we understand each other," she said.

"Ed, check the security camera tapes. See if they picked up anybody besides Francis," Jack instructed. "Bobbie, keep Elizabeth company for a minute. I'll be right back."

Ed nodded and left for the small security video room, where screens showed the yard and doors.

Jack walked to the hallway, opened a locked drawer, pulled out his Walther P99, and took out two extra clips. He placed it behind his back and returned to the living room.

Elizabeth's report that Gecht was following her gave Jack cause for concern. He knew he was taking a risk by talking with her before calling the police, but he still needed to ask her a few more questions.

"Elizabeth, could you go on the record and testify in court about what you and James found?" Jack asked.

"I can't. You will find out why later."

"What do you mean?"

"James was born to do one thing, and I was born to do another. We were a team," she said. "He collected evidence and wanted you to write about these things in the hope that it would stop the phosphate company from polluting the environment so much." She paused. "In his memory, I want to do what he asked me to do."

"What is that?"

"Give you all the evidence he collected," Elizabeth said.

"But you won't go on the record or testify about these documents?" Jack asked.

"Listen," Elizabeth said, "I want to make a deal with you. This Gordon Gecht—you want him dead, I want him dead. What if I kill him for you?"

Just then, the phone rang.

"Elizabeth, do you mind if I get this?" asked Jack, ensuring he wouldn't upset her.

"Go ahead," she said.

He picked up the phone, relieved that she'd come to trust him.

"Jack, this is Lt. Stevens. Are you all right?"

"Yes, why?"

"We found the bodies of Cross and Decker. They've been murdered in their apartments," Lt. Stevens said.

"Is that right?" said Jack, trying to act normally so Elizabeth wouldn't become agitated.

"Are you all right? Anything unusual?"

"I'm doing an interview right now. Can I call you back later?" said Jack, not wanting to turn in Elizabeth.

"Chief wanted to make sure you aren't in danger. We now have four murders—all connected to Granger Station, all since Gordon Gecht arrived," Lt. Stevens said.

"You don't have to worry. Ed's here with Francis."

"Good. Officers saw a woman enter Cross's apartment and leave in a car. We followed her, but she lost us."

Jack didn't react.

"As a precaution, we're sending a squad car to watch your

place. Be careful," Lt. Stevens said.

"We will, thanks," Jack replied. "Bye."

"You could have turned me in? Why didn't you?" Elizabeth asked with admiration in her eyes.

Jack slid the phone back into its cradle. "I could have."

"But you didn't," she said, watching him closely. "James was right about you."

Jack looked up. "About what?"

"About trusting you." She paused. "The question is whether you trust me."

Jack didn't answer right away. He looked at Bobbie, who stared intensely at Elizabeth.

"Gecht is coming, and as you know, he's dangerous," Elizabeth continued.

"So am I," Jack said in a powerful, emotional voice.

She met his eyes—unflinching. "Me too. That's why this will work."

"What will work?" Jack asked, wondering if she knew.

"You know."

Jack nodded. He didn't know exactly what she meant, but he smiled anyway.

"Elizabeth, I need to ask you. We need to be honest with each other. Did you have anything to do with these murders the past week?"

"You keep asking me that. You don't want to know," she said. "We're friends, aren't we?"

Jack stared at her for a long second. Who was this Elizabeth Brewster? Was she a grieving sister, a vengeful killer, or a complete psychopath? He didn't know.

On the one hand, she seemed friendly to him and Bobbie, almost reasonable. On the other hand, she appeared unhinged, unwilling to acknowledge the murders she clearly implied she had committed.

As Jack hesitated, Ed pulled out his Glock 17 and held it by his side. Jack waved him off.

"Can I trust you? I want to know," said Jack, beginning to sense from her body language that she was telling the truth about her desire to help.

"I mean no harm to you, your brother, Bobbie, or Francis," she said. "You all were helping James."

"Tell me this. Why did James change his name from David Kane?" Jack asked. "What's your real name?"

"I'm Elizabeth Kane. You'll have all the answers to your questions soon," she said.

Suddenly, the lights flickered and went out. A few seconds later, they came back on. The wind had been blowing hard off and on for the past hour, but it began to ease.

"Everybody, stay calm. Ed, what's happening?" Jack asked.

Ed raced into the security control room next to the kitchen at the back of the house.

"Somebody's moving out by the fence," he said. "Jack, Gordon Gecht is here."

Chapter 40:
Elizabeth's Storm

Later Tuesday night, July 20, 1982

The full moon was rising, its light dimmed by dark, fast-moving clouds as Gordon Gecht, dressed in an all-black outfit, moved away from two unconscious officers in the patrol car parked across from Jack's house. The wind howled as he stepped over the curb and onto the property.

It seemed different than last time for the highly skilled assassin. He remembered the ease with which he had lured Kendall to his former employer's house two years before, knocked him out, drugged him, and injected him with a heavy dose of crack cocaine. That Jack had survived was a miracle.

As Hurricane Amos approached the coastline, Gecht felt uneasy. He'd first confronted Kendall on a warm, calm evening in Sarasota. The howling wind, sporadic bursts of rain, the flickering power in the neighborhood, and the storm's unsettling sounds filled him with concern tonight.

Then he remembered that afternoon in Bogotá 18 months ago when he shot Kendall and was closing in for the kill. But at the last moment, Kendall managed to fire off a lucky shot. This time, he assured himself, Kendall wouldn't be so lucky.

Ahead, a tall steel fence and an electric-powered gate surrounding the house rattled in the wind. He suspected Kendall's house security system would have many surprises for average burglars, so he'd brought a few surprises himself.

Security cameras were positioned in key locations facing the front driveway gate. To avoid detection, he moved to the back driveway gate on the other side of the house until he spotted a security guard battling against the wind and walking away from him inside the fence.

He quickly returned to the front gate and prepared to force it open using the small crowbar in his backpack.

Suddenly, the security guard turned and walked toward him. He put the crowbar away and pulled a small wind-up bird from his backpack. He tossed it by an oak tree inside the fence. When it hit the ground, it chirped, a simple ploy to attract attention. But the wind was too loud, and the guard didn't take the bait.

Gecht decided to be more direct. He took out the crowbar and slid it along the iron gate, hitting three rails. This time, the guard heard the sound, said something into a small two-way radio, pulled out his weapon, and cautiously approached.

Gecht took out a compressed air gun loaded with a poison dart. As the wind whipped against him, he braced himself, waited for the guard to get closer, then shot him in the arm.

Francis yelped, staggered, and then collapsed, unconscious. Seizing the opportunity, Gecht removed his crowbar again, pried open the gate, and slipped into the yard.

Gecht quickly went to the main electrical box and cut off the house's power. He walked around the house and approached the front door. Removing a small piece of explosive from his backpack, he placed it on the handle, then lit the fuse and stepped back. The explosion sounded louder than a .45-caliber gunshot. He then tossed a smoke bomb into the foyer and stepped through the door.

*　*　*

Inside the house, Ed noticed the amber alert light flashing, and he saw the video feed of Francis collapsing. A shadow moved across the yard before disappearing into the darkness.

The wind continued to howl outside, rattling the windows as Hurricane Amos drew closer to the city.

Jack steadied himself against the vibrations of the house. "Bobbie, go into the upstairs safe room and call the police. Ed, take these infrared goggles. Here's a pair for you, too, Elizabeth. Now, we'll lure him into the living room and set the trap," said Jack. "Follow me."

Jack and Ed hid in the downstairs safe room on the other side of the living room at the back of the house. Elizabeth didn't follow Jack into the safe room. She entered the dining room on the right front side of the house, hid behind a cabinet, and waited to see what unfolded.

"Welcome, Gordon," said Jack, speaking into a microphone connected to a small wireless speaker in the living room facing the hallway.

Jack continued. "I've been expecting you. Why did it take you so long?"

"I was busy in Bogotá. It was nice seeing your wife again,

by the way," said Gecht as he made his way toward the sound of Jack's voice.

"You and I have things to discuss about Becky and her friend Michelle. And then there is the night at Michael's house on Siesta Key when you gave me a rather nasty headache. Remember?" said Jack, trying to lure Gecht into the living room.

"I thought we'd settle things in Bogotá at the warehouse, but you had to get the cops involved. It was quite a gun battle. Did you like my little .32 caliber gift to you?" Gecht asked with a snicker.

"I seem to recall I gave you a little gift, too," Jack replied.

"It was just a scratch," Gecht countered as he twisted on his Ruger Mk II's silencer—force of habit—while the storm's noise drowned out everything else.

"At least I evened the score with your employer, Robert Mackey. Now it's your turn," Jack said.

Gecht heard Jack's voice and cautiously followed it down the hall.

"Becky begged me not to shoot her and promised me everything," Gecht said with an evil smile. "She told me you would save her by giving me the $5 million. Do you still have it for me? Never mind—I only want the original documents Brewster's sister gave you. Give them to me, and you all can live."

Jack seethed with anger. He wanted to wring Gecht's neck right then. Ed steadied his arm and held him back. "Stick with the plan," he whispered.

"I have an idea: why don't we stop wasting time and talk over this arrangement for the documents I have in my hands?" Jack said.

"So, you do have them. Good," said Gecht, standing still

and listening for sounds of movement in the house.

"Just tell me the truth, and we have a deal: Granger hired you, and you killed James Brewster, correct?" Jack asked.

As Gecht slowly made his way down the hall, he checked around every corner and in each room. He stood by the entrance to the living room and waited for the moment.

"I did. Granger paid me top dollar in cash. I killed him," Gecht said. "It was easy. He never saw it coming, just like you."

Gecht, so confident of his kill, quickly turned into the living room, took aim at the dim figure sitting on the sofa, and fired two shots in the chest and twice in the head. The body fell to the floor, and Gecht took several steps toward it, looking puzzled.

Just then, as Jack and Ed came out of the safe room with their guns, six shots rang out.

Gecht's body shivered with the impact of the gunshots on his back. The would-be assassin fell face forward with a surprised look.

Without a word, Elizabeth Brewster walked up to him and shot him a seventh time in the head, just as he had killed her brother.

The tape recorder kept running as Elizabeth stood there, still pointing her gun at Gecht. Jack turned off the recorder. He had the evidence, and Gecht was dead.

"Ed, better check on your man outside and on the other officers. Bobbie, you can come out," Jack said. "Elizabeth, you can put down your gun now. It's over."

"It's over?" she asked. "Over?"

"Yes, Gordon Gecht is dead. You killed him to avenge your brother and my wife, Becky," Jack said as he calmly walked over to inspect the body.

Elizabeth lowered her Sig P22 and looked at Jack with a strange smile.

"It's over?" she repeated, eyes glazed. She then stared deeply into Jack's eyes. "Promise me you will expose Granger's corruption."

"I will," Jack said solemnly. "I owe you and your brother a lot."

Elizabeth smiled and dropped her gun. She lowered her head, and as she raised it again, her expression shifted from seriousness and intelligence to a silly, disorganized grin.

Bobbie gasped at the drastic change in Elizabeth's demeanor.

Jack understood what that meant—her mind was no longer present. Was it real or a ruse? He wasn't sure. It didn't matter. He wasn't going to pass judgment or sentence. Others would do that. He approached her and gently kissed her on the cheek.

"Goodbye, Elizabeth," he said softly.

Just then, Lt. Stevens and Detective Terry entered the house, the wind following them. Their rain-soaked uniforms testified to the storm's outer bands reaching the coast. They looked around and saw Gecht on the floor with bullet holes and blood across his back.

"Jack, what's going on here?" demanded Lt. Stevens, looking at the dead body and then turning to Elizabeth. "Who is this?"

Jack heard the questions but was thinking of Becky, James, and Elizabeth as she stood there motionless, her gaze unfocused, still with a slight smile.

"Ask her," said Jack as he switched back on the tape recorder. "She'll tell you everything."

"Miss, are you all right?" Detective Terry asked.

Despite the growing storm outside, Elizabeth stood there, motionless, with that unusual smile, looking across the living room to a picture on the wall of Sarasota Bay and a dolphin breaking the water's surface.

She spoke quietly.

"Sarasota is so beautiful—the water, the sun, the sky, the sea life. This is how life should be for families. Nothing like Bartow when I was growing up with James and my parents.

"Phosphate mining destroyed our natural beauty by ripping gaping holes in the landscape, creating towering gypstacks and slime ponds containing radioactive elements and heavy metals that polluted our water and air. Where we once had beautiful prairies and forests teeming with trees, plants, and vegetation, we now have mountains of toxic waste that poison our lungs and eyes."

Then, in a flat voice, looking straight ahead with glazed eyes, she said, "My name is Elizabeth Kane, daughter of Chester and Roxanne Kane of Bartow, Florida, sister of David Kane.

"Phosphate company owners and those who made destructive decisions for profit killed my parents and my dear brother. They didn't deserve to live."

As she spoke, the policemen, Jack, Bobbie, and Ed, stood silently and listened in amazement to Elizabeth's confession as the wind and rain pounded the house.

"You may want to know how many I have killed. Let me count. I'll start with this asswipe. Granger hired him to kill my brother. Now he's dead. Three other asswipes were also involved in killing my brother. They're dead too.

"Did I not mention the asswipe in Bartow? Oh, maybe you haven't found him yet. He seems to have fallen into a pond of phosphoric acid, one of his own making. He may have sprung a leak with a bullet hole in his head. Oh my."

She looked directly at Lt. Stevens and Detective Terry. "Will you take me away now? I seem to be having an unusual urge to kill more asswipes who make phosphate.

"Thank you, officers."

With that last remark, Elizabeth Kane stopped talking.

Lt. Stevens nodded, and Detective Terry read Elizabeth her Miranda rights. "Elizabeth Kane, I charge you with the murders of Pierre Grousland, Herbert Cross, and Louis Decker. You have the right to remain silent. Anything you say can and will be used against you in a court of law. You have the right to an attorney. If you cannot afford one, an attorney will be provided at no cost. Do you understand these rights as I have explained them?"

Elizabeth didn't respond. She was handcuffed and led to a squad car in the pouring rain.

Jack, Ed, and Bobbie watched silently from the front door. Dressed in dark green camouflage parkas, Col. Hanks and three military friends stood by the police cars as the rain fell around them. Jack had called them earlier, explained his plan, and they had come as backup, only to enter the house if signaled by a beeper call from Jack.

Outside, the wind tore off small tree branches and pulled up loose debris, but Elizabeth remained calm and detached as she bent down to enter the squad car. She paused and looked intensely at Jack one last time for help. Jack saw tears in her eyes before she was pushed into the vehicle.

Jack knew that look, an emotional mix of helplessness, sadness, fear, and finality. Despite what she had done, he felt sorry for her.

Later, after she was processed at the Sarasota County Jail, she sat in her cell, remaining silent, not uttering another word until her trial four months later.

Chapter 41:
No Escaping a Category 5

Wednesday, **July 21, 1982**

As Hurricane Amos's roar intensified, Jack and Bobbie huddled downstairs in the safe room of his Sarasota home. The Category 5 storm was 50 miles offshore, traveling eight miles per hour, and projected to make landfall 15 miles north of Bradenton Beach at dawn.

"We've done everything possible to prepare for this," Jack said, glancing at their supplies—food, water, flashlights, and a battery-powered radio.

"I know you built your house with all the security systems and other protections against Gordon Gecht, but are you sure staying overnight at a crime scene is the best idea?" Bobbie asked.

"That was in the living room. The police have other worries. Besides, my house was also built for hurricanes," Jack said. "We're safer here. Now, it's just a matter of hoping for the best."

Bobbie sighed, exhaustion and anxiety etched across her face. "Fine, as long as I'm with you. But I don't know how we'll sleep tonight—not after Elizabeth, and now with Amos practically knocking on our door."

"Elizabeth," Jack said, thinking about how she would ride out the hurricane in her jail cell. "She'll probably get more sleep than any of us with the meds they are giving her."

He looked back at Bobbie. "How are you doing?"

"I was thinking about James and how you told me he worried about a hurricane like this," she replied.

Jack nodded. "I can still hear his words. I quote, 'If a strong hurricane hits Granger Station, those weak gypstack walls won't hold. Toxic wastewater will flood everything—destroying homes, poisoning land, and devastating lives."

"Do you think his prediction will come true?"

"From the sound of this storm, it's looking that way," Jack said. "Only time will tell."

As they talked, Amos's wind roared outside like a freight train barreling past, a deep, guttural howl punctuated by sharp, high-pitched whistles as it found gaps in the brick house. Sheets of rain lashed against the walls and windows, sounding like thousands of nails peppering the glass. Occasionally, a bone-jarring boom echoed as trees or telephone poles snapped.

Jack couldn't yet tell Bobbie, but he still hadn't processed that Gecht, his archenemy and the one responsible for Becky's brutal murder, was dead. It was finally done—he didn't have to watch his back anymore. Gecht was gone.

But it wasn't Jack who had killed Gecht—it was Elizabeth.

While he appreciated the finality of her actions, he hadn't fully come to terms with the fact that someone else had delivered the justice he so desperately sought.

He kept his conflicted feelings to himself, knowing that admitting them to her might make her uneasy. Justice had been served, but actual closure felt just out of reach.

Jack realized he couldn't do anything more. Becky was gone, and so was Gecht. His thoughts drifted to James and why he and Elizabeth dedicated their lives to exposing the phosphate industry's dirty secrets.

Bobbie looked over at Jack. He hadn't said anything in five minutes and had a strange expression.

"Jack, what is it? Are you all right?" she asked.

"Just thinking. You mentioned James. I was thinking about him," he replied. "Gecht killed Becky and James. Elizabeth eliminated Gecht. We don't have to worry about him, but we've got to make sure James's story gets out."

"We will," said Bobbie. "Just tell me what you want."

"I never met anyone like James. He was the least selfish, most down-to-earth, and smartest person I ever knew. He could have done so much with his life as a doctor and engineer, but he was committed to exposing the evils of the phosphate industry, no matter the cost."

"We've got to make it through this storm, and then we can start writing about it."

"I've been thinking. As a reporter, I owe it to James, Elizabeth, their family's legacy—and the public—to expose Granger Phosphate's corruption and the grave dangers phosphate mining poses to our health and environment," Jack said. "It's what we must do to honor James."

"I'm with you," Bobbie replied as she moved closer to him.

He put his arm around her, and they listened to the deafening sounds of the horrific storm.

Hour after hour, the storm battered the house. They talked quietly—about James and Elizabeth, about court dates and trials, about how they'd cover whatever damage the hurricane left behind. They listened to the radio and wondered about friends, family, and the neighborhoods they knew by heart.

At 2 a.m., the power went out, plunging their two-story brick house into darkness. Bobbie lit candles while Jack turned on a camp lantern and checked the flashlights. The silence afterward felt heavier than the noise.

"I should've pushed harder," Jack said finally. "We should've run the story sooner."

Bobbie sat on the loveseat, her legs tucked beneath her. She hadn't taken off her shoes. Neither of them had touched the coffee she'd made hours ago, which was still warm in a Thermos.

"You didn't kill him," she said.

"That's what I tell myself," Jack replied. He turned toward her. "Johnny, when I was young. Charlie. Sarah. Becky. Michelle. Now, James." He shook his head. "Is it worth it? Exposing the truth when so many people have to die?"

Bobbie didn't want to interrupt, but she hadn't heard that first name before. "Who's Johnny? Another source?"

"No, Johnny was a neighborhood friend who was killed by a drunk driver while riding his bike to my sixth birthday party. I'll tell you that story one day," Jack said, his voice faltering.

"Please do," she gently urged him.

"About James...I keep wondering how things would be different if I'd spent more time looking for him that Friday, when the exposé was held. Pushed Wiseman harder. Ignored

Gantz and went straight to Mr. Lindsay to argue my case." His voice dropped. "And now I look at you, and all I can think is—you could be next."

"I'm not just your colleague, Jack," she said quietly. "I'm not just your close friend, either."

He studied her, as if she were a set of facts he'd been avoiding. "I know," he said. "That's the problem."

She stood and crossed the room, stopping a few feet away. "I need to say this, even if it scares you off." She took a breath. "I have felt for a while that what we have is more than a casual relationship."

"I feel it too," Jack said after a moment. "That's what scares me."

"Because of Becky."

He nodded. Jack shifted uneasily, listening to the wind batter the shutters.

"I'm going to say something I've carried around the past two years," he murmured. "It used to feel like a passing thought, but tonight...I wonder if it's true."

Bobbie leaned closer. "What is it?"

"I used to think she left me because we disagreed about her drug use and drinking, the late-night partying, and her secrecy about it," Jack said.

"She was out of control, you used to say," Bobbie agreed.

"Now that I've had time to think it through, I think the main reason she left me was something we never resolved: children. She knew I wanted them, and she never did."

Bobbie frowned softly. "But why? Children can be such a joy."

Jack sighed. "I always thought it had something to do with her mother. She never said it outright, but she couldn't stand being around her. Did you know she was an only child?"

"No," Bobbie said, after a pause. "But now that you mention it...that does explain a lot."

"All along, I thought she couldn't stop drinking or using, but she didn't want children. She said it many times," Jack said, pausing, his voice faltering. "I thought my love for her, and time, would fix whatever hesitancy she had."

Bobbie absorbed this without judgment. "I didn't know any of this."

"No one knew," Jack said. "Some days, I don't even know who I'm grieving: the woman she was—beautiful, funny, charming, and charismatic at times—or the life we never had."

"I've always wanted children," Bobbie said. "Not someday. Always."

The words didn't wound him. They opened something. A future he'd stopped letting himself imagine.

"I don't know how to do this," Jack said. "Care about someone and not destroy them by being who I am."

Bobbie rested her hand lightly on his arm. "You don't destroy people. You expose the truth. Sometimes it's harsh. Sometimes it comes too late. But it matters."

He covered her hand with his. It felt steady. Right.

"I don't want to lose anyone else," he said.

"Then don't close the door before they even step inside," she replied.

Outside, a siren wailed and faded. The radio crackled— *Amos sustaining winds of one hundred eighty miles per hour.*

They sat side by side as the storm pressed closer—two people not making promises, not walking away either—waiting for the worst of the weather to pass, together.

During the long night, they dozed off occasionally, waking

up startled as the thunder boomed, the lightning crackled, and the wind roared.

As the minutes and hours passed, they felt the tension rise amid the ongoing uncertainty about the storm's strength and whether their modern, hip-designed hurricane roof would withstand Amos's impact.

Outside, the hurricane sounded like a jet engine revving higher and higher, howling, screaming, and hissing as it drew closer. The windows rattled, the ceiling vibrated, and the roof moaned. Trees cracked like bowling pins, and buildings' metal siding shrieked as their sides were ripped out.

When he was younger, Jack had experienced two major hurricanes, Donna and Betsy, but Amos's growing fury was far greater than anything he had ever experienced.

At about 6 a.m., the southernmost eye of Amos passed over Jack's house as the storm's center began to make landfall on Bradenton Beach. The winds abruptly subsided, leaving an eerie calm in their wake.

"Listen," said Bobbie, her ears still throbbing from hours of constant roar. "What do you hear?"

"Nothing," said Jack as he bent his neck back, looked at the ceiling, and turned his head from side to side as if testing the silence. "We must be in the eye."

"Do you want to go outside for a few minutes?"

"Sure, let's take a look. We probably have 15 to 20 minutes."

They walked into the house and cautiously opened the front door. The world outside was surreal. The wind was gone, leaving the trees bent and broken.

Jack scanned the yard, noting the debris scattered across the lawn—tree branches, leaves, and several downed palm trees in the island median on their boulevard and a collapsed fence in a neighbor's yard.

"I don't think I've ever seen anything like this," Bobbie said, stepping carefully off the front steps. The air was moist and felt heavy.

"It's like the world is holding its breath," Jack whispered as he gazed across the damage in the yards and at the dark clouds moving fast across the morning sky.

They ventured a few steps farther, their shoes crunching on shattered branches and debris. Bobbie pointed toward the street. "Look at the neighbor's car. The windshield's completely smashed."

Jack nodded grimly. "We'll need to check on them after this is over."

He glanced back at the house, instinctively keeping track of their escape route. "We shouldn't stay out here too long. The other side of the storm is coming, and it'll hit just as hard."

Bobbie sighed, rubbing her arms against the damp chill in the air. "It's just so strange. After all that noise, this silence feels...wrong."

"It won't last," Jack said.

As if on cue, the wind picked up slightly, a low moan that grew louder with each passing second.

"That's our signal," Jack said, placing a hand on Bobbie's back and gently guiding her toward the house.

They hurried inside and secured the door behind them. The faint, unsettling calm outside was already beginning to unravel.

"Time to go back to safety," Jack said firmly.

Bobbie nodded as the first gusts of the returning wind rattled the house again. The storm wasn't finished with them yet.

Further north, Amos wreaked havoc everywhere, tearing off roofs, uprooting trees, and causing widespread destruction.

After slamming into Bradenton Beach with sustained winds of 195 mph and gusts over 200 mph, Amos tore into Palmetto, barreled into Terra Ceia and Hillsborough Bay, and made a second landfall in the small town of Gibsonville.

Amos's destructive force proved too much for Granger Station's fragile infrastructure. The gypstack walls, already weakened by years of neglect, collapsed under the storm's 25 inches of rainfall and hurricane-force winds. The earthen dikes crumbled, unleashing a torrent of radioactive and toxic wastewater into surrounding neighborhoods and Terra Ceia Bay.

"The rain pushed the gypstack beyond its breaking point," the state-appointed manager, Stuart Locker, later explained. "We knew the risks, but the storm left us no time."

Three smaller holding ponds at Granger Station also overflowed, spilling more toxic water into the environment. Jack Kendall's next-day article described it as a "20-foot white wave of phosphate wastewater rolling over homes and into the bay."

Piney Point, another fertilizer plant near Terra Ceia, fared no better. Two containment walls collapsed under Amos's relentless pressure, spilling millions of gallons of toxic wastewater across farmland and roadways and into Bishop Harbor. Combined with Granger Station's breaches, the twin disasters released more than 500 million gallons of toxic phosphate slime into Tampa Bay.

Jack's articles, published using emergency backup power

at the *Herald-Tribune*, described the destruction of homes, businesses, neighborhoods, and waterways.

As Hurricane Amos plowed inland, its path of destruction extended to six additional phosphate facilities in Central Florida, including the massive Riverview plant.

Riverview alone discharged 400 million gallons of sludge into Hillsborough Bay after its gypstacks failed. By the time the storm exited Florida near Daytona Beach, it had left behind more than 3 billion gallons of toxic wastewater.

Rivers such as the Peace, Myakka, Manatee, Alafia, and Little Manatee carried phosphate sludge miles downstream, turning once-pristine waterways into hazardous zones. Fish kills, poisoned marshes, and contaminated water systems were among the immediate effects.

Jack reported staggering damage. Tampa Bay and the surrounding waters turned greenish-yellow as millions of dead fish, manatees, and dolphins floated to the surface. The storm surge inundated entire coastal areas, leaving roads and homes covered in debris and phosphate-laden silt.

Governor Bob Graham acted swiftly, lobbying the EPA to designate affected areas as Superfund hazardous waste zones. "This disaster has exposed the phosphate industry's chronic neglect and the dangers of weak regulations," Graham said. "We must address these gypstacks before they destroy our environment and jeopardize our aquifer."

Jack wrote a follow-up column that resonated deeply with the public's feelings.

"Hurricane Amos exposed the state's phosphate industry's weak regulations and environmental dangers. More than three billion gallons of toxic and radioactive wastewater have been released into waterways and the sensitive aquifer, killing marine life, decimating local fisheries, and damaging the livelihoods of thousands of people."

"There is a public need for stronger oversight and meaningful reform. Government and industry should compromise and devise a plan to prevent future disasters like this," Jack wrote. "The public's patience with the industry's empty promises has run out."

For Jack, Bobbie, and the *Herald-Tribune*, the combination of Hurricane Amos, the greed of a phosphate company like Granger, the murder of James Brewster, and the deaths of dozens of others from the storm was a call to action.

The battle had begun.

Epilogue:
The Bone Valley Phosphate Murders

November 1982

Jack assisted Bobbie with her stories about the murder of James Brewster by Gordon Gecht and the revenge murders of Pierre Grousland, Herbert Cross, Louis Decker, and Harold Maynard by Elizabeth Kane.

They wrote a series of articles titled the "Bone Valley Phosphate Murders," which won them a Pulitzer Prize the following year for local reporting.

Jack's stories further exposed Granger's corruption, the mismanagement of the gypstack and fertilizer plant before the hurricane, and the resulting environmental catastrophe.

The Granger corporate documents revealed the corruption. The late James Brewster's evidence, along with that of Daniel Rumsfeld, Manny Hernandez, and other plant workers and experts, provided the context, while Jack offered the narrative.

Elizabeth Kane's trial was among the most sensational in Florida's recent history, drawing national attention to the Bone Valley phosphate industry's dark underbelly. Every day, the courtroom was packed with citizens, reporters, supporters and opponents of the phosphate industry and of the defendant. Protesters gathered outside, some holding signs condemning Granger and other phosphate companies for environmental crimes, while others called for justice for the victims of Elizabeth's revenge killings.

The prosecution portrayed Elizabeth as a cold-blooded vigilante who methodically carried out her murders. They recounted the deaths of Grousland, Cross, Decker, and Maynard in chilling detail, highlighting the calculated brutality of her actions. Her injection of thallium and phosphoric acid wastewater into victims and her meticulous planning were offered as evidence of premeditation.

The defense, however, focused on Elizabeth's mental state, arguing that her lifelong bipolar disorder, a growing schizoaffective disorder, years of trauma, and the devastating loss of her family drove her to a breaking point.

Jack Kendall was called to testify, recounting the interviews he'd conducted with James and Elizabeth Brewster about their motivation to expose Granger and phosphate companies for the deaths of their parents. He also testified about Gordon Gecht's statements that he killed James and was hired by Granger.

Expert witnesses described Elizabeth's actions as the result of mental illness and profound psychological anguish, trauma, and loss stemming from both personal tragedy and moral outrage.

Diagnosed with bipolar disorder at age 13, she experienced frequent mood swings, ranging from euphoric highs to deep lows. By her mid-20s, she began exhibiting signs of schizoaffective disorder, including abnormal thoughts, paranoia, and auditory hallucinations.

After her parents died, Elizabeth managed her condition with medication and support from James. However, after James's death, she stopped taking her pills. Obsessed with revenge, she began a killing spree targeting phosphate executives.

In the courtroom, the defense painted a vivid picture of Elizabeth's deteriorating mental state in the days leading up to her crimes.

The defense revealed journal entries from her manic phases, in which Elizabeth described hearing her brother's voice urging her to act and seeing vivid imagery of her parents calling for justice. Doctors explained that these hallucinations were symptomatic of a worsening schizoaffective disorder.

Her plea of not guilty by reason of insanity rested on the argument that Elizabeth's actions were not premeditated in the legal sense but were driven by her disordered mind.

Elizabeth was calm and composed during cross-examination, yet her piercing gaze unnerved witnesses and spectators. She spoke little during the trial but detailed her pain in journal entries, writing about her love for her family and her belief that she was waging a war for justice against an industry that had ruined countless lives.

One of the highlights of the trial came when Chief Tom

Bagley testified that Elizabeth's killing of Gordon Gecht saved the lives of Jack, Ed, and Bobbie.

Although the prosecution argued that this did not excuse her actions, it generated sympathy among the jurors, who attributed part of Elizabeth's mental state to the murderer, Gordon Gecht.

After two weeks of testimony, the jury deliberated for three days before signaling to the judge that they had reached a decision. Elizabeth was found not guilty by reason of insanity. She was sentenced to life without parole at the Florida State Hospital, a psychiatric institution in Chattahoochee.

For many, Elizabeth's trial was as much about her tragedy as it was about the broader corruption and environmental devastation she sought to expose.

Before being escorted from the courtroom, Elizabeth stood and addressed the court, her voice steady and resolute. "I am only guilty of avenging the murder of my brother and the deaths of my parents by corrupt phosphate companies! You can put me away, but mining phosphate and producing fertilizer will continue to kill and poison the environment!"

She paused, cleared her throat, and looked directly at Jack.

As Elizabeth's piercing gaze met his, Jack tightened his grip on his notepad. A rush of emotions flooded through him; her words were full of defiance and grief, yet there was more to them. He understood that Elizabeth was challenging him to complete his investigation into the phosphate industry and expose everything she and her brother had given their lives for.

She then stared ahead. "I am the daughter of Chester and Roxanne Kane and the sister of David Kane."

Afterword

I covered phosphate mining as a reporter at the *Bradenton Herald* in the early 1980s.

My interactions with phosphate company executives during interviews, meetings, or plant tours were generally positive. They answered my questions, for the most part, straightforwardly and sincerely.

I sometimes disagreed with company executives, government officials, and environmental and consumer groups during interviews about the scientific or technical aspects of phosphate mining, production, or transportation. But I never felt bullied or intimidated by anyone in the industry.

While the plot and characters related to the Granger Phosphate Co. in this book are fictional, the controversy surrounding phosphate mining, phosphoric acid, and fertilizer production is factual.

Over the past decade, two phosphate disasters have befallen the Tampa Bay and Bradenton environments.

In 2016, a 45-foot-wide sinkhole opened beneath a gypstack at Mosaic's New Wales phosphate fertilizer plant in Mulberry, releasing 215 million gallons of wastewater into the Floridan aquifer system. It took two years to seal the opening.

On March 25, 2021, leaks were discovered in the containment wall of a 67-acre holding pool at Piney Point, where radioactive phosphogypsum was stored.

Ultimately, more than 215 million gallons of nutrient-rich, moderately radioactive wastewater containing numerous toxic heavy metals were discharged into Tampa Bay.

Meanwhile, more than 270 million gallons of wastewater at Piney Point are expected to be pumped over time into a deep injection well 3,000 feet into the Floridan aquifer to prevent another catastrophic gypstack wall failure. Piney Point contains more than 400 million gallons of toxic wastewater.

Phosphate spills and environmental disasters have been occurring for much longer. Although the devastation from past spills is strikingly similar, the current effects are far more significant because a much larger population depends on clean water.

Beyond the spills of the past 50 years, my inspiration for writing this novel began in high school, when I read Rachel Carson's landmark 1962 environmental book, *Silent Spring*. Carson's book ushered in the modern environmental movement and heightened awareness of the natural world.

The U.S. Environmental Protection Agency was established in 1970, when I was a high school sophomore. That same year, the Clean Air Act was signed into law, and the Clean Water Act was enacted in 1972, when I graduated.

Several months earlier, on Dec. 3, 1971, the worst phosphate spill in Florida's history occurred when nearly two billion gallons of phosphate slime poured into the 105-mile-long Peace River from a giant clay pond near Bartow in Polk County, the heart of Bone Valley.

The phosphate wastewater and sludge turned the Peace River white, killing seagrass and 90 percent of the fish, including snook, tarpon, and more than two dozen other species. The slime traveled downstream and emptied into Charlotte Harbor near Fort Myers. As landowners and local politicians noted, the spill marked the fourth time in 10 years that the Peace River had been poisoned by phosphate slime.

While Cities Service Co. said an earthen dam broke, environmentalists and some politicians believed the spill was intentional. The phosphate company was thought to have needed more storage space for its phosphogypsum sludge.

Despite the conjecture, the actual cause of the phosphate spill was never satisfactorily explained.

The State of Florida sued Cities Services for $20 million to help with the cleanup of the Peace River and to address the region's economic damage.

It took me hours of online research to discover this fact, but six years later, in 1977, the state quietly settled for a paltry $290,000.

This meager settlement reinforced the belief, in many people's minds, that the phosphate industry in Florida was all-powerful. It could poison the land, air, and water, kill millions of fish, cause pain and anguish to citizens, and get away without paying a genuine price for mismanagement, corruption, or greed.

In September 2024, a federal judge found the current owner of Piney Point, HRK Holdings LLC, liable for the 2021 toxic wastewater discharge into Tampa Bay. However, the $846,000 judgment is unlikely to be collected, as HRK has been under bankruptcy protection since 2012.

After the 1971 Peace River spill, the Sarasota County Commission spent millions on legal fees to keep phosphate mining as far from the fast-growing tourist, cultural, and retirement haven as possible.

This was one of the many true stories I cited in *Bone Valley*. All are true except for Granger Station.

Later, while a student at the University of Florida, I learned that one of the English Literature professors, Harry Crews, had written a novel titled *Naked in Garden Hills*.

In unforgettable prose, Crews graphically described the ravages of phosphate mining in Florida and its impact on the unusual people of the fictional town of Garden Hills. It struck a nerve with me because I had studied environmental science in my first two years of college.

Driving back and forth between Gainesville and my hometown of Sarasota, I often passed a large phosphate fertilizer plant in Riverview, along Tampa Bay. I wondered what happened at the industrial plant that constantly emitted white smoke from its smokestacks. I was also curious about what was inside what I considered Florida's highest mountain.

After speaking with my professors, I learned that the "mountain" is a 200-foot-tall, half-acre-long gypsum containment pond.

One day, as I passed the plant, I was curious. When I returned to Gainesville, I called to request a tour of the plant, which was then owned by Gardinier Inc. The Riverview plant is now owned by Tampa-based Mosaic Co., the world's largest phosphate company, which also operates four other phosphate mines in Florida.

One of the Riverview managers was gracious enough to give a two-hour tour of the facility to a single college student. I ended up writing a paper for a school report.

During the tour, we drove past a greenish, toxic holding pond where the manager told me highly concentrated fertilizer-processing wastewater was stored.

I asked him whether the plant had ever had problems with the toxic pond. He told me a plant worker had accidentally driven a pickup truck into it. I asked him what happened. He replied dryly, "We fired him."

After I graduated from UF and began covering the phosphate industry, I learned that employees at phosphate companies are as dedicated and hardworking as those in any other industry.

But they also make mistakes and bad decisions, and they cover up or downplay problems. Occasionally, they can lie, misrepresent, be evasive and unhelpful, greedy, or even corrupt, just like other companies I have covered over the years in the healthcare industry.

It is up to the free press, honest politicians and regulators, astute citizens, and environmental watchdog groups to stay vigilant in their work, especially as hurricanes intensify amid a warming planet.

-30-

Other Jack Kendall Books

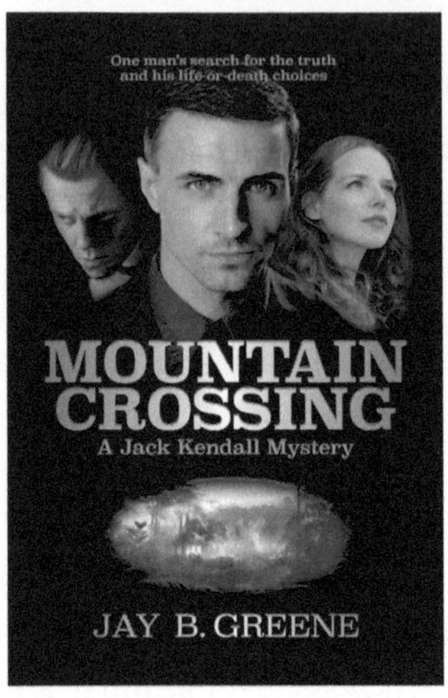

Mountain Crossing—Investigative reporter Jack Kendall is devastated after witnessing a suicide while on assignment. His life begins to unravel when his wife, Becky, disappears, leaving only a cryptic letter. Driven to uncover the truth, Jack's investigation reveals Becky's ties to a dangerous global cocaine ring. With help from Sarah, an enigmatic woman linked to his wife's disappearance, Jack ventures into Jamaica's Blue Mountains. Guided by haunting dreams of a mysterious angelic figure, Jack confronts perilous secrets about Becky's hidden life. This gripping debut in the Jack Kendall Mystery series is a compelling tale of love, betrayal, and survival.

Other Jack Kendall Books

Becky—Becky Kendall and Michelle Talley have fled their traumatic past in Jamaica, taking control of $5 million in drug profits. But they are pursued by Gordon Gecht, a ruthless enforcer determined to reclaim the money he believes is rightfully his. When estranged husband Jack Kendall arrives in Bogotá to uncover the truth about Becky, he becomes entangled in a deadly game of betrayal and survival. As old wounds resurface and trust becomes hard to find, Jack races against time to expose Gecht's crimes. Becky is a tense journey through danger, resilience, and the relentless pursuit of justice—set against the gritty backdrop of 1980s Colombia.

Other Jack Kendall Books

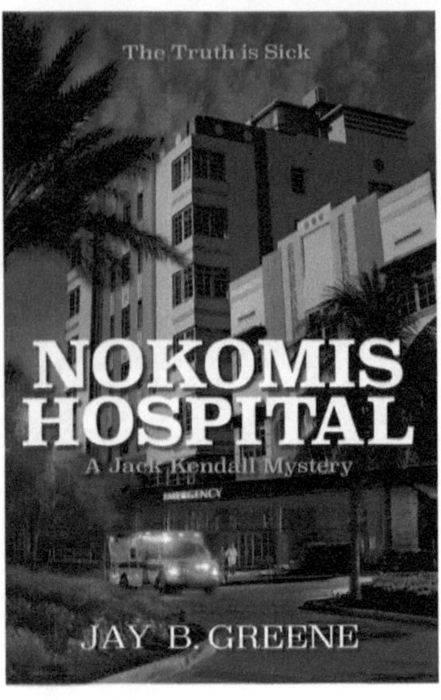

Nokomis Hospital—In the fourth book, Jack Kendall suspects financial troubles and healthcare fraud when his wife, Bobbie, is admitted to Nokomis Hospital after she is treated in the ER for pre-eclampsia. While Bobbie has a successful C-section and delivers healthy twins, Jack learns from several employees during her three-day stay that charismatic CEO Mike Lard has conspired with other top executives and board members to embezzle millions of dollars that threaten the non-profit hospital's future. Join Jack as he discovers the lengths—and crimes—the executives go to cover up their illegal acts.

Other Jack Kendall Books

Coming Next: **Breakthrough Lies**—When sixteen-year-old **Julie France**, granddaughter of a powerful Manatee County Commissioner, is seized from her home and forced into *Breakthrough*—a controversial teen drug rehabilitation program—her desperate mother turns to investigative reporter **Jack Kendall** for help. Inside the Sarasota facility, Julie's younger brother, **Steve**, already confined there for a month, faces humiliation, isolation, and emotional manipulation in the name of "tough love." When program enforcers claim that Julie must also be admitted to protect her brother's recovery, she becomes the next victim of *Breakthrough's* coercive methods.

As Jack digs deeper, he uncovers a tangled web of abuse, corruption, and political protection linking the so-called treatment center to Florida's most powerful political families.

Tim and Peggy Smith Space Adventures

Danger From Space—After Tim Smith gains psychic powers from a mysterious space rock, his visions reveal an alien threat. As a NASA astrophysicist, Tim foresees the arrival of a corrupted alien mothership from the Kuiper Belt. With Earth reeling from climate change, Tim and his wife, Peggy, rally a group of survivors to confront the invaders. Racing to reset the ship's AI, they unlock alien technology that could cleanse the planet, offering humanity a chance to rebuild and thrive among the stars. *Danger From Space*, the debut novel in the Tim and Peggy Space Adventure series, is a thrilling tale of survival, unity, and the fight for Earth's future.

Tim and Peggy Smith
Space Adventures

Flight to the Stars—Five years after an alien attack, Earth is recovering from climate disasters and the AI War. At their Sarasota bioshelter, Tim and Peggy Smith are raising their extraordinary twins, Ethan and Lila—two-and-a-half-year-olds with psychic abilities and wisdom far beyond their years. When a strange pulse is detected from a wormhole beyond Saturn, Tim assembles the *Horizon's* crew—trusted NASA colleagues, old friends, and Terra Novan allies. Their mission: investigate the phenomenon and stop whatever lies beyond from threatening Earth. To survive, Tim, Peggy, and their children must unite human ingenuity, Terra Novan technology, and new allies. Failure could mean not only the fall of Earth but also the collapse of the Milky Way. *Flight to the Stars* delivers a heart-pounding journey of danger, discovery, and the limitless reach of courage.

How to Contact Jay B. Greene

Visit my website, review my books, and
sign up for my newsletter at
www.jaybgreene.com

- Early sneak peeks at upcoming books.

- Bonus chapters, deleted scenes, blogs,
  exclusive children's stories, short stories,
  and newspaper articles I wrote over the years.

- Insider updates on my novels, including the
  investigative reporter Jack Kendall mysteries
  and the family space opera Tim and Peggy
  Smith Space Adventures.

- Special offers and giveaways.

- Author insights, personal notes, and
  healthcare policy blogs.

Love My Books? Leave a review and share it with your
friends!
Your reviews on Amazon, Barnes and Noble, or independent bookstore websites help other readers discover the
series, and they mean the world to me as an author.

Thanks again for reading, and I hope you'll join Jack
Kendall, or Tim and Peggy, on their thrilling adventures!

Pursue the Truth, **Jay B. Greene**

About the Author

Jay B. Greene was born, raised, and lives in Sarasota. He studied environmental science and journalism in college, graduating from the University of Florida. His passion for storytelling led to a 40-year career covering health care, government, crime, and the environment for newspapers across multiple states. *Bone Valley* is the third installment in the Jack Kendall Mystery series. Greene is also the author of *Mountain Crossing, Becky, Nokomis Hospital,* and *Danger From Space* and *Flight to the Stars*, the first two books in the Tim and Peggy Smith Space Adventure trilogy. In 2026, Jack will return in *Breakthrough Lies*, and Tim and Peggy will conclude their space adventures in *Children of the Stars*.